Introduction by Rob Roehm

Edited by Rob Roehm and Paul Herman

THE
Robert E. Howard
FOUNDATION PRESS

For Glenn Lord (1931-2011), preserver of Howard's typescripts and manuscripts, godfather of Howard studies, and the greatest fan that ever lived.

Copyright © 2012, 2024 Robert E. Howard Properties Inc. Robert E. Howard™ and related logos, names, characters and distinctive likenesses thereof are trademarks or registered trademarks of Robert E. Howard Properties Inc. unless otherwise noted. All rights reserved.

ISBN: 978-1-955446-10-5 (Paperback)
ISBN: 978-1-955446-20-4 (Hardcover)
ISBN: 978-1-955446-28-0 (eBook)

Published by the REH Foundation Press, LLC by arrangement with Robert E. Howard Properties Inc.

https://rehfoundation.org
https://rehfpress.com

Cover illustration copyright © 2024, Mark Wheatley.

https://markwheatleygallery.com

Book prepared for publication by Ståle Gismervik, Savage Studios.

Version 2.0 - Ultimate Edition.

Acknowledgments

All of the Howard stories, poems, letters and portions thereof contained in *Pirate Adventures* come from Howard's original typescripts, manuscripts, and carbons. Virtually all of them were scanned from the Glenn Lord collection, now at the University of Texas, Austin; the Robert E. Howard collection at Texas A&M University; or the typescript collection at Cross Plains Library.

Thanks to Patrice Louinet for tracking down the owner of the Howard photographs and sharing his copies. Thanks also to Rusty Burke for his knowledge of the books that Howard may have read.

CHANGES FROM THE 1ST EDITION: This Ultimate Edition adds the earliest known draft of "Black Vulmea's Vengeance."

Furthermore, the poems have been updated to reflect the new standardized versions as they now appear in the Collected Poetry volumes, ensuring consistency across the Ultimate Editions.

Contents

Humor

Robert E. Howard (at right) playing "make believe" with his Cross Plains neighbors Leroy and Faustine Butler.

The Pirate

I was born in Devonshire, close by Bristol Bay,
Used to watch the ships go out, sittin' on the quay
Thought I'd be a sailor when I was a man,
Always wandered sea-ward, never liked the land.
Fishin' from the old wharfs, wanderin' on the lea,
Drinkin' in the glorious breeze blowin' from the sea.
Watchin' ships a-passin', listenin' to their hail,
Scannin' the horizon for a liftin' sail.

–Robert E. Howard

Introduction

by Rob Roehm

In "Robert E. Howard as a Boy," a short piece published in the *Cross Plains Review* shortly after Howard's death in June 1936, Mrs. T. A. Burns describes an encounter with a young Howard near Burkett, Texas, where the Howards lived in 1918-19. Robert is out playing with his dog, Patches, who disturbs Mrs. Burns while she is reading in a clearing. Howard apologizes, saying that he and his dog "like to come here where there are big rocks and caves so we can play 'make believe.' Some day I'm going to be an author and write stories about pirates and maybe cannibals."

Howard was 12-13 years old when the family lived in Burkett. If Mrs. Burns' memory can be trusted, this must be the time Howard refers to three years later in a high school essay, "Some People Who Have Had Influence Over Me":

> First and foremost in this list appear, of course, my parents. But there are others. Captain Kidd, for instance. Reading his biography and fiction based on his eventful life, caused me to determine, at an early age, to lead a life of piracy on the high seas. Tales of Blackbeard and Morgan clinched my resolve.
>
> But the influence of another man finally overbalanced this idea. I have forgotten his name but he was an author. He wrote an authentic book about piracy and by some means I secured it. I devoured it with avidity but was shocked to find that it contained a harrowing account of the deaths of Kidd, Blackbeard, and other noted gentlemen.
>
> These accounts grieved me deeply. I felt as if I had lost some old and trusted friends. Also my determination to follow in Kidd's footsteps was weakened. I began to perceive that there might be disadvantages attached to piracy. At the back of the

> aforesaid book there was an illustration which shattered my hopes entirely. It portrayed a pirate of my acquaintance just after his execution. He was fastened to the mast of a man-o-war, by a great spike which was driven through his head into the wood. The huge blood spattered head of the spike stood out from the center of his forehead and his villainous features were streaked with blood and twisted with the awful agony that had been his before death came to his release.
>
> This gruesome picture haunted me for days and caused me, once and for all time, to give up any thoughts of sailing the Spanish Main under the skull and crossbones.

By the time he was writing this paper, dated February 7, 1922, Howard's interests had moved beyond the piratical, but it seems clear that he read a good deal on the subject. The title of the book mentioned above remains a mystery, but Rusty Burke posits that it may have been *The Pirates Own Book* (1837), by Charles Ellms, which features a picture of "The head of Benavides stuck on a pole," though this doesn't exactly fit Howard's description above. Another title that is not mentioned in Howard's surviving papers is Robert Louis Stevenson's *Treasure Island*, though based on Howard's poem "Flint's Passing," it's certain he was at least aware of it. Other pirate-related titles on Howard's bookshelf include Jeffrey Farnol's *Black Bartlemy's Treasure* and *Martin Conisby's Vengeance*. *Drake's Quest*, by Cameron Rogers, and the *Bounty Trilogy*, while not specifically pirate novels, were also among Howard's reading material.

Howard's interest in the subject is also clear by the number of stories and poems—even photographs—he produced along those lines. One of his early efforts, "The Treasure of Henry Morgan," may have been inspired by a reading of Washington Irving's *Tales of a Traveller*, which contains "Kidd the Pirate." Compare the opening of Howard's story (see the Treasure of Henry Morgan) with the following from Irving's:

> They [the pirates] took advantage of the easy access to the harbor of the Manhattoes, and of the laxity of its scarcely-organized

> government, to make it a kind of rendezvous, where they might dispose of their illgotten spoils, and concert new depredations. Crews of these desperadoes, the runagates of every country and clime, might be seen swaggering, in open day, about the streets of the little burgh; elbowing its quiet Mynheers; trafficking away their rich outlandish plunder, at half price, to the wary merchant, and then squandering their gains in taverns; drinking, gambling, singing, swearing, shouting, and astounding the neighborhood with sudden brawl and ruffian revelry.

Possible influences aside, Howard's tales of the sea were never as successful as the yarns that appeared in *Weird Tales* or *Action Stories*; none of the items contained in the present collection were published until after the Texan's death; of course, this was not for lack of trying. In 1928, Howard submitted "The Isle of Pirates' Doom" to *Argosy*, *Adventure*, and *Red Blooded*—to no avail. In 1929 he sent it to *Romance*, a pulp magazine that carried tales by some of Howard's favorite authors from *Adventure*. It was rejected again, and he filed it away in his trunk.

Also in 1929, "The Blue Flame of Vengeance," a piratical tale featuring Solomon Kane, was shopped around. It went to *Argosy* and *Adventure* but was rejected by both. There is no record of whether or not Howard sent the story to *Weird Tales*, but due to its lacking a weird element, it seems unlikely. In 1932, when Howard was attempting to crash into other markets, he rewrote the story into its present form, changing the hero to Malachi Grim and the title to "Blades of the Brotherhood." There is no record to show to which magazines this story was offered, if any.

While Howard was unsuccessful in selling straight pirate yarns, he did incorporate many of the elements into his other work, perhaps most notably in the Conan stories "Queen of the Black Coast," published in 1934, and "The Black Stranger," which remained unpublished at the time of Howard's death. "The Black Stranger" may have been rejected by *Weird Tales*' editor Farnsworth Wright in February or March 1935. Undaunted, Howard rewrote it into "Swords of the Red Brotherhood" and sent it to his agent, Otis

Adelbert Kline, who received it on May 28, 1935. Now featuring Terence Vulmea, the tale remained unsold and did not see print until 1976. Another Vulmea story, "Black Vulmea's Vengeance," appeared in *Golden Fleece* for November 1938, more than two years after Howard's death.

The tales collected herein were not commercial successes for their author, though many of them do display the poetic prose and narrative drive that are the earmarks of Howard's fiction. Recognizing this—and no doubt trying to cash in on the "Howard Boom"—in 1976, a small collection containing the Vulmea series and "The Isle of Pirates' Doom" was published by Donald M. Grant; the collection was reissued in the years that followed by several paperback publishers. Now, thanks to the persistence of Glenn Lord and the kindness of his widow, we are able to present all of Howard's stories, poems, and fragments inspired by his long ago admiration for Captain Kidd.

These include three never before published items from the Glenn Lord Estate: the untitled fragment beginning "Help! Help!,"* a list of characters, and a stray page that appears to be from an earlier draft of "The Treasure of Henry Morgan"; the new text is appended to the story here.

* This fragment is part of a humorous boxing tale that also appears in Fists of Iron, Round 2 (REHF Press 2014)

Pirate Adventures

A Pirate Remembers

From the scarlet shadows they come to me,
   Shades of the dust-dead past,
Like drifting fogs of the restless sea
   From the silent Nameless Vast.
Ghostly and grey in the dying day
   Their spectral ranks are massed.

With their lank, dank hair, and their eery stare,
   Phantom and fiend and ghost —
Skeletons limned in a haunted sky,
   Footfalls light where the dim bats fly,
Stealthy shadows — yet none but I
   Am 'ware of the weird host.

Their light tread whispers on every hand
   When I walk through the shadows' rack
And I hear the mumble of fleshless jaws
   In the dark behind my back.

Red shades of many a buccaneer
   Whose bones rust in the sea,
Grisly phantoms who gape and leer
   That died on the gallows tree.
And they haunt my brain with their dim refrain:
   "As we are, thou shalt be."

A Buccaneer Speaks

I've broken the laws of man and God,
I've flung my gauntlet forth to the world.
I've turned from the ways that in youth I trod —
Yonder the Skull Flag flies unfurled.

I laugh at Death and I mock at Life.
Through seas of blood I have steered my prow.
I've known the glories of crimson strife
And I've tattooed the cross-bones on my brow.

I've bared my breast to the sea-wind's force;
Sailed red ways beyond seamen's ken.
I've scattered red ruin along my course,
Of ravished women and slaughtered men.

I've steered in the teeth of bloody dawns
And I've raced the sunset o'er crimson seas.
I've sailed where abyss-red Hell yawns,
And I've battled the bergs where the star beams freeze.

I've seized my wish at the hilt of the sword
And held my own by the point of the blade,
Spite of the foe or my own wild horde,
Were it gold of man or beauty of maid.

I've had my pleasure in slaughter and wreck,
And all undaunted my end shall be,
With the broken sword on a bloody deck
Or the raven's croak on the gallows tree.

The Isle of Pirates' Doom

The First Day

The long low craft which rode offshore had an unsavory look and, as I lay close in my covert, I was glad that I had not hailed her. Caution had prompted me to hide myself and observe her crew before I made my presence known, and now I thanked my guardian spirit; for these were troublous times and strange craft haunted the Caribees.

Truth, the scene was a fair and peaceful one enough. I lay among green and fragrant bushes on the crest of a slope, which ran down before me to the broad beach. Tall trees rose about me and their ranks swept away on either hand. Below on the shore, green waves broke on the white sand and above all lay the blue sky like a dream. But like a serpent in a rose bed lay that black sullen ship, anchored just outside the shallow water.

She had an unkempt look, a slouchy, devil-may-care appearance of rigging which speaks not of an honest crew or a careful master. Anon rough voices floated across the intervening space of water and beach, and once I saw a great hulking fellow slouching along the rail, lift something to his lips and then hurl it overboard.

Now the crew was lowering a longboat, heavily loaded with men, and as they laid hand to oar and drew away from the ship, their coarse shouts and the replies of they who remained on the decks came to me, though the words were blurred by reason of the distance.

I lay in my covert wishing for a telescope that I might discern the name of the ship, and presently the longboat drew in close to the beach. There were eight men in her: seven great rough fellows and the other a slim, foppishly clad varlet who wore a cocked hat who did no rowing. Now as they approached, I perceived that there was argument between them, and seven of them roared and bellowed at the dandy, who, if he answered at all, spoke in a tone so low that I did not hear.

The boat swept through the light surf and, as she beached, a huge hairy rogue in the bows heaved up and plunged at the fop, who sprang up to meet him. I saw steel flash and heard the larger man bellow, then the other leapt nimbly out, splashed through the wet sand and legged it inland as fast as he might, while the other rogues streamed out in pursuit, yelling and brandishing weapons. He who had begun the brawl halted a moment to make the longboat fast, then took up the chase also, cursing at the top of his bull's voice, the blood trickling down his face.

The man in the cocked hat was leading by several paces when they reached the first fringe of trees. He vanished among them and the rest followed, and for awhile I could hear the alarums and bellowings of the chase, till the sounds faded in the distance.

Now I looked again at the ship. Her sails were filling and I could see men in the rigging. As I watched, the anchor came aboard and she stood off—and from her peak broke out the Jolly Roger. Truth, 'twas no more than I had expected.

I worked my way further back among the bushes on hands and knees, and then stood up. A gloominess of spirit was upon me, for when the sails had first hoven in view, I had looked for rescue. Instead of proving a blessing, the ship had disgorged eight ruffianly buccaneers on the island for me to cope with.

I wondered at the reason for this as I slowly made my way between the trees. No doubt these men had been marooned by their comrades—a procedure very common among the bloody Brothers of the Main.

I know not what I might do, since I was unarmed and these rogues would doubtless consider me an enemy—as, in truth, I was to all their ilk. My gorge arose against running and hiding from them, but I saw naught else to do. Nay, 'twould be rare fortune were I able to escape them at all.

Meditating thus, I had traversed a considerable distance inland and had heard naught of the pirates, when I came to a small glade. Tall trees, crowned with lustrous green vines and gemmed with small exotic-hued birds flitting through their branches, rose about it. The musk of tropic growths filled the air and the stench of blood was there also. A man lay dead in the glade.

Flat on his back he lay, his seaman's shirt drenched with the gore which had ebbed from the wound below his heart. He was one of the Brethren of the Red Account, no doubt of that. He'd never shoes to his feet, but a great ruby glimmered on his finger, and a costly silken sash girdled the waist of his tarry pantaloons. Through this sash were thrust a pair of flintlock pistols and a cutlass lay near his hand.

Here were weapons, at least. So I drew the pistols from his sash, noting that they were charged, and having thrust them in my waistband, I took his cutlass also. He would never need weapons again and I had good thought that I might very soon.

Then as I turned from despoiling the dead, a soft mocking laugh brought me round like a shot. The dandy of the longboat stood before me. Faith, he was smaller than I had thought, though supplely and lithely built. Boots of fine Spanish leather he wore on his trim legs, and above them tight britches of doeskin. A fine crimson sash, with tassels and rings to the ends, was round his slim waist, and from it jutted the silver butts of two pistols. A blue coat with flaring tails and gold buttons gaped open to disclose the frilled and laced shirt beneath, and the cocked hat I had noticed rode on the owner's brow at a jaunty angle, golden hair showing beneath.

"Satan's throne!" said the wearer of this finery. "There is a great ruby ring you've overlooked!"

Now I looked for the first time at the face. It was a delicate oval, with red lips that curled in mockery, large grey eyes that danced—only then did I realize that I was looking at a woman and not a man. One hand rested saucily on her hip, the other held a long ornately-hilted rapier—and with a twitch of repulsion I noted a trace of blood on the blade.

"Speak, man!" cried she impatiently. "Are you ashamed to be caught at your work?"

Now I doubt not that I was a sight to inspire little respect, what with my bare feet and my single garment, sailor's pantaloons, and them stained and discolored with salt water. But at her mocking tone my anger stirred.

"At least," said I, finding my voice, "if I must answer for robbing a corpse, someone else must answer for making it."

"Ha, I struck a spark then, eh?" she laughed in a hard way. "Satan's Fiends, if I'm to answer for all the corpses I've made, 'twill be a wearisome reckoning."

Thereat my gorge rose.

"One lives and one learns," said I. "I had not thought to meet a woman who rejoiced in cold-blooded murder."

"Cold-blooded, say you!" she fired up then. "Am I then to stand and be butchered like a sheep?"

"Had you chosen the proper life for a woman you had had no necessity either to slay or be slain," said I, carried away by my revulsion. And I then regretted what I had said for it was beginning to dawn on me who this girl must be.

"So, so, self-righteous," sneered she, her eyes beginning to flash dangerously. "So you think I'm a rogue! And what might you be, may I ask; what do you on this out-of-the-way island and why do you come a-stealing through the jungle to take the belongings of dead men?"

"My name is Stephen Harmer, mate on *The Blue Countess*, Virginia trader. Seven days ago she burned to the waterline from a fire that broke out in her hold and all her crew perished save myself. I floated on a hatch and eventually raised this island, where I have been ever since."

The girl eyed me half thoughtfully, half mockingly, while I told my tale, as if expecting me to lie.

"As for taking weapons," I added, "it's but bitter mead to bide among such rogues as yours without arms."

"Name them none of mine," she answered shortly, then even more abruptly: "Do you know who I am?"

"There could be only one name you could wear—what with your foppery and cold-blooded manner."

"And that's—?"

"Helen Tavrel."

"I bow to your intuition," she said sardonically, "for it does not come to my mind that we have ever met."

"No man can sail the Seven Seas without hearing Helen Tavrel's fame and, to the best of my knowledge, she is the only woman pirate now roving the Caribees."

"So, you have heard the sailors' talk? And what do they say of me, then?"

"That you are as bold and heartless a creature as ever walked a quarter-deck or traded petticoats for breeches," I answered frankly.

Her eyes sparkled dangerously and she cut viciously at a flower with her sword point.

"And is that all they say?"

"They say that though you follow a vile and bloody trade, no man can say truthfully that he ever so much as kissed your lips."

This seemed to please her for she smiled.

"And do you believe that, sir?"

"Aye," I answered boldly, "though may I roast in Hades if ever I saw a pair more kissable."

For truth to tell, the rare beauty of the girl was going to my head, I who had looked on no woman for months. My heart softened toward her; then the sight of the dead man at my feet sobered me. But before I could say more, she turned her head aside as if listening.

"Come!" she exclaimed. "I think I hear Gower and his fools returning! If there be any place on this cursed island where one may hide a space, lead me there, for they will kill us both if they find us!"

Certes I could not leave her to be slaughtered, so I motioned her to follow me and made off through the trees and bushes. I struck for the southern end of the island, going swiftly but warily, the girl following as light-footed as an Indian brave. The bright-hued butterflies flitted about us and in the interwoven branches of the thick trees sang gay-winged birds. But a tension was in the air as if, with the coming of the pirates, a mist of death hung over the whole island.

The underbrush thinned as we progressed and the land sloped upward, finally breaking into a number of ravines and cliffs. Among these we made our way and I marveled at the activity of the girl, who sprang about and climbed with the ease of a cat, and outdid me who had passed most of my life in ship's rigging.

At last we came to a low cliff which faced the south. At its foot ran a small stream of clear water, bordered by white sand and shadowed by waving fronds and tall vegetation which grew to the edge of the sand. Beyond, across this narrow rankly grown expanse there rose other higher cliffs, fronting north and completing a natural gorge.

"Down this we must go," said I, indicating the cliff on which we stood. "Let me aid you—"

But she, with a scornful toss of her head, had already let herself over the cliff's edge and was making her way down, clinging foot and hand to the long heavy vines which grew across the face of it. I started to follow, then hesitated as a movement among the fronds by the stream caught my eye. I spoke a quick word of warning—the girl looked up to catch what I had said—and then a withered vine gave way and she clutched wildly and fell sprawling. She fell not far and the sand in which she lighted was soft, but on the instant, before she could regain her feet, the vegetation parted and a tall ruffian leaped upon her.

I glimpsed in a single fleeting instant the handkerchief knotted about his skull, the snarling bearded face, the cutlass swung high in a brawny hand. No time for her to draw sword or pistol—he loomed over her like the shadow of death and the cutlass swept downward—but even as it did I drew pistol and fired blindly and without aim. He swerved sidewise, the cutlass veering wildly, and pitched face down in the sand without a sound. And so close had been her escape that the sweep of his blade had knocked the cocked hat from the girl's locks.

I fairly flung myself down the cliff and stood over the body of the buccaneer. The deed had been done involuntarily, without conscious thought, but I did not regret it. Whether the girl deserved saving from death—a fact which I doubted—or not, I considered it a worthy deed to rid the seas of at least one of those wolves which scoured it.

Helen was dusting her garments and cursing softly to herself because her hat was all awry.

"Come," said I, somewhat vexed thereat, "you are lucky to have escaped with a skull uncloven. Let us begone ere his comrades come at the sound of the shot."

"That was a goodly feat," said she, preparing to follow me. "Fair through the temples you drilled him—I doubt me if I could have done better."

"'Twas pure luck guided the ball," I answered angrily, for of all faults I detest in women, heartlessness is the greatest. "I'd no time to take aim—and had I had such time, I might not have fired."

This silenced her and she said no more until we reached the opposite cliffs. There at the foot stretched a long expanse of solid stone and I bade her walk upon it, as did I. So we went along the line of the cliff and presently came to a small waterfalls, caused by a stream tumbling over the cliff's edge to join the one in the gorge.

"There's a cave behind that falls in the cliff," said I, speaking above the chatter of the water. "I discovered it by accident one day. Follow me."

So saying, I waded into the pool which whirled and eddied at the cliff's foot, and ducking my head, plunged through the falling sheet of water with the girl close behind. And we found ourselves in a small dark cavern which ran back until it vanished in the blackness, and in front the light ebbed in faintly through the sliding silver screen the falling water made. This was the hiding place I had discovered, and for it I had been making when I met the girl.

I led the way back into the cavern until the rattle of the falling stream died to a murmur and the girl's face glimmered like a rare white flower in the thick darkness.

"Damme," says she, beating the water from her coat with the cocked hat, "you lead me in some cursed inconvenient places, Mr. Harmer; first I fall in the sand and soil my garments, and now they are wet—will not Gower and his gang follow the sound of the pistol shot and find us, tracking our footprints where we bent down the bushes crossing from cliff to cliff?"

"No doubt they will come," answered I, "but they will be able to track us only to the cliff where we walked a good way on stone which shows no footprint. They will not be able to say if we went up or down or whither. There is not one chance in a hundred of them ever discovering this cavern and, at any rate, 'tis the safest place on the island for us."

"Do you still wish you had let Dick Comrel kill me?" she asked.

"He was a bloody pirate, whatever his name might be," I answered. "No, you're too comely for such a death, no matter what your crimes."

"Your compliments take the sting from your accusations, and your accusations rob your compliments of their roses. Do you hate me?"

"No, not you, but the red trade you follow. Were you in some other walk of life 'tis joyed I would be to look on you."

"Zounds," said she, "but you are a queer young fellow, in truth. One moment you talk like a courtier and the next like a chaplain. What are your feelings toward me to make you speak in so inconsistent a manner?"

"I am fascinated and repelled," said I, for the dim white oval of her face floated before me and her nearness made my senses reel. "As a woman you attract me, as a pirate you rouse a loathing in me. God's truth, but you are a very monster, like that Lilith of old, with the face of a beautiful maiden and the body of a serpent."

Her soft laugh lilted silvery and mocking in the shadows.

"So, so, broadbrim. You saved my life, though methinks you grudge the act, and I will not run you through the body as I might have done otherwise. For such words as you have just said like me not. Are you wondering how I came to be here with you?"

"They of the Red Brotherhood are like hungry wolves and range everywhere," I answered. "I've yet to sight an island of the Main unpolluted by their cursed feet. So 'tis no wonder to me to find them here, or to find them marooning each other."

"Marooned? John Gower marooned from his own ship? Scarcely, friend. Hark ye. The craft from which I landed is *The Black Raider*, on The Account as you know. She sails to intercept a Spanish merchantman and returns in two weeks.

"Black be the memory of the day I shipped on her! For a more rascally, cowardly crew I have never met. But Roger O'Farrel, my captain aforetime, is without ship at present and I threw my lot with Gower—the swine! Yesterday he forced me to accompany him ashore, and on the way I gave my opinion of him and his dastardly henchmen. Thereat they were little pleased and bellowed like bulls but dared not start fighting in the boat, lest we all fall among the sharks.

"So the moment she beached, I slashed Gower's ape-face with my rapier point and outfooted the rest and hid myself. But it was my bad fortune to come upon one alone—he rushed at me and swung with his blade, but I parried it and spitted him with a neat riposte just under the heart. Then came you, Righteousness, and the rest you know. They must have scattered all over the isle, as testifieth Comrel.

"But now I will tell you why John Gower came ashore with seven men. Heard you ever of the treasure of Mogar?"

"No."

"I thought not. The legend goes that when the Spaniards first sailed the Main, they found an island whereon was a decaying empire. The natives thereof lived in mud and wooden huts on the beach, but they had a great temple of stone, a remnant of some forgotten, older race, and therein was a great treasure of precious stones. The Dons destroyed this race, but first the natives hid their hoard so thoroughly that not even a Spanish nose could smell it out, and they the Dons tortured died unspeaking.

"So the Spaniards sailed away empty-handed, leaving all traces of the Mogar kingdom utterly effaced, save the temple which they could not destroy.

"The island was off the beaten track of ships, and, as time went by, the tale was mostly forgotten, living only as a sailor's yarn. Such men as took the tale seriously and came to the island were unable to find the temple.

"But on this voyage there shipped with John Gower a man who swore that he had set foot on the island and had looked on the temple. He said he had landed there with the French buccaneer de Romber and that they found the temple, just as it was described in the legend.

"But ere they could search for the treasure, a man-o'-war hove in sight and they were forced to run for it. Nor ran far ere they fell afoul of a frigate who blew them out of the water. Of the boat's crew who were with de Romber when he found the temple, only this man who shipped with Gower remained alive.

"He refused to tell the location of it or to draw a map but offered to lead Gower there, in return for a large share of the gems. So upon sighting the island, Gower bade his mate, Frank Marker, sail to take a merchantman we had word of some days agone, and Gower himself came ashore—"

"What! Do you mean—"

"Aye! On this very island rose and flourished and died the lost kingdom of Mogar, and somewhere among the trees and vines hereon lies the forgotten temple with the ransom of a dozen emperors!"

"The dream of a drunken sailor," I said uncertainly. "And why tell me this?"

"Why not?" said she, reasonably enough. "We are in the same boat and I owe you a debt of gratitude. And we might find the treasure ourselves, who knows? The man who sailed with de Romber will never lead John Gower to the temple, unless ghosts walk, for he was Dick Comrel, the man you killed!"

"Listen!" A faint sound had come to me through the dim gurgle of the falls.

Dropping on my belly, I wriggled cautiously toward the water-veiled entrance and peered through the shimmering screen. I could make out dimly the forms of five men standing close to the pool.

The taller one was waving his arms savagely and his rough voice came to me faintly and as if far away.

I drew back, even though knowing he could not see through the falls, and as I did, I felt silky curls brush against my shoulder and the girl, who had crawled after me, put her lips close to me to whisper, under the noise of the water.

"He with the cut face and the fierce eyes is Captain Gower; the lank dark one is the Frenchman, La Costa; he with the beard is Tom Bellefonte; and the other two are Will Harbor and Mike Donler."

I had heard all those names and knew that I was looking on as red-handed and black-hearted a group as ever walked deck or beach. After many gestures and rough talk which I could not understand, they turned and went along the cliff, vanishing from view.

Back where we could talk in ordinary tones and be heard, the girl said:

"Damme, but Gower is in a rare rage! He will have to find the temple now by himself, since your pistol ball scattered Dick Comrel's brains. The swine! He had better be putting the width of the Seven Seas between himself and me! Roger O'Farrel will pay him for the way he has treated me, I wager you, even if I fail in my vengeance."

"Vengeance for what?" I asked curiously.

"For disrespect. He sought to treat me as a woman, not as a buccaneer comrade. When I threatened to run him through, he cursed me and swore he would tame me some day—and made me come ashore with him."

A silence followed and suddenly she said:

"Zounds! Are we to stay pent up here forever? I grow hungry!"

"Bide you here," said I, "and I will go forth and procure some fruit which grows wild here—"

"Good enough," she replied, "but I crave more than fruit. By Zeus! There is bread and salt pork and dried beef in the longboat and I am of a mind to sally forth and—"

Now I, who had tasted no Christian food in more than a week, felt my mouth water at the mention of bread and beef, but I said:

"Are you insane? Of what good is a hiding place if it be not used? You would surely fall into the hands of those whom we are trying to escape."

"No, now is the best time for such an attempt," said she, rising. "Hinder me not—my mind is made up. You saw that the five were together—so there is no one at the boat for the other two are dead."

"Unless the whole gang of them returned to the beach," said I.

"Not likely. They are still searching for me, or else have taken up the hunt for the temple. No, I tell you now is the best time."

"Then I go with you, if you are determined," said I, and together we dropped from the ledge in front of the cavern, splashed through the falls and waded out of the pool.

I looked about, half expecting an attack, but no man was in sight. Silence reigned, save for the occasional raucous plaint of some jungle bird. I looked to my weapons. One of the pistols I had taken from the dead buccaneer was empty, of course, and the priming of the other was wet.

"The locks of mine are wrapped in silk," said Helen, noticing my activities. "Here, draw the useless charge and reload them."

And she handed me a waterproof horn flask with compartments for powder and ball. So I did as she said, drying the weapons with leaves.

"I am probably the finest pistol shot in the world," said the girl modestly, "but the blade is my darling."

She drew her rapier and slashed and thrust the empty air.

"You sailors seldom appreciate the true value of the straight steel," said she. "Look at you with that clumsy cutlass. I could run you through while you were heaving it up for a slash. So!"

Her point suddenly leaped out and a lock of my hair floated to the earth.

"Have a care with that skewer," said I, annoyed and somewhat uneasy. "Save your tierces and thrusts for your enemies. As for a cutlass, it is a downright weapon for an honest man who knows naught of your fine French tricks."

"Roger O'Farrel knows the worth of the rapier," said she. "'Twould do your heart good to see it sing in his hand, and how that he spits they who oppose him."

"Let us be going," answered I, shortly, for her hardness rasped again on me, and it irked me somehow to hear her sing the praises of the pirate O'Farrel.

"We waste time in child's talk. Let us get this crazy adventure over with."

So we went silently up through the gorges and ravines, mounting the north cliffs at another place, and so proceeded through the thick trees until we came to the crest of the slope that led down to the beach, and peering from ambush, saw the longboat lying alone and unguarded.

No sound broke the utter stillness as we went warily down the incline. The sun hung over the western waters like a shield of blood, just ready to set, and the very birds in the trees seemed to have fallen silent. The breeze had lain and no leaf rustled on any branch.

We came down to the longboat and, working swiftly, broke open the kegs and made a bundle of bread and beef. My fingers trembled with haste and nervousness, for I felt we were riding on the crest of a precipice—I was sure that the pirates would return to their boat before nightfall, and the sun was about to go down.

And even as this thought came to me, I heard a shout and a shot, and a bullet hummed by my cheek. I looked. Mike Donler and Will Harbor were running down the beach toward us, cursing and bellowing horrible threats. They had come upon us from among the lofty rocks further down the shore, and now were on us ere we had time to draw a breath.

Donler rushed in on me, wild eyes aflame, belt buckle, finger rings and cutlass blade all afire in the gleam of the sunset. His broad breast showed hairy through his open shirt, and I leveled my pistol and shot him through the chest, so that he staggered and roared like a wounded buffalo. Yet such was his terrible vitality that he came reeling on in spite of this mortal hurt and slashed at me with his cutlass. And I parried the blow and split his skull to the brows with my own blade, and he fell dead at my feet, his brains running out on the sand.

Then I turned to the girl, whom I feared to be hard pressed, and looked just in time to see her disarm Harbor with a dextrous wrench of her wrist, and run him through the heart so that her point came out under his shoulder.

For a fleeting instant he stood erect, mouth gaping stupidly, as if upheld by the blade, then blood gushed from that open mouth and, as she withdrew her sword with a marvelous show of wrist strength, he toppled forward, dead before he touched earth.

Helen turned to me with a light laugh.

"At least, Mr. Harmer," quoth she, "my 'skewer' does a cleaner and neater job than does your cleaver. Bones and blades! I had no idea there was so much brain to Mike Donler."

"Have done," said I somberly, repelled by her words and manner. "This is a butcher's business and one I like not. Let us begone; if Gower and the other two be not behind these, they will come shortly."

"Take up the pack of food, imbecile," said she sharply. "Have we come this far and killed two men for nothing?"

I obeyed without speaking, though truth to tell, I had little appetite left, for my soul was not with such work as I had just done. So as the ocean drank the westering sun and the swift southern twilight fell, we made our way back toward the cavern under the falls. After we had topped the slope and lost sight of the sea except such as glimmered between the trees in the distance, we heard a faint shout, and knew that Gower and the remainder of his men had returned.

"No danger now until morning," said my companion. "Since we know that the rogues are on the beach, there is no chance of coming upon them unexpectedly in the wood. And they will scarcely venture into this unknown wilderness at night."

So after we had gone a little farther, we halted, set us down and supped on the bread and beef, washing it down with draughts from a clear cold stream. And I marveled at how daintily and with what excellent manners this pirate-girl ate.

When she had finished and washed her hands in the stream, she tossed her golden curls and said:

"By Zeus, this hath been a profitable day's work for two hunted fugitives! Of the seven buccaneers which came ashore early this morn, but three remain alive! What say you—shall we flee them no more, but come upon them and trust to our battle fortune? Three against two makes not such great odds."

"What say you?" I asked bluntly.

"I say nay," said she frankly. "Were it any man but John Gower I might say differently. But this Gower is more than a man—he is as crafty and ferocious as any wild beast, and there is that about him which turns my blood to ice. He is one of the two men I have ever feared."

"Who was the other?"

"Roger O'Farrel."

Now she had a way of pronouncing that rogue's name as if he were a saint or a king, and for some reason this rasped on my nerves greatly. So I said nothing.

"Were Roger O'Farrel here," she prattled on, "we should have naught to fear, for no man on all the Seven Seas is his equal and even John Gower would shun the issue with him. He is the greatest navigator that ever lived and the finest swordsman, and hath the manners of a cavalier, which in truth he is."

"Who is this Roger O'Farrel?" I asked, then brutally, "Your lover?"

At that, quick as a flash, she struck me across the face with her open hand so that I saw stars. We were on our feet, and I saw her face crimson in the light of the moon which had come up over the black trees.

"Damn you!" she cried. "O'Farrel would cut your heart out for that, were he here! From your own lips I had it that no man could call me his!"

"So they say, indeed," said I bitterly, for my cheek was stinging, and my mind was in such a chaotic state as is difficult to describe.

"They say, eh? And what think you?" There was danger in her tone.

"I think," said I recklessly, "that no woman can be a plunderer and a murderess and also virtuous."

It was a cruel and needless thing to say. I saw her face go white, I heard the quick intake of her breath and the next instant her rapier point was against my breast, just under the heart.

"I have killed men for less," I heard her say in a ghostly, faraway whisper.

I looked down at the thin silver line of death that lay between us and my blood froze, but I answered:

"Killing me would scarcely change my opinion."

An instant she stared at me, then to my utter bewilderment, she dropped her blade, flung herself face down on the earth and burst into a torrent of sobs. Much ashamed of myself, I stood over her, uncertain, wishing to comfort her, yet afraid the little spitfire would stab me if I touched her. Presently I was aware of words mingling with her tears.

"After all I have done to keep clean," she sobbed, "this is too much! I know I am a monster in the sight of men—there is blood on my hands. I've looted and cursed and killed and diced and drunk, till my very heart is calloused. My only consolation—the one thing to keep me from feeling utterly damned—is the fact that I have remained as virtuous as any girl. And now men believe me otherwise. I wish—I—I—were dead!"

So did I for the instant, and I also, for never in my life have I felt such unutterable shame. What I had said had been certainly no act of a man, and now I felt as if the girl had dropped her mask of hard recklessness to reveal a surprizingly sensitive soul. Her words carried the tang of sincerity, and, truth to tell, I had never really doubted her. But such emotions were moving dimly in the depths of me that I feared and resented while not recognizing, and they prompted me to think hard thoughts and utter bitter words that were not sincere.

Now I dropped to my knees beside the weeping girl and, raising her, made to wipe her eyes.

"Keep your hands off me!" she ordered promptly, jerking away. "I will have naught to do with you, who believe me a bad woman."

"I don't believe it," I answered. "I most humbly crave pardon. It was a foul and unmanly thing for me to say. I have never doubted your honesty, and I said that which I did only because you had angered me."

She seemed somewhat appeased.

"As for Roger O'Farrel," said she, "he is twice as old as either of us. He took me off a sinking ship when I was a baby and raised me like his own daughter. And if I took to the life of a rover, 'tis not his fault, who would have established me like a fine lady ashore had I wished. But the tang of adventure is in my blood and though Fate made a woman of me, I have lived a man's life.

"If I am hard and cold and heartless, what else might you expect of a maid who grew up among daily scenes of blood and violence, whose earliest remembrances are of sinking ships, crashing cannon and the shrieks of the dying? I know the rotten worth of my companions—sots, murderers, thieves, gallows-birds—all save Captain Roger O'Farrel.

"Men say he is cruel and it may be so. But to me he is ever kind and gentle. And moreover he is a fine upstanding man, of high aristocratic blood and hath the courage of a lion!"

I said nothing against the buccaneer, whom I knew to be the disinherited black sheep of a powerful Irish family, but I experienced a strange sensation of pleasure to learn from her lips just what their relationship was to each other.

And a scene long forgotten suddenly flashed in my mind: a boatload of people sighted off the Tortugas and taken aboard—the words of one of the women, "And it's Helen Tavrel we have to thank, God bless her! For she made bloody Hilton put all we a-boat with food and water, when the fiend would ha' burned us all with our ship. Woman pirate she may be, but a kind heart she hath for all that—"

After all, the girl was a credit to her sex, considering her raising and surroundings, thought I, and felt strangely cheerful.

"You'll try to forget my words," said I. "Now let us be getting toward our hiding place, for 'tis like we will have need of it tomorrow."

I helped her to her feet and gave her rapier into her hand. She followed me then without a word and no conversation passed between us until we reached the pool beside the cliff. Here we halted a moment.

Truth, it was a weird and fantastic sight. The cliffs rose stark and black on either side, and between them whispered and rustled the thick shadows of the fronds. The stream sliding over the cliff before us glimmered like molten silver in the moonlight, and the pool into which it slipped shimmered with long bright ripples. The moon rode over all like a broad buckler of white gold.

"Sleep in the cavern," I commanded. "I will make me a bed among these bushes which grow close by."

"Will you be safe thus?" she asked.

"Aye; no man is like to come before morning, and there are no dangerous beasts on the island, save reptiles which lurk among the swamps on the other side of it."

Saying no more then, she waded into the pool and vanished in the silver mist of the fall, and I parted the bushes near at hand and composed myself for slumber. The last thing I remembered, as I fell asleep, was an unruly mass of golden curls, below which danced a pair of brooding grey eyes.

The Second Day.

Someone was shaking me out of my sound slumber. I stirred, then awoke suddenly and sat up, groping for blade or pistol.

"My word, sir, you sleep deep. John Gower might have stolen upon you and cut out your heart and you not aware of it."

It was early dawn and Helen Tavrel was standing over me.

"I had thought to wake before dawn," said I, yawning, "but I was weary from yesterday's work. You must have a body and nature of steel springs."

She looked as fresh as if she had but stepped from a lady's bedroom. Truth, there are few women who could endure such exertions, sleep all night on the bare sand of a cavern floor and still look elegant and winsome.

"Let us to breakfast," said she. "Methinks the fare is a thought scanty, but there is pure water to go with it, at least, and I believe you mentioned fruit?"

Later, as we ate, she said in a brooding manner:

"It stirs my blood most unpleasantly at the thought of John Gower coming into possession of the Mogar treasure. Besides Roger O'Farrel, I have sailed with Hilton, Hansen and le Ban between times, and Gower is the first captain to offer me insult."

"He is not like to find it," said I, "for the simple reason that there is no such thing on this island."

"Have you explored all of it?"

"All except the eastern swamps which are impenetrable."

Her eyes lighted.

"Faith, man, were the shrine easy to find, it had been looted long ere now. I wager you that it lies somewhere amid that swamp! Now listen to my plan.

"It is yet awhile before sunup and as it is like Gower and his bullies drank rum most of the night, they are not like to be up before broad daylight. I know their ways, and they alter not, even for treasure!

"So let us go swiftly to this swamp and make some exploration therein."

"I repeat," said I, "it is tempting Providence—why have a hiding place if we use it not? We have been very fortunate so far in evading Gower, but if we keep running hither and yon through the woods we must eventually come on him."

"And if we cower in our cave like rats, he will eventually discover us. Doubtless we can explore the swamp and return before he fares forth, or if not—he has naught of woodcraft but blunders along like a buffalo. We can hear them a league off and elude them. So there is no danger in hiding awhile in the woods if need be, with always a safe retreat to run to as soon as they have passed. Were Roger O'Farrel here—" She hesitated.

"If you must drag O'Farrel into it," said I with a sigh, "I must agree to any wild scheme you put forward. Let us be started."

"Good!" she cried, clapping her hands like a child. "I know we will find treasure! I can see those diamonds and rubies and emeralds and sapphires gleaming even now!"

The first grey of dawn was lighting and the east was growing brighter and more rosy as we went along the cliffs and finally went up a wide ravine and entered the thicker growth of trees that ran eastward. We were taking the opposite direction from that taken the day before. The pirates had landed on the western side of the island and the swamp lay on the eastern.

We walked along in silence awhile, and then I asked abruptly:

"What sort of looking man is O'Farrel?"

"A fine figure with the carriage of a king," She looked me over with a critical eye. "Taller than you, but not so heavily built. Broader of shoulder, but not so deep of chest. A cold, strong handsome face, smooth shaven. Hair as black as yours in spite of his age, and fine grey eyes, like the steel of swords. You have grey eyes, too, but your skin is dark and his is very white.

"Still," she continued, "were you shaved and clad properly, you would not cut a bad figure, even beside Captain O'Farrel—how old are you?"

"Twenty-seven."

"I had not thought you that old. I am twenty."

"You look younger," I answered.

"I am old enough in experience," quoth she. "And now, sir, we had best go more silently, lest by any chance there be rogues among these woods."

So we stole cautiously through the trees, stepping over trailers and making our way through undergrowth which rose thicker as we progressed eastward. Once a large, mottled snake wriggled across our path and the girl started and shrank back nervously. Brave as a tigress when opposed to men, she had the true feminine antipathy toward reptiles.

At last we came to the edge of the swamp without having seen any human foe and I halted.

"Here begins the serpent-haunted expanse of bogs and hummocks which finally slopes down into the sea to the east," said I. "You see those tangled walls of moss-hung branches and vine-covered trunks which oppose us. Are you still for invading that foul domain?"

The only reply she made was to push impatiently past me.

Of the first few rods of that journey, I like not to remember. I hacked a way through hanging vines and thickly grown bamboos with my cutlass, and the farther we went, the higher about our feet rose the stinking, clinging mud. Then the bamboos vanished, the trees thinned out, and we saw only rushes towering higher than our heads, with occasional bare spaces wherein green stagnant pools lay in the black bubbling mud. We staggered through, sinking sometimes to our waists in the water and slime. The girl cursed fervently at the ruin it was making of her finery, and I saved my breath for the labor of getting through. Twice we tumbled into stagnant pools that seemed to have no bottom, and each time were hard put to get back on solid earth—solid earth, said I? Nay, the treacherous shaky, sucking stuff that passed for earth in that foul abomination.

Yet we progressed, ploughing along, clinging to the yielding rushes and to rotten logs, and making use of the more solid hummocks when we could. Once Helen set her foot on a snake and thereat shrieked like a lost soul; nor did she ever become used to the sight of them, though they basked on every log and writhed across every hummock.

I saw no end to this fool's journey and was about to say so, when above the rushes and foul swamp growth about us I saw what seemed to be hard soil and trees just beyond. This I imparted to Helen, and she exclaimed for joy and rushing forward, promptly fell into a pool which sucked her under except for her nose. Fumbling under the nasty water, I got a good grip on her arms and managed to draw her forth, cursing and spluttering. By that time I had sunk to my waist in the mud about the pool, and it was with some desperation that we fought our way toward the higher earth.

At last our feet felt a semblance of bottom under the mud and then we came out on solid land. Tall trees grew there, rank with vines, and grass flourished high between them, but at least there was no bog. I, who had been all around the swamp's edges, was amazed. Evidently this place was a sort of island, lapped on all sides by the mire. One who had not been through the swamp would think as I had thought: that nothing lay therein but water and mud.

Helen was excited, but ere she would venture further, she stooped and attempted to wipe some of the mud from her garments and face. Truth, we were both a ludicrous sight, plastered with mire and slime to the eyebrows.

More, in spite of the silk wrappings, water had soaked into Helen's pistols, and mine also were useless. The barrels and locks were so fouled with mud that it would take some time to clean and dry them so they might be recharged from her horn flask, which still contained some powder. I was in favor of halting long enough to do this, but she argued that we were not likely to need them in the midst of the swamp, and that she could not wait—she must explore the place we had found and learn if the temple did in truth stand there.

So I gave in and we went on, passing between the great boles of the trees, where the branches intertwined so as to almost shut out the light of the sun which had risen some time before. Such light as filtered through was strange, grey and unearthly, and the tall grass waved through it like thin ghosts. No birds sang there, no butterflies hovered, though we saw several snakes.

Soon we noticed signs of stonework. Sunk in the earth and overgrown by the rank grass lay shattered paves and tiles. Further on we came to a wide-open stretch which was like a street. Great flagstones lay, evenly placed, and the grass grew in the crevices between them. We fell silent as we followed this strange street, for long forgotten ghosts seemed to whisper about us, and soon we saw a strange building glimmering through the trees in front of us.

Silently we approached it. No doubt of it; it was a temple, squarely built of great stone blocks. Wide steps led up to its floor, and up these we went, swords drawn, still and awed. On three sides it was enclosed by walls, windowless and doorless, on the fourth by huge squat columns which formed the front of the edifice. Tiling, worn smooth by countless feet, made up the floor, and in the middle of the great room began a row of narrow steps which led up to a sort of altar. No idol stood there; if there had ever been one, no doubt the Spaniards destroyed it. No carvings decorated wall, ceiling or column. The keynote of the whole seemed grim simplicity, a sort of terrible contempt for man's efforts at beautifying and adorning.

What strange people had built that shrine so long ago? Some terrible, somber people who died ages before the brown skinned Caribs came to rear up their transient empire, surely. I glanced up at the altar which loomed starkly above us. It was set on a sort of platform built solidly from the floor. A column rose from the center of this platform to the ceiling, and the altar seemed to be part of this column.

We went up the steps. For myself, I was feeling not at all at ease, and Helen was silent and slipped her firm little hand into mine, glancing about nervously. A brooding silence hung over the place, like a monster of some other world lurked in the corners ready to leap upon us. The evident terrible antiquity of the temple oppressed us and bore us down with a sense of our own futile smallness and weakness.

Only the quick nervous rattle of Helen's small heels on the stone steps broke the stillness, yet I could picture in my mind's eye the majestic and somber rites of worship which had been enacted here in bygone years. Now, as we reached the platform and bent over the altar, I saw deep dark stains on its surface and heard the girl shudder involuntarily. More shadows of horror out of the past, and had we known, the horror of that grim shrine was not yet over.

Turning my attention to the solid column which rose behind the altar, my gaze followed it up to the roof. This seemed to be composed of remarkably long slabs of stone, except for the space just above the altar. There a single huge block showed, of a different stone than that which composed the rest of the temple. It was of a somber yellowish hue, shot with red veins, and was of a monstrous size. It must have weighed many tons, and I was put to it to guess by what means it was held in place. But at last decided that the column which rose from the platform upheld it in some manner, for this entered the ceiling beside the great block. From the ceiling to the platform was, I should say, some fifteen feet, and from the platform to the floor, ten.

"Now that we are here," said the girl, rather breathlessly, "where is the treasure?"

"That's for us to find," said I. "And before we begin to search, let us prepare our pistols, for the saints alone know what lies before us."

Down the stair we went again, and partway down, Helen halted, an uneasy look in her eyes.

"Hark, was that a footfall?"

"I heard nothing; belike 'tis your imagination conjuring up noises."

Still she insisted she heard something and was for hurrying out into the open as quickly as might be. I reached the floor a stride or so before her and turned to speak across my shoulder, when I saw her eyes go wide and her hand flew to her blade. I whirled to see three menacing shapes bulking among the columns—three men, smeared with mud and slime, with weapons gleaming in their hands.

As in a flying dream I saw the fierce burning eyes of John Gower, the beard of the giant Bellefonte, and the dark saturnine countenance of La Costa. Then they were on us.

How they had kept their powder dry as they crossed that filthy swamp I know not, but even as I drew blade, La Costa fired and the ball struck my right arm, breaking the bone. The cutlass dropped from my numb fingers, but I stooped and, catching it up in my left hand, met Bellefonte's charge. The giant came on like a wild elephant, roaring, his cutlass whirling like a flame. But the desperate fury of a cornered and wounded lion was mine. And, crashing on his guard as a smith hammers an anvil, until the clash of our steel was an incessant clangor, I drove him across the room and beat him to his knees. But he partly parried the blow that felled him, so that my cutlass, glancing from his blade to his skull, turned in my hand and struck flat instead of edgewise, stunning and not killing. At that instant, La Costa clubbed a musket and laid my scalp open so that I fell and lay in my own blood.

Of how Helen fared I was partly told later, and partly saw, dimly, as I lay dazed and unable to rise.

At the first alarum she had attacked Gower and he had met her with his blade held in a posture for defense rather than attack. Now this Gower was a rare swordsman, able to hold his own for a time against even such a skill as was Helen's, though his weapon was a heavy cutlass, which blade is unsuited for tricky work.

He had no wish to slay her, and even so he had more craft than to leave himself wide open to her thrust by slashing at her. So he parried her first few tierces, retreating before her while La Costa sought to steal upon her from behind and pinion her arms. But ere the Frenchman could accomplish his design, Helen feinted Gower into a wide parry that left him open. Then and there had John Gower died, but luck was not with us that day, and Helen's foot slipped as she thrust for his black heart. The point wavered and only raked his ribs, and ere she could recover her balance, Gower shouted and struck down her sword, dropping his own to seize her in his huge arms.

She fought even then, clawing at his face, kicking his shins and striving to shorten her grip on her sword so as to use it against him, but he only laughed. And having wrenched the rapier out of her hand, he held her helpless as a baby while he bound her with cords. Then he carried her over to a column and, standing her upright against it, made her fast—she raving and cursing in a manner to make one's blood run cold.

Then, seeing that I was struggling to arise, he ordered La Costa to bind me. The Frenchman answered that both my arms were broken and Gower commanded him to bind my legs, which he did, and dragged me over near the girl. And how the Frenchman made this mistake I know not, unless it were that because of the blow on my head, I seemed unable as yet to use my limbs, so he assumed my left arm broken also, besides my right.

"And so, my fine lady," said John Gower in his deep menacing voice, "we end where we began. Where you got this brawny young savage, I know not, but methinks he is in a sad plight—but there is work to do at present after which I may ease his hurts."

Dazed as I was, I knew that he meant not by saving but by slaying me, and I heard Helen's quick intake of breath.

"You beast!" she cried. "Would you murder the boy?"

Gower gave a cold laugh and turned to Bellefonte, who was just now rising in a muddled sort of way.

"Bellefonte, is your brain yet too addled for our work?"

"Nay," snarled the giant. "But may I roast in Hades if I ever felt such a bash, I would—"

"Get the tools," ordered Gower, and Bellefonte slouched out to return presently with picks and a great sledgehammer.

"I will tear this cursed building to pieces or find what I look for," quoth John Gower. "As I told you when you asked the reason for loading the sledge into the longboat, my pretty Helen. Comrel died ere he could tell us just where this temple lay, but from the hints he had let drop from time to time, I guessed that it lay on the eastern side of the isle, and when we came hither this morn and saw the swamp, I felt our search was done. And truth it was, and our search for you also, as I found when I stole up to the columns and peeked between 'em."

"Methinks we waste time," broke in Bellefonte. "Let us be tearing down something."

"All a waste of time," said the somber Frenchman moodily. "Gower, I say again that this is a fool's quest, bound to end but evilly. This is a haunt of demons; nay, Satan himself hath spread his dark wings o'er this temple and 'tis no resort for Christians! As for the gems, a legend hath it that the ancient priests of these people flung them into the sea, and I, for one, believe that legend."

"We shall soon see," was Gower's imperturbable reply. "These walls and pillars have a solid look, but persistence and appliance will crumble any stone. Let us to work."

Now strange to say, I have neglected to make mention of the quality of the light in the building. On the outside there was a clear space, no trees growing within several yards of the walls on either side. Yet so tall were those trees which grew beyond this space, and so close their branches, that the shrine lay ever in everlasting shadow, and the light which drifted through between the columns was dim and strange. The corners of the great room seemed veiled in grey mist and the humans moving about appeared like ghosts—their voices sounding hollow and unreal.

"Look about for secret doors and the like," said Gower, beginning to hammer along the walls, and the other two obeyed, Bellefonte eagerly, La Costa otherwise.

"No luck will come of this, Gower," the Frenchman said as he groped in the dimness of the furthest corner. "This daring of heathen deities in heathen shrines—*nom de Dieu!*"

We all started at his wild shriek and he reeled from the corner screaming, a thing like a black cable writhing about his arm. As we looked aghast, he crashed down in the midst of the tiled floor and there tore to fragments with his bare hands the hideous reptile which had struck him.

"Oh Heavens!" he screeched, writhing about and staring up at his mates with wild, crazed eyes. "Oh, Grand Dieu, I burn, I die! Oh, saints, grant me ease!"

Even Bellefonte's steel nerves seemed shaken at this terrible sight, but John Gower remained unmoved. He drew a pistol and flung it to the dying man.

"You are doomed," said he brutally. "The venom is coursing through your veins like the fire of Hell, but you may live for hours yet. Best end your torment."

La Costa clutched at the weapon as a drowning man seizes a twig. A moment he hesitated, torn between two terrible fears, then as the burning of the venom shook him with fiercer stabbings, he set the muzzle against his temple, gibbering and yammering, and jerked the trigger. The stare of his tortured eyes will haunt me till Doomsday, and may his crimes on earth be forgiven him for if ever a man passed through Purgatory in his dying, it was he.

"By God!" said Bellefonte, wiping his brow. "This looks like the hand of Satan!"

"Bah!" Gower spoke quick and impatiently. "'Tis but a swamp snake which crawled in here. The fool was so intent upon his gloomy prophesying that he failed to notice it coiled up in the darkness of the corner, and so set his hand in its coils. Let not this thing shake you—let us to work, but first look about and see if any more serpents lurk here."

"First bind up Mr. Harmer's wounds, if you please," spoke up Helen, a quaver in her voice to tell how she had been affected. "He is like to bleed to death."

"Let him," answered Gower without feeling. "'Twill will save me the task of easing him off."

My wounds, however, had ceased to bleed, and though my head was still dizzy and my arm was beginning to throb, I was nowhere near a dead man, and was beginning to work stealthily at my bonds with my left hand when the pirates were not looking. Truth, I was in no condition to fight, but were I free, I might accomplish something. So I, lying on my side, slowly drew up my feet behind me and fumbled at the cords on my ankles with strangely numb fingers, while Gower and his mate poked about in the corner and hammered on the walls and columns.

"By Zeus, I believe yon altar is the key of this mystery," said Gower, halting his work at last. "Bring the sledge and let us have a look at the thing."

They mounted the stair like two rogues going up the gallows steps, and their appearance in the dim light was as men already dead. A cold hand touched my soul and I seemed to hear the sweep of mighty batlike wings. An icy terror seized me, I know not why, and drew my eyes to the great stone which hung broodingly above the altar. All the horror of this ancient place of forgotten mysteries descended on me like a mist, and I think Helen felt the same for I heard her breath come quick and hard.

The buccaneers halted on the platform and Gower spoke, his voice booming like a hollow mockery in the great room, re-echoing ghostily from wall to ceiling.

"Now, Bellefonte, up with your sledge and shatter me this altar."

The giant grunted doubtfully at that. The altar seemed merely a solid square of stone, as plain and unadorned as the rest of the fane, and a part of the platform as it was part of the column behind it. But Bellefonte lifted the heavy hammer and the echoes crashed as he brought it down on the smooth surface.

"Again!"

Sweat gathered on the giant's brow with the effort, and the great muscles stood out on his naked arms and shoulders as he heaved up the sledge and smote again and yet again. Gower cursed and Bellefonte swore that it was waste of strength cracking a solid rock, but at Gower's urging, he again raised the hammer. He stood with his legs spread wide, arms above his head and bent backward, hands gripping the handle. Then with all his power he brought it down and the hammer handle splintered with the blow; but, with a shattering crash, the whole top of the altar gave way and the fragments flew in all directions.

"Hollow, by Satan!" shouted John Gower, smiting fist on palm. "I suspected as much! Yet who would have thought it, with the lid so cleverly joined to the rest that no crack showed at all? Strike flint and steel here, man, the inside of this strange chest is as dark as Hades."

They bent over it and there was a momentary flash, then they straightened.

"No tinder," snarled Bellefonte, flinging aside his flint and steel. "What saw ye?"

"Naught but one great red gem," said Gower moodily. "But it may be that there is a secret compartment below the bottom where it lies."

He leaned over the altar-chest and thrust his hand therein.

"By Satan," said he, "this cursed gem seems to cling fast to the bottom of the chest, as though it were fastened to something—a metal rod from the feel—ha, now it gives and—"

Through his words came a muffled creak as of bolts and levers long unused—a rumble sounded from above and we all looked up—. And then the two buccaneers beside the altar gave a deathly cry and flung up their arms as down from the roof thundered the great central stone, and column, altar and stair crashed into red ruin.

Stunned by the terrible earthquake-like noise, the girl and I lay, eyes fixed with terrible fascination on the great heap of shattered stone in the middle of the temple, from under which oozed a river of dark red.

At last after what seemed a long time, I, moving like a man in a trance, freed myself and unbound the girl. I was very weak and she put an arm about me to steady me, and so we went out of that temple of death, and once in the open, never did free air and light seem so fair to me, though the air was tainted with the swamp reek and the light was strange and shadowy.

There a wave of weakness flooded body and brain and I fell to the earth and knew no more.

And Last

Someone was laving my brow and at last I opened my eyes.

"Steve, oh, Steve, are you dead?" someone was saying; the voice was gentle and there was a hint of tears.

"Not yet," said I, striving to sit up, but a small hand forced me gently down.

"Steve," said Helen, and I felt a strange delight in hearing her call me by my first name, "I have bandaged you as good as might be with such material as I had—stuff torn from my shirt, but methinks we should be out of this low dank place and in a fresher part of the island. Do you think you can make it?"

"I'll try," said I, though my heart sank at the thought of the swamp.

"I have found a road," said she. "When I went to look for clean water, I found a small spring, and also stumbled upon what was once a fine road, built with great blocks of stone set deep in the mire. The mud overlaps it now some few inches and rushes grow thereon, but 'tis passable, so let us be gone."

She helped me to my feet and, with one arm about me, guided my uncertain steps. We crossed the ancient causeway in this manner and I found time to marvel again at the nature of that strange old race who had built so strongly and had so terribly protected their secrets.

The journey seemed terribly long, through the swamp and again through the thick jungle, but at last my eyes, swimming with torment and dizziness, saw the ocean glimmering through the trees, and soon we sank down beside the longboat on the beach, both exhausted. Yet Helen would not rest as I urged her, but took a case of bandages and ointment from the boat and dressed my wounds. With a keen dagger she found and cut out the bullet in my arm, and I thought I would die thereat, and then made shift at setting the broken bone. I wondered at her dexterity, but she told me that from early childhood she had aided in dressing hurts and setting broken limbs—that Roger O'Farrel tended thus to all his wounded himself, having attended a medical university in his youth, and he imparted all his knowledge to her.

Still she admitted that the setting of my arm was a sad job of it, with the scant material she had, and she feared it would give me trouble. But while she was talking I sank back and became unconscious—for I had lost an incredible amount of blood—and it was early dawn of the next day before I came to my full senses.

Helen, while I lay senseless, had made me a bed of soft leaves, spreading over me her fine coat, which I fear me was none too fine now, what of the blood and stains thereon. And when I came to myself, she sat beside me, her eyes wide and sleepless, her face drawn and haggard in the early grey of morn.

"Steve, are you going to live?" asked she, and I made shift to laugh.

"You have scant opinion of my powers if you think a pistol ball and a musket stock can kill me," I answered. "How feel you—exhausted?"

"A thought. And remarkably meditative. I have seen men die in many ways, but never a sight to equal that. Their death shrieks will haunt me to my death. How think you their end was brought about?"

"All seems mazed and vague now," said I, "but methinks I remember seeing many twisted and broken metal rods among the ruins. From the way the platform and stair shattered, I believe that the whole structure was hollow, like the altar, and the column also. And that a crafty system of levers was run through them up to the roof, where the great stone was held in place by bolts or the like. I believe that the gem in the altar was fastened to a lever which, working up through the column, released that stone."

She shuddered.

"Like enough. And the treasure—"

"There never was any. Or if there was, the Caribs flung it into the sea and, knowing some curse lay over the temple, pretended that they had hidden it therein, hoping the Spaniards would come to harm while searching for it. Certainly that thing was not the work of Caribs, and I doubt if they knew just what sort of fate lay in wait there. But, certes, any man could look on that accursed shrine and instinctively feel that doom waited there."

"Another dream turned to smoke," sighed she. "La, la, and me a-wishing for rubies and sapphires as large as my fist!"

She was gazing out to sea as she spoke, where the waves were beginning to redden in the growing light. Now she sprang erect.

"A sail!"

"The Black Raider> returning!" I exclaimed.

"No! Even at this distance I can tell the cut of a man-o'-war! She is making for this island."

"For fresh water, no doubt," said I.

Helen stood twisting her slim fingers uncertainly.

"My fate lies with you. If you tell them I am Helen Tavrel, I will hang between high tide and low, on Execution Dock!"

"Helen," said I, reaching up and taking her small hand, "my opinion of you has changed since first I saw you. I still maintain the Red Trade is no course for a woman to follow, but I realize the circumstances which forced you into it. No woman, whatever her manner of life, could be kinder, braver, and more unselfish than you have been. To the men of yonder craft you shall be Helen Harmer, my sister, who sailed with me."

"Two men have I feared," said she with lowered eyes; "John Gower because he was a beast, Roger O'Farrel because he was so fine and noble. One man I have respected—O'Farrel. Now I find a second man to respect without fearing. You are a bold, honest youth, Steve, and—"

"And what?"

"Nothing," and she seemed confused.

"Helen," said I, drawing her gently closer to me, "you and I have gone through too much blood and fire together for anything to come between us. Your beauty fascinated me when first I saw you, later the sterling worth of your soul which lay beneath your reckless mask. Each soul has its true mate, little comrade, and though I fought the feeling, and strove to put it from me, fondness was born in my bosom for you and has steadily grown. I care not what you may have been, and I am but a sailor, now without a ship, but let me tell yonder seamen when they land that you are, not my sister, but my wife-to-be—"

A moment she leaned toward me, then she drew away and her eyes danced with the old jaunty fire.

"La, sir, are you offering to marry me? 'Tis very kind of you indeed, but—"

"Helen, don't mock me!"

"Truth, Steve, I am not," said she, softening. "But I had never thought of any such a thing before. La, I must be growing up with a vengeance! Fie, sir, I am too young to marry yet, and I have not yet seen all of the world I wish to. Remember, sir, I am still Helen Tavrel."

"I care not; marry me and I will take you from this life."

"Not so fast," said she, tracing patterns in the sand with her finger. "I must have time to think this thing over. Moreover, I will take no step without Roger O'Farrel's consent. I am only a young girl after all, Steve, and I tell you truth, I have never thought of marrying or even having a lover.

"Ah, me, these men, how they press a poor maid!" laughed she.

"Helen!" I exclaimed, vexed yet amused. "Have you no care for me at all?"

"Why, as to that," she avoided my gaze, "I really feel a fondness for you such as I have never felt for any other man, not even Roger O'Farrel. But I must mull over this and discover if it be true love!"

Thereat she laughed merrily aloud, and I cursed despairingly.

"Fie, such language before your lady love!" she said. "Now hear me, Steve, we must seek Roger O'Farrel, wherever he may be, for I am like a daughter to him, and if he likes you, why, who knows? But you must not speak of marrying until I am older and have had many more adventures. Now we shall be true comrades as we have been hitherto."

"And a comrade must allow an honest kiss," said I, glancing seaward where the ship came sweeping grandly.

And with a light laugh she lifted her lips to mine.

A Song of the Anchor Chain

Let down, let out the anchor chain,
   The gulls are dipping low,
A faint wind rattles stays in vain —
   Oh, let the anchor go.
A yellow mist is lying,
   A broken wind is sighing
And Captain Gower's dying —
   Oh, let the anchor go!

Carven with ivory rough and rare,
   Warped with the sea salt spray,
Glowered the captain's cabin where
   The dying buccaneer lay.

He sought to dream of flying ships
   And winds that waver and dart,
But the rattle of death was under his lips
   And Hell was in his heart.

And ever the vision rose and fled:
   A craft on the outward tack,
And a ghostly skipper who swayed and said:
   "No man of our crew came back."

And ever a vision followed fast —
   A ship with a tattered sail
Idly flapping a broken mast —
   And a plank was over the rail.

Gower dreamed of the gallows-tree —
   In a sloop like a lurching gull
He sailed a weird white haunted sea
   Where each wave was a skull.

Gower clutched at a flask of rum,
   And dreamed of a bloody moon,
And he heard the evilly muttering drum
   In the jungle barracoon.

He heard the whimper of naked slaves
   And the crack of the driver's whip
And the wailing of women and brawny braves
   Pent in the hold of the ship.

He dreamed of low long ships that run
   From the guns of a man-o'-war,
And a crimson road from the rising sun
   To the coast of Calabar.

He saw on the waste of a windy sea,
   Strange death lights glimmer and slant
And he sailed for the port of Eternity
   With the sailor's echoed chant:

"Let down, let out the anchor chain,
   "The wind is rising slow,
"It's far to Rio and the Main,
   "Oh, let the anchor go.
"Oh, turn her bows for Gades
   "To greet the wharf side ladies,
"And Gower's gone to Hades.
   "Oh, let the anchor go."

Blades of the Brotherhood

Chapter .1.

The blades crossed with a vicious clash, showering blue sparks. Across the flickering steel lines hot eyes burned into each other—hard black eyes and volcanic blue eyes. Breath hissed between locked teeth; feet scruffed the sward in quick short play.

The black-eyed swordsman feinted and thrust as quick as a snake strikes. The other parried with a half turn of a steely wrist and his counter was like the flash of summer lightning.

"Hold, gentlemen!" the blades were struck up and a portly man stood between the combatants, jeweled rapier in one hand, cocked hat in the other. "Have done! Honor is satisfied. Sir George is wounded."

The black-eyed man, with an impatient gesture, put behind him his left arm from which blood was streaming.

"Stand aside!" he cried furiously. "A wound—a scratch! It decides nothing. This must be to the death."

"Aye, stand aside, Sir Rupert," said the victor, his eyes sparks of blue steel. "The matter between us can be settled only by death."

"Put up your steel, you young cockerels!" snapped Sir Rupert. "As magistrate I command it! Sir physician, come and look to Sir George's wound. Jack Holland, sheath your blade, sirrah! I'll have no bloody murders in this district an my name be Rupert d'Arcy."

Young Holland said nothing, but he dropped his point to the earth and with head half lowered stood silent and moody, watching the company from under frowning black brows.

Sir George had hesitated, but one of his seconds whispered urgently in his ear, and he sullenly handed his sword to the speaker and gave himself up to the ministrations of the physician.

It was a bleak setting. A low-level land, sparsely grown with sickly grass, now withered, ran to a wide strip of white sand, strewn with bits of drift wood. Beyond the sand the sea washed grey and restless, a dead thing upon whose leaden waste the only sign of life was a single sail hovering in the distance. Inland, across the bleak moors there could be seen in the distance the drab cottages of a small village.

With the desolation of the landscape the splash of color and passionate life there on the beach contrasted violently. The pale autumn sun flashed on blue steel, silver buckles, and the gilt-work on Sir Rupert's cocked hat.

Sir George's seconds were helping him in his coat, and Holland's friend, a sturdy young man in home spun, was urging him to don his. But the latter impatiently put him aside, and stepped forward, with his sword still in his hand.

"Sir George Blanard!" his voice rang fierce with passion. "Look to yourself! A scratch in the arm will not blot out the insult whereof you know! The next time we meet there will be no magistrate to save your rotten hide!"

The nobleman whirled with a black oath, and Sir Rupert started forward with a roar, "Sirrah! How dare you!"

Holland snarled in his face and turning his back, strode away, sheathing his sword with a vicious thrust. Sir George made as if to follow him, his dark face contorted, but again his friend whispered in his ear, motioning seaward, where the single sail hung as if suspended in the sky. Blanard eye's followed the gesture and he nodded grimly.

Holland strode along the beach in silence, bareheaded, hat in one hand, his coat slung over his arm. The chill wind brought coolness to his sweat-plastered locks, but not to his turmoiled brain.

His second, Randel, followed him in silence. As they progressed along the beach, the scenery became more wild and rugged; gigantic rocks, grey and moss grown, reared up along the shore and straggled out to meet the waves in grim jagged lines. Further out a dangerous reef sent up a low and continuous moaning.

Jack Holland halted, dashed his hat to the ground and cursed long, fervently and deep throated. Randel listened awedly to his passionate expressions of regret that he had failed to sink his point to the hilt in the black heart of that swine, that jackal, that damned rogue, Sir George Blanard!

"Calm yourself, Jack!" honest Randel squirmed uneasily. He was Holland's closest friend, but he did not understand the black furious moods into which his comrade sometimes fell. "You drubbed him fairly. He got the worst of it all around. After all, you'd hardly kill a man for what he did—"

"No?" cried Holland passionately. "Not kill a man for a foul insult? Well, not a man but a base rogue of a nobleman whose heart I'll see before the moon wanes! Do you realize that he publicly slandered Ellen Garvin over his drinking cup in the common tavern? Why—"

"So I understand," sighed Randel, "having heard the details no less than a score of times. Also I know that you threw a cup of wine in his face, broke his crown, upset a table on him and kicked him twice or thrice. Faith, Jack, you've done enough for any man. Sir George is highly connected; you are but the son of a retired sea captain—though you've distinguished yourself for valor abroad. Be careful, lest you bring harm to yourself."

Holland's teeth snapped viciously. "Leave me to my folly, Dick. My blood is too hot to be reasoned with. He knew Ellen was my betrothed, yet he sat there and insulted her in my very teeth! He has monies, lands, titles; I am a poor man and a poor man's son, who carries his fortune in his sheath at belt side. Had I, or Ellen, been of high birth, he had respected—"

"Pshaw!" broke in Randel. "When did the man ever respect anything? His black name is well deserved. He respects his own desires."

"And now he desires Ellen Garvin," growled Holland. "Dick, I would not appear churlish, but you had best leave me for a space.

I'm no fit companion, and I need solitude and the cold breath of the sea to cool my burning blood."

"You'll not seek Sir George—" Randel hesitated.

Jack made a gesture of impatience.

"But his bullies are of unsavory repute—"

Holland grinned wolfishly. "Never fear; if he strikes back *that way* 'twill be in the darkness of night—not in open day."

Randel walked away toward the village, shaking his head dubiously, and Holland strode on along the beach, each step taking him further into a dim realm of wastelands and waste waters. The cold greyness of the scene brought no calmness to his soul. He muttered profanely as he strode.

A powerful voice broke in on his curses.

"Young man, your words are as sounding brass and tinkling cymbals, full of sound and fury, signifying nothing."

Holland whirled, hand at hilt. On a great grey boulder sat a stranger who rose, unwrapping a wide black cloak and laying it over his arm. Inches taller than Holland, who was well above medium height, there was no surplus flesh on his spare frame, yet he did not look frail. His broad shoulders, deep chest and long rangy limbs spoke of strength and endurance—bespoke the swordsman as plainly as did the long rapier at his belt. There was something wolflike about his lean hardness.

His face was rather long, smooth shaven and of a strange dark pallor that was almost corpselike. But his eyes gleamed with dynamic life, cold as the North Sea.

The stranger's somber garb was unbroken by any gleam of gold or gem. His black slouch hat was featherless, his rapier hilt without jewels. The only hint of color about him was a shimmering green silk sash knotted about his lean waist; from it jutted a dirk hilt and the butts of two pistols.

"How come you here, clad like a Puritan, and armed to the teeth?" asked Holland bluntly. "How is it I saw you not until you spoke?"

"I came as all honest men come, young sir," the deep voice answered, as the speaker wrapped his wide black cloak about him and reseated himself on the boulder, "on my two legs. As for the other—men engrossed in their own affairs to the point of taking the Name in vain, see neither their friends—to their shame; nor their foes—to their harm."

"Who are you?"

"Men call me Malachi Grim."

Holland started violently. "Grim? Of the Brotherhood?"

"Perchance I have been associated overmuch with divers ungodly men in the past," answered the other guardedly. "But what make you of yonder ship standing off and on as she hath done since yesterday's daybreak?"

Holland shook his head. "She lies too far out. I can make naught of her."

The somber eyes bored into his, and Holland had a feeling that that cold gaze might plumb the distance and read the very name painted on the distant bows.

"I have seen her before," said Grim. "I know the cut of her rigging. I would like to meet the master of yon craft."

Holland said nothing. There was no harbor thereabouts, but a ship might, in calm weather, run close ashore and anchor just outside the reef. This ship might well be a smuggler; the type was common on that coast.

"Have you ever heard of one Jonas Hardraker, whom men called the Fishhawk?"

Again Holland started, scanning the stranger's face narrowly; the brooding eyes were inscrutable.

"That bloody pirate? The last I heard of him, he was purported to be cruising the Caribees."

Grim shrugged his wide shoulders. "Lies travel ahead of a fast craft. The Fishhawk cruises where his ship is, and where that is, only his master Satan knows."

He stood up, wrapping his cloak more closely about him.

"The Lord hath led my feet into many strange places, and over many grim paths," said he somberly. "And hark'ee, lad, for by the fires of hell, there is no hotter fire than the blue flame of vengeance which burneth a man's heart night and day without rest until he quench it in blood.

"Well—the Lord is my staff and my guide, and methinks he hath delivered mine enemy into mine hands."

And so saying, Grim strode away with long catlike strides, leaving Holland to gape after him in bewilderment. Was this stranger indeed that strange wanderer, whom, men said, a fanatical hatred for Spain had led to follow a crimson sea-path? Already the deeds of Malachi Grim on the war-torn Main had become half mythical. Holland shrugged his shoulder and turned toward the distant village.

Chapter .2.

Jack Holland awoke suddenly, sat up in bed and stared about him. Outside the moon had not risen but in his window a head and a pair of broad shoulders were framed black in the starlight. A warning, "Shhhh!" came to him like a serpent's hiss.

Slipping his sword from the scabbard which hung on the bed-post, Holland rose and approached the window. A bearded face set with two small bright eyes looked in at him. The man was breathing deeply as if from a hard run.

"Bring tha' swoord, lad, and follow me! 'E's got she!"

"How now? Who's got who?"

"Sir Garge!" came the chilling whisper. "'E sent she a writin' wi' yer name onto it, biddin' 'er come to the Rocks, and his rogues grabbed she—"

"Who, in God's name?" ripped out Holland, a grisly suspicion rising in his mind.

"Ellen Garvin!"

The room reeled. Holland had anticipated a treacherous attack on himself; he had not thought Blanard villain enough to strike at the girl.

"Where is she now?" he was snatching at his garments in fumbling haste.

"They tooken she to 'is 'ouse, sur."

"And who are you?"

"No' but poor Sam as tends stable down to the tavern, sur. I see 'em grab she."

Dressed and bare sword in hand, Holland stepped through the broad window.

"I thank you, Sam," said he. "If I live, I'll remember this."

Sam showed wolfish fangs in a wide grin. "I'll go wi' 'e. I've a grudge or twain to settle wi' Sur Garge!" He flourished a wicked bludgeon.

"Come then. We'll go straight to the swine's house."

Sir George Blanard's ancient manor house, in which he lived alone except for a few evil-visaged servants and several more evil cronies, stood a mile or so from the village, close to the beach. A great lowering bulk of a house, its oaken panels stained with age, many ill tales were told about it, and of the villagers, only such ruffians as enjoyed the owner's confidence, had ever set foot in it. No wall surrounded it, only ragged hedges and a few straggling trees. The moors ran to the back of the grounds and the front faced a wide strip of sandy beach which lay between the house and the boulder-torn surf. It was said that there were curious caves among the rugged and barren rocks at the water's edge, but Sir George's habit of discharging muskets at trespassers discouraged exploration of that section of the beach.

No light showed in the huge house as Jack Holland and his strange follower made their way across the dank moor. A thin mist had blotted out most of the stars, and through it the great black house reared up dark and ominous, surrounded by dark, bent ghosts which were hedges and trees. Seaward, all was veiled in a grey shroud, but once Holland thought he heard the muffled clank of a mooring chain. He wondered if a ship could be anchored outside that venomous line of breakers. The grey sea moaned restlessly as a sleeping monster might moan without waking.

"The windy, sur," came from Sam in a fierce whisper. "No lights—'e's there, just the same!"

Together they stole silently into the shadow of the huge bulk. Holland found time to wonder at the apparent absence of guards. Blanard was not a man to be negligent in such matters. He tried a window cautiously. The heavy shutters swung open with surprizing ease. Even as they did so, suspicion crossed his brain like a lightning flash—all this was too easy! Too sure! He whirled, just in time to see the bludgeon in Sam's hand descending. There was no time to thrust or duck. He had a fleet confused impression of the man's eyes glittering beastlike in the shadows, then the world crashed into utter blackness.

Chapter .3.

A red glow was in Jack Holland's eyes, and he blinked repeatedly. His head ached sickeningly, and the glare hurt his eyes. He shut them, hoping it would cease, but the merciless radiance beat through the lids, into his throbbing brain, it seemed. A confused medley of voices bore dimly on his ears. He tried to raise his hand to his head, but was unable to stir. Then it all came back with a rush and he was fully and poignantly conscious.

He was bound hand and foot, lying on the dank dirt floor of a vast cellar, piled high with squat casks and kegs and black sticky-looking barrels. The roof was braced with heavy oaken timbers, and from one of these hung a lanthorn from which emanated the glow that hurt his eyes. This light illumined the cellar, but filled its corners with flickering shadows. A flight of broad stone stairs came down into the cellar at one end, and a dark tunnel-like opening showed at the other end.

There were many men in the cellar. Twisting his head, Jack recognized the dark mocking countenance of Blanard, the bestial face of the traitor Sam, two or three bullies from the village tavern. The rest he did not know. Brawny men, with earrings, nose rings and tarry breeches, they were indubitably seamen, but their garb was grotesque. No honest seaman, these, with bright bandannas bound about their heads, and their breeks upheld with silken sashes. No stockings to their legs, yet many wore silver-buckled shoes. Great gems gleamed on their horny fingers, and dangled from heavy gold hoops serving as earrings. Not an honest sailorman's knife among them, but jewel-hilted Spanish and Italian daggers. Their girdles bristled with broad cutlasses and pistols. Their speech was wild and reckless as their appearance, as they guzzled rum from leathern jacks and cast dice on cask heads. Pirates! Their trade was evident enough.

Holland thought of the ship he had seen before sundown, and the rattle of anchor chains in the mist. One of the crew turned toward him, and Holland's eyes were held like a magnet on this man.

The fellow was scantily but gaudily clad, ornate with silken sash, silver buckles and gilded tassels. Dagger hilts and pistol butts, scintillant with jewels, jutted from his girdle. From each golden earring hung a ruby whose crimson sparkle contrasted with the dark face.

A cocked hat, worn over a gay bandanna, was thrust carelessly back from the high narrow forehead. A pair of cold grey eyes danced recklessly with changing sparks of light and shadow. A knife-bridged beak of a nose hooked over a thin gash of a mouth, and the cruel upper lip was adorned with long drooping mustachios, like a Manchu mandarin's.

"George, our guest wakes!" this man shouted with a cruel slash of laughter in his voice. The rest ceased their games to turn and stare. Blanard's face darkened and he indicated his left arm, the bandage showing through the silken sleeve.

"You spoke truth, Holland, when you said with our next meeting no magistrate should interfere—"

"*Jack!*"

The sudden agonized cry cut the din like a knife. Holland, with his blood congealing to ice, wrenched frantically over and, craning his neck, saw a sight that almost stopped his heart. A girl was bound by her wrists to an oaken support, kneeling on the dirt floor, straining helplessly towards him, her face white, her golden locks in tousled disarray.

"My God!—Ellen!" burst from Holland's anguished lips. A brutal shout of laughter echoed his horrified exclamation.

"Drink a health to the loving pair!" roared the tall captain, lifting a frothing jack. "Drink to the lovers, lads—!"

"You damned black swine!" raved Holland, struggling to his knees. "You cowards, you poltroons, you dastards, you white-livered curs! God's devils, if my hands were but free! Loose me, an the pack of you have a drop of manhood between you all! Loose me, and let me at your swine throats with my bare fingers! If I make not corpses of jackals, then blast me for a cowardly knave!"

"Judas!" spoke one of the buccaneers admiringly. "The lad hath the good right guts, even so! And what a flow o' speech, keelhaul me! Blast my liver, cap'n, but—"

"Be silent," cut in Sir George harshly, his hate eating like a rat at his heart. "Holland, you had your chance when I deigned to draw blade against you. You won that cast. I win this. The sea has hidden better bodies than yours. As for the wench, she shall bide here in this cellar until I am wearied of her—"

"Hadst better be wearied of her by the time I return in three months," broke in the captain with a sort of fiendish joviality. "If I take a corpse to sea this trip—which Satan knoweth is a plaguey evil cargo!—I must have a fairer passenger the next time."

Blanard smiled darkly. "So be it. In three months she is yours—unless she dies before that time. You sail just before dawn with the red ruin I intend to make of Holland, wrapped in canvas, and you sink the remains so far out at sea they will never wash ashore. That we have agreed. Then in three months you may return for the girl."

Holland's heart shriveled within him as he listened to this frightful program.

"How come you here, lass?" he asked weakly.

"A man brought a missive," she whispered, faint with fear. "Your name was signed. It bade me come to the Rocks. I came; these men seized and bore me here through a long evil tunnel."

"Two fools!" gloated Blanard. "Oh, you were passing easy to trick, both of you—"

"Belay," spoke up a dark, lean saturnine pirate, evidently first mate. "'Tis perilous enough putting in this way to get rid of the loot. What if they find the girl here and she tips 'em the lay? Where'd we find a market this side the Channel for the North Sea plunder?"

"Be at ease, Allardyne," answered the captain. "Was't ever a melancholy knave. They'll think the wench and the lad eloped together. Her father is against him, George says. None of the villagers will ever see or hear of either of them again, and they'll never look here. You're downhearted because we're so far from the Main. Blast your hide, haven't we threaded the Channel before?"

"Aye," mumbled Allardyne, "but I'll feel safer wi' these waters far behind. The day o' the Brotherhood is passin' in these climes. I feel evil in my bones. Death hovers over us like a black cloud, and I see no channel to steer through."

The pirates moved uneasily. "Avast, man, that's ill talk."

"It's an ill bed, the sea bottom," answered the other gloomily.

"Brace up!" laughed the captain, slapping his despondent comrade resoundingly on the back. "Execution Dock's a foul berth, but we're well to wind'ard of *that*. Drink to the bride! Ha! George's *and mine*—"

"*What's that?*" the mate's head jerked up.

Silence fell while eyes rolled toward the stair and thumbs stealthily felt the edge of blades. The captain shrugged his mighty shoulders.

"I heard nothing."

"I did. A scream and a fallin' carcass—I tell you, Death's walkin' tonight!"

"Allardyne," said the captain with a sort of still passion as he knocked the neck from a bottle, "you are become a very old woman, starting at shadows. Take heart from me!"

"Better if *you* went wi' more heed," answered the gloomy one direly. "Takin' breakneck chances, night and day—and wi' a human wolf on your trail day and night. Have you forgot *him?*"

"Bah!" the captain laughed scornfully, raising the bottle to his lips. "The trail's too long for even—"

A black shadow feel across him and the bottle slipped from his fingers to shatter on the floor. As if struck by a premonition, the pirate paled and turned slowly. All eyes sought the stone stairway which led down into the cellar. None had heard a door open or shut, but there on the steps stood a tall figure dressed all in black save for a bright green sash about the waist. Under heavy black brows, shadowed by a low-drawn slouch hat, cold eyes gleamed like burning ice. Each hand gripped a cocked pistol. Malachi Grim had come at last.

Chapter .4.
The Quenching of the Flame.

"Move not, Jonas Hardraker," said Grim tonelessly. "Stir not, Jem Allardyne. George Blanard, John Harkley, Black Mike, Bristol Tom—keep your hands in front of you. Let no man touch weapon lest he die suddenly."

There were nearly twenty men in that cellar, but in those black muzzles there was sure death for two, and none wished to be first to die. None moved. Only the mate Allardyne, with his face like snow on a winding sheet, gasped, "Grim! I knew it! Death's in the air when he's near! I told you he came like a shadow and slew like a ghost!"

Grim's somber eyes chilled him into silence. "You remember me of old, Jem Allardyne. You knew me before the brotherhood of free buccaneers turned into a bloody gang of cutthroat pirates. I had dealings with your former captain, as we both remember—in the Tortugas and again off the Horn. An evil man as thou art, and one whom hellfire doubtless hath devoured—to which end I aided him with a pistol ball in the midriff.

"As to my subtlety, your true pirate is as blind as a ox. Those you set to watch the house saw me not as I stole through the thick fog, and the bold rover who guarded the cellar door died suddenly with only a short squeal, like a struck hog."

Hardraker burst out with a furious oath. "What do you here?"

Malachi Grim regarded him with a stare that was blood-chilling in its bleak certitude of doom.

"You know well why I have followed you from the Main to this shore," Grim's voice was toneless, but deep feeling hummed behind it. "John Ord was my comrade, since we were boys together. He sailed to pound the Dons for the glory of God. But you, you bloody dog, thought only of loot and throat-slitting. So you, whom he trusted, crushed his head as he slept in his bunk, with a traitor's blow of a hatchet. Before dawn every honest man of the crew was overside, a feast for the sharks, and you were running up the Jolly Roger at the masthead, you and the scum John Ord had shipped unwittingly. So you gained a ship for your bloody deeds—but retribution hath dogged thy heels ever since, and hath at last caught up with thee!"

As he spoke his voice rose with the biblical phraseology, and the last sentence was thundered forth like a physical impact. Nothing is more terrible than the sight of a man of icy nerves and iron control suddenly losing that control and flaming into a withering blast of murderous fury. For a fleeting instant Grim was a fearful image of primitive, incarnate passion; then the storm passed and he was himself again—cold as chilled steel, deadly as a cobra.

One black muzzle centered on Hardraker's breast, while the other menaced the rest of the crew.

"Make your peace with God, pirate," said Grim tonelessly.

For the first time Hardraker blenched. "Great God," he gasped, paling. "You'd not shoot me down like a dog?"

"That will I, Jonas Hardraker, and with a joyous heart," answered Grim. "Are you not a stench in the nostrils of God, and a black smirch on the books of mankind? Shrink you from your doom, you black coward?"

With an effort the pirate pulled himself together.

"Why, I shrink not. But it is you who are the coward."

The cold eyes clouded momentarily. Grim seemed to retreat within himself, to withdraw himself still further from human contact. He poised there on the stairs like some brooding unhuman thing—like a great black condor, somber with terrible potentialities.

"You are a coward," continued the pirate recklessly, realizing that he had touched the one weak spot in Grim's armor—vanity. "If you give me no chance to defend myself, men will name you poltroon."

"Praise or blame of man is vanity," said Grim somberly. "Men know I am no coward."

"But not I!" shouted Hardraker triumphantly. "An you shoot me down I'll go into hell knowing you are a dastard! And my men will know!"

Grim started as if stung—his finger trembled on the trigger. Then he said shortly, "Name your weapons."

Hardraker grinned wolfishly. "Knives!" his strong white teeth snapped viciously as he said it.

Grim turned his gaze to the crew. "Throw down your weapons." Sullenly they obeyed. "Now loose the girl and the lad." This was also done, and Holland stretched his numbed limbs, felt the cut in his scalp, now clotted dried blood, and took the frightened Ellen in his arms.

"Let the girl go," he whispered, but Grim shook his head.

"She could never get by guards outside the house."

He motioned Holland to stand part way up the stairs, with Ellen behind him. He gave Jack the pistols and swiftly undid his sword belt and cloak, laying them on the lower step. "Watch them all," he muttered. "I'll take care of the Fishhawk. If any other reaches for a weapon, shoot quick and straight. If I fall, flee up the stairs with the girl. But my brain is afire with the blue flame of vengeance, and I shall not fall!"

The two men now approached each other, the pirate armed with a long Turkish dagger, held point upward, Grim with his dirk, which he gripped like a rapier. It was a strange nightmare scene that was lighted by the guttering lanthorn swinging from the beam; the pale youth with his pistols on the stone stair with the shrinking girl behind him, the fierce hairy faces ringed about the walls, eyes glittering—the gleam on the dull blue blades—the tall figures in the center circling each other while their shadows changed and shifted, keeping pace with their motions.

"Come in and fight, Broadbrim," taunted the pirate, yet giving ground.

"I am coming, offal," said Grim somberly. "There be many fires, scum,"—how deadly blue the blades shimmered in the lanthorn light!—"But, save the fires of hell, all fires may be quenched by—*blood!*"

He struck as a wolf leaps. Hardraker parried the thrust and, springing in, struck upward. Grim's downturned point deflected the blade and with a dynamic coil and release of steel-spring muscles, the pirate bounded backward out of reach. Grim came on in a relentless surge, thrusting like lightning for face and body, and for an instant the pirate was too busy parrying the strokes to launch a counterattack.

This could not last; a knife fight is necessarily short and deadly. The nature of the weapons prevents any long-drawn play of fencing skill. Now Hardraker suddenly caught Grim's knife-wrist and at the same time ripped savagely for the belly. Grim, at the cost of a badly cut hand, caught the uplunging wrist and checked the point an inch from his body. There for an instant they stood like statues, glaring into each others' eyes.

Grim had shifted his grip on his dirk to suit the emergency. At first grips, Hardraker had forced his knife hand upward. Now he held his dirk poised above the pirate's breast, point downward. The Fishhawk's knife-hand was held low, point upward; he sought to strain against Grim's arresting left hand and braced arm, until he could rip open the wanderer's belly.

So there they strained, man to man, until the muscles stood out in tortured knots all over them, and sweat beaded their foreheads. The veins swelled in Hardraker's temples. In the watching ring breath hissed sharply between clenched teeth.

Slowly but surely Grim began to force Hardraker backward. The locked hands of the men did not change in their relative positions, but the pirate's whole body began to sway. His thin lips split in a ghastly grin of superhuman effort, like a grinning skull, in which there was no mirth. He bent like a tree whose roots are ripped up and which falls slowly. His breath hissed and whistled, as back and down he went, inch by inch, until his back was pressed hard against an oaken tabletop.

Hardraker's right hand still gripped his dagger; his left hand was still locked on Grim's right wrist. Now Grim, holding the dagger at bay with his left, began to force his own knife-hand downward, inch by inch. The veins stood out in blue cords on his temples; the muscles swelled and coiled like tortured steel cables in the pirate's slowly bending left arm, but slowly the dirk descended. From Hardraker's slavering lips burst a terrible scream. He dropped his dagger, seeking to tear loose his right hand from that vise-like grip. Grim's hand lurched downward—the dirk point sank into the breast. On the stairs Ellen Garvin turned away, pressing her face against the dank wall to shut out sight—covered her ears to shut out sound.

Hardraker's screams were not the cries of a coward afraid of the dark, but the blind unconscious howling of a man in his death agony. He did not release his grip on his slayer's wrist, holding death at bay to the bitter end. As Grim had forced the point to his breast, so he forced it through his heart—inch by inch. Until death and a gush of crimson choked the shrieks and loosed the knotted thews.

Silence lay like a white shroud over all. Grim wrenched his dirk clear and a thin trickle of seeping blood followed sluggishly, then ceased. He swished the blade through the air to shake off the clinging red drops, and as it flashed in the lanthorn light, it seemed to Jack Holland to glitter like a blue flame—a flame quenched in scarlet.

Grim reached for his rapier. At that instant Holland saw the man Sam stealthily lift a pistol and aim it at Grim. Sight and action was as one. At the crash of Holland's shot Sam screamed and reared upright, his pistol exploding in the air. As he flung out his arms in his death throes, the pistol barrel struck the lanthorn and shattered it, plunging the cellar into sudden blackness.

Instantly the darkness crashed into sound, strident and blasphemous. Kegs toppled, men fell over each other and swore soulfully, steel clashed and pistols cracked as men found them with groping hands and fired at random. Somebody howled profanely as one of these blind bullets found a mark. Holland had the girl by the arm and was half leading, half carrying her up the dark stairs. He slipped and stumbled, but eventually reached the head of the steps, and flung open the heavy door. A faint light which this opening let in showed him a man just behind him, and a dim flood of figures scrambling blasphemously up the lower steps. He swung round the other pistol, when Grim's voice spoke.

"'Tis I—Grim. Out swiftly with the lass!"

Holland obeyed and Grim, leaping out after him, slammed the oaken door in the faces of the yelling horde which surged up from below. He dropped a strong bolt in place and stepped back. From inside sounded muffled yells, hammerings and shots, and in places the wood of the door bulged and splintered outward as bullets chunked into the other side.

"And now what?" Holland turned to the tall buccaneer, noting a bizarre figure that lay at his feet—a dead pirate with earrings and sash, whose sword and musket lay beside him. Undoubtedly the sentry whose watch Grim's silent sword had ended.

The buccaneer casually shoved the corpse aside with his foot and motioned for his companions to follow him. He led the way up a short flight of wooden steps, down a dark hallway and into a dim oak-paneled chamber where a candle burned on a table.

"There are guards without," he said, "some five or six men. I slipped between them as I came, but now I think the moon is out and we must be wary. We are safe from those in the cellar, at present. I will look through an outer window, and see if I can spy those who watch outside."

Left alone in the chamber Holland looked at Ellen with love and pity. It had indeed been a hectic night for a girl unused to violence. Her dilated eyes were almost starting from her head, and she spoke stammeringly as she mechanically arranged her rumpled garments and tousled hair.

"Oh, Jack, whatever shall we do? This is a judgment sent on us, I know, because I've yearned for excitement betimes. Oh, yes, I have, Jack, and wish I'd been birched for it. If we ever get safely home again—*ohhhh!*"

Her pink mouth flew wide to emit a piercing scream. Simultaneously came the scrape of a rusty bolt.

Holland wheeled. A black opening gaped in the wall where formerly had stood only one of the regular panels. In it stood Sir George Blanard, eyes blazing, garments disheveled, pistol leveled.

Holland flung Ellen aside and threw up his weapon. The two shots crashed together. Holland felt the bullet cut the skin on his ear like a white-hot razor-edge. A bit of cloth flew from Sir George's shirt-bosom, and with a sobbing curse he went down. Then as Holland turned back to the horrified girl, Blanard reeled up again. He was drinking in the air with great gasps as if his breath had been driven out of him, but he did not seem hurt, and no spot of blood showed on his garments.

Frozen with amazement—for he knew the ball had struck squarely—Holland stood gaping, the smoking pistol dangling in his fingers, until Sir George knocked him sprawling with a hard buffet of his fist. Then as he sprang up again, raging, Blanard snatched the girl and, dragging her in a brutal grip, leaped back through the opening with her. The secret panel slammed shut, and her pitiful lamentations muffled and ceased. Malachi Grim, returning as fast as his long legs could carry him, found Holland raving and bruising his bare fists against a blank wall.

A few gasping words, interlarded with wild blasphemies and scorching self-reproaches, gave Grim the key to the situation.

"The hand of Satan is over him! Full in the breast I shot him, yet he took no hurt! Oh, fool and drooling imbecile that I am—I stood there like a graven image, while he—"

"I might have known this den would have secret ways," snapped Malachi. "Of course this doorway lets into a tunnel leading to the cellar. Stay!" as Holland would have attacked the panel with the dead seaman's cutlass which Grim had brought. "Even if we got into the cellar, they will shoot us like rabbits, and the girl will be no better off for our folly.

"You saw that dark opening in the end of the cellar? It must be a tunnel which leads to the rocks along the seashore. Blanard has long been in league with smugglers and pirates. Spies have never seen any bundles or bales carried into the house or out, therefore it follows that there needs must be a tunnel connecting cellar with sea. Therefore, it likewise follows that these rogues, with Sir George who can never bide in England after this night, will run through the tunnel and take to ship. We will go across the beach and meet them as they emerge."

"Then in God's name let us hasten!" begged Holland. "Once on that hellish craft we can never get Ellen again!"

"Your wound bleeds again," muttered Grim with a worried glance.

"No matter; on, for God's sake!"

Chapter .5.

Holland followed Grim out of the silent house. The fog had faded and the moon was clear, showing the black rocks across the beach, and beyond them the long evil-looking ship riding at anchor outside the foam line of the breakers. There were no guards outside the house. Whether they took alarm at the noise inside and fled, there was no knowing. But the companions saw no one. Along the beach the Rocks rose black and sinister, like jagged dark houses, hiding whatever was going on in the sand at the water's edge.

Recklessly they raced across the barren level. Grim showed no signs that he had just gone through a terrible grueling grind of life and death. He might have been made of steel springs. But Holland reeled as he ran, dizzy from exertion, excitement and loss of blood.

As they approached the Rocks, the sound of fierce voices instilled caution in their movements. Holland, almost in delirium, was for leaping across the barriers and falling on their enemies, but Grim restrained him. Together they crept forward and, lying flat on their bellies on a jutting ledge, they looked down.

The clear moonlight showed them that the pirates on board the ship were preparing to weigh anchor.

On the sand below stood a small group of men, their blades flashing in the moonlight. Already a longboat full of rogues was pulling away to the ship, while another boat crew rested impatiently on their oars, while their leaders argued out a question on shore. Evidently the flight through the tunnel had been made with no loss of time. Had not Sir George halted to seize the girl, in which act luck had been incredibly with him, all the rogues would have been aboard ship. The watchers could see the small cave, revealed by the rolling back of a large boulder, which was the mouth of the tunnel.

Sir George and Jem Allardyne stood facing each other in hot debate. Ellen, bound hand and foot, lay at their feet. At the sight Holland made to rise, but Grim's iron grip withheld him.

"I take the girl aboard!" rose Blanard's angry voice.

"And I say *no!*" came Allardyne's answering rasp. "No good'll come of it! Women stirs up trouble and strife between men—maybe Hardraker could have managed 'em, but I can't, nor you either. And he's layin' in his blood in yon cellar. Bring that wench aboard and we'll have a dozen gullets slit afore sunrise. Cut her throat here, I says, and—"

He reached for the girl. Sir George struck aside his hand and drew his rapier, but Holland did not see that. Throwing aside Grim's restraining hand, he leaped recklessly from the ledge. At the sight the pirates in the boat raised a shout, and evidently thinking themselves to be attacked by a larger party, laid to their oars, leaving their mate and patron to shift for themselves.

Holland, striking feet first in the soft sand, went to his knees from the impact, but bounding up, his cutlass flamed in the moonlight. Allardyne went down with his skull cleft, and Sir George parried Holland's second ferocious slash.

A cutlass is clumsy and not suited for fencing—no weapon to match a rapier in a skilled hand. Still, for a few seconds Holland kept the nobleman on the defensive by the sheer fury of his desperate onslaught; then, in spite of his raging hate, he began to weaken. Blanard, a cold smile on his dark face, touched him again and again, on cheek, breast and leg, not deep wounds, but stinging scratches which, bleeding, inexorably drained his strength.

Judging the time had come, Sir George feinted swiftly, started his finishing thrust. His foot slipped in the shifty sand, he lost balance, lunged wildly, leaving himself wide open. Holland, seeing this dimly through blood-blinded eyes, sprang in with one last desperate effort, striking with all his waning power. The keen edge crunched against Blanard's side, but instead of cleaving through his ribs, the blade shivered like glass. Holland reeled back, dazed, the useless hilt falling from his nerveless hand.

Sir George recovered himself and thrust with a mad cry of triumph. But even as the point sang toward Holland's defenseless heart, a great shadow fell between, and Blanard's hissing blade was brushed aside.

Holland, crawling away like a snake with a broken back, saw Malachi Grim looming like a black cloud over Sir George Blanard, while the buccaneer's long rapier, inexorable as doom, forced the nobleman to break ground.

In the light of the moon which frosted the long quick blades with silver, Holland watched that fight as he leaned over the fainting girl and tried with fumbling hands to loosen her bonds. He had heard of Malachi Grim's swordplay. Now, born sword-lover that he was, he found himself wishing Grim faced a more worthy foe.

For though Sir George had a reputation as a deadly duelist, Grim merely toyed with him. With a great advantage in height, weight, strength and reach, Grim had yet the advantages of speed and skill. He fought with an economy of motion and lack of heat which robbed his play of some brilliance—he made no wide spectacular parries or long breathtaking lunges. But every motion he made was the right one; he was never at a loss, never excited—a combination of ice and steel. On the Continent, Holland had seen more flashy fencers than Grim, but he realized as he watched that he had never seen one who was as technically perfect, nor as instinctively the swordsman—a matter beyond the mere perfection of technique.

It seemed to him that Grim could have transfixed his adversary at the first pass, but such was not the buccaneer's intention. As he kept the nobleman on the defensive he talked in a passionless tone, never losing the play for an instant, as if tongue and arm worked far apart.

"No, no, young sir, you need not leave your breast open. I saw Jack's blade shatter on your side, and I will not risk my steel, strong and pliant as it is. Well, I have worn steel mail under my shirt also, at times, though methinks 'twas scarce as strong as yours, to so turn a bullet at close range. However, the Lord in his infinite justice and mercy hath so fashioned man that his vitals be not all locked up in his brisket. Would you were handier with the steel, Sir George. I take shame in slaying you—but when a man sets foot on an adder, he asks not its size or age."

These words were delivered in a serious and sincere manner, not in a sardonic fashion, and Holland knew that Grim did not mean them as taunts. Sir George was white faced; now his hue grew ashy under the moon. His arm ached with weariness and was heavy as lead; still this great devil in black pressed without stay.

Suddenly Grim's brow clouded, as if he had an unpleasant task to do and would do it quickly.

"Enough!" he cried in his deep vibrant voice which thrilled and chilled his hearers. "This is an ill deed—let it be done quickly!"

What followed was too quick for the eye to analyze. Holland caught a flashing hint of a feint—a sudden blinding flurry of bright steel—Sir George Blanard lay dead at Malachi Grim's feet without twitching. A slight trickle of blood seeped from the side of his head.

"Through the temple and into the brain," said Grim moodily, cleansing his point on which shone a single drop of blood. "He knew not what took him and died without pain. God grant all our deaths be as easy. But my heart is heavy within me, for he was little more than a youth, albeit an evil one, and not my equal with the steel. Well, the Lord judge between him and me on Judgment Day."

Ellen, coming out of her swoon, whimpered in Holland's arms. A strange glow was spreading over the land, and a peculiar crackling came to their ears.

"Satan! The house burns!"

Flames leaped from the black roof of the Blanard manor house. The departing pirates must have set a blaze, and now it sprang into full fury, dimming the moon. The sea shimmered gorily in the scarlet glare and the pirate ship, beating out to open sea, seemed to ride in a sea of blood, her sails redly reflecting the glow.

"She sails in an ocean of blood and her sails are bright with gore!" cried Grim, like an ancient prophet. "Death and destruction follow her and hell cometh after! Red be her ruin and black her doom!"

Then with a sudden change in mood, he bent over Holland and the girl.

"I would bide and dress your wounds, lad," said he, "but methinks they are not serious, and I hear the rattle of many hoofs across the moors. Doubtless men come to investigate the fire, and your friends will soon be about you—"

"But you?" cried Ellen, rising to her knees, and seeking to catch his hand.

"Verily, a man's mistakes follow him to the ends of the earth," he replied with the suggestion of a sigh. "My way hath sometimes lain over ungodly paths and amongst sinful companions. 'Twere better that I go quietly now before yonder folk arrive—among which may be king's officers and magistrates and suchlike inquisitive vermin, so—"

"But who are you? Whence come you? Whither do you go?"

"I am a landless man," an almost mystic look flashed in the cold eyes. "I come out of the sunset, and into the sunrise I go. I seek—my soul's salvation, mayhap. My work here is done; the man of blood is dead. But there be other evil men encumbering the good green earth. I work the will of God, and for such as work that will, there is no rest nor peace. Farewell!"

"Wait!" cried Ellen, reaching out her white arms.

But the tall form had vanished in the darkness and no sound came back of his going.

Buccaneer Treasure

(Line breaks added by the editor.)

This is a story that I heard from the lips
    of a drunken tramp
Down by the wharfs in Mike's saloon,
    in the light of the smoky lamp.
From his tousled hair his strange eyes stared,
    glimmering, shot with blood;
His rags hung loose and his tattered shoes were caked
    with the wharfside mud.

With his twitching hands and his rasping laugh
    he gazed like an idol grim
With a drunken leer o'er the stein of beer
    that I had bought for him.
"Look here," said he, "I'll tell ye a tale —
    a story strange, d'ye hear?
"No man has heard it from me before —
    I've held it many a year.

"Some twenty years ago it was,
    I found myself a-float
"From the shattered deck of a fog-bound wreck —
    at sea in a sailless boat.
"Me and the mate — the other boats
    they lost us in the fog.
"Still was the day and dim and grey,
    the sea like curdled grog.

"The silence shuddered o'er the waves,
we scarcely dared to speak.
"We might have rowed for half a day —
it might have been a week.
"The mate had got the water-keg
and kept it to his hand,
"A pistol resting on his knee
to keep him in command.

"He sat unmoving in the bows,
his gaze an insane stare.
"At first he'd let me have a drink
and then he wouldn't share.
"I rowed until my strength gave out
and as he sat he slept;
"I shipped the oars; each second he dozed,
closer to him I crept.

"My thirst was like a raging fiend;
I leaped with lifted knife;
"He woke — his pistol grabbed —
too late; my dagger drank his life.
"I seized the keg — gods! it was good! —
I guzzled long and deep,
"Then flung my victim overside,
lay down and fell asleep.

"I might have slept for half a day,
I might have slept a year,
"But when I woke the fog had broke,
the sea was sapphire clear.
"The sea was clear and strange to see.
it lay like a girl asleep.
"Though strange it be yet I could see
uncounted fathoms deep.

"As I were mazed I lay and gazed
through emerald depths untold.
"The eastern sky was rosy red,
the sun was rising gold.
"The lazy waves they swung the bow
with a gentle sway and lift.
"I laid the oars across the thwarts
and the boat I let it drift.

"I watched and saw strange shadows stray
for fathoms down below;
"Like shimmery, gossamer things of dreams
I watched them come and go.
"And then sometimes, like fairy chimes
or a golden Chinese gong,
"Strange music echoed across the sea
like tones of a wordless song.

"Through the golden day as mazed I lay,
like jade without a flaw,
"The sea lay clear to my wondering eyes
and strange were the sights I saw.
"I gazed on wonders of ages gone
as my boat went drifting o'er
Gem-set towers and strange sea flowers
a-bloom on the ocean floor.

"Galleys of cities long forgot,
dragon-ships and triremes;
"Beneath the bows of my drifting boat
they glided like hazy dreams.
"Spires and castles swam into view,
lost cities met my glance,
"And ever the shadows swayed and fled
like things of a deep sea dance.

"At last I saw them plain and clear
    and I swear I do not lie!
"The shadows were mermaids, that I saw,
    beautiful, swift and shy.
"Their hair was wavy and long and gold,
    their bodies whiter than snow;
"Through the wondrous sheen of the ocean green
    they sported to and fro.

"The sun was close to the western sea
    when the fairest maid of the mer
"Swam by me, beckoning with her hand,
    and I set my course by her.
"I scarcely needed to touch an oar,
    in a merry laughing throng
"The sea-girls swarmed on every hand
    and hurried my boat along.

"The sun was touching the western sea,
    gold on a sea of blue,
"When riding the green waves motionless,
    a galley loomed to view.
"Barnacles crusted her ancient strakes,
    her tall mast held no sail;
"I found a rusty anchor chain
    and clambered across the rail.

"So ancient was she I gaped and gazed
    in wonder, craning my neck;
Skeletons sat at the rotting oars
    and lay on the sun-warped deck.
"A steel-bound chest on the main bridge stood
    and a skeleton lay thereon.
"From the size of the bones he must have been
    a giant of thews and brawn.

"All in and out among his ribs
    the clinging sea moss twined
"And decked the bare, sea-rotting skull
    that once had held a mind.
"Those bones were old as Time itself,
    sun-warped, broken and grey.
"I flung them down upon the deck
    and the chest's lock pried away.

"But I knew by the sword cuts and the marks
    as I flung back the lid
"I had found the treasure that seamen seek,
    the treasure of Captain Kidd!
"Glimmers of diamonds met my eyes,
    rubies that shone like stars;
"Gleam and glitter of virgin gold,
    shimmer of silver bars.

"I thrust my hands in the kingly hoard
    where the doubloons rare lay massed —
"When an icy breath like a thing of Death
    like a shadow whispered past.
"I turned me round, my eyes a-blink,
    half-blind from the treasure shine —
"The short hair prickled at my neck
    and a cold hand touched my spine.

"For I will swear that I saw there
    a sight to cold the blood,
"The skeleton like a living man
    before me rose and stood!
"The fleshless, toothless jawbones moved
    and yet he spoke no word,
"But they upon the deck uprose
    and the bones of the rowers stirred.

"The rotten oars began to creak
 and sway each in its groove,
"The arm bones creaked and bent and swayed —
 the galley began to move!
"The galley leaped like a fleeing deer,
 straight into the west she sped
"As the scarlet sun in a sea of blood
 sank with a blaze of red.

"The crimson waves cleft to her prow
 and in behind her spun.
"And I saw a world of lurid flames
 behind the setting sun.
"In wild amaze I watched them blaze,
 leap up and die and flare
"Beyond the rim of the fiery sea
 like things of a wild nightmare.

"No worldly fires could fling such flame
 and I knew what befell--
"As faster and faster the galley sped —
 she was bearing me into Hell!
"Shrieking I hurled me across the rail,
 I clambered into the boat;
"With shaking hands I loosed the chain
 and pushed her far afloat.

"But the galley altered not her pace,
 'twas as she fled the night;
"Marveling there I watched her fly,
 fast dwindling from my sight.
"Till far away like some foul bird
 she stood against the flare,
"Then vanished in the red sunset
 and Hell that waited there.

"The stars came blinking o'er the sea,
slow came a slender moon
"And I found that I clutched in my shaky hand
a tarnished gold doubloon.
"The blue waves barely rocked the boat
beneath the silver moon;
"All night she drifted with the tides
as I lay half in a swoon.

"And sometime 'tween the dusk and dawn,
after the moon had slid
"Across the skyline, there came to me
the ghost of Captain Kidd.
"He wore his pistols and great sea boots
as when he trod the deck,
"But shackles clung to his hairy arms
and the noose was on his neck.

"And he told me how, as a living man,
he had sailed to unknown climes
"And had found that galley upon the sea,
adrift since ancient times.
"And put thereon his chest of loot
and a grisly bargain made
"With Satan himself, and with men's blood
he sealed his part of the trade.

"And Satan guards his servant's gold
with a magic grim and fell
"And none may seize that blood-stained loot
lest they be hurled to Hell.
"From his bearded lips I had the tale,
ere the weary stars had fled
"And he faded like a wisp of smoke
before the dawn broke red.

"How many days my boat did drift,
  I swear I cannot say,
"But I came to upon the deck
  of a trader from Bombay.
"I told them not my weird tale,
  they would have deemed me crazed.
"Indeed I scarce believe myself,
  all was so strange and mazed.

"But sure it was no lunacy,
  no daftness of the moon,
"For in a pocket of my clothes
  I found a gold doubloon.
"For many a year I've sailed the seas
  but nevermore have seen
"That frightful galley all afloat
  upon that sea of green.

"Around the world for twenty years
  I've sailed the driving brine;
"Some day I'll sight that ship again
  and her plunder will be mine.
"I'm weary, worn, bent by toil,
  I've neither wife nor friends,
"But never shall I quit the trails
  that lead to far sea ends.
"That treasure haunts my restless dreams;
  I see the gleaming hoard.
"A tramp? Ha! Ha! Some day I'll live '
  like some blue-blooded lord."

This was the story that he told,
 that drunken, strange-eyed tramp,
And as he finished, a thing that gleamed
 in the light of the smoky lamp
He laid upon the drink-stained bar.
 Before each curious stare
A glittering thing of Spanish gold,
 a doubloon glinted there

Swords of the Red Brotherhood

Chapter .1.
The Painted Men.

One moment the glade lay empty; the next, a man poised tensely at the edge of the bushes. There had been no sound to warn the red squirrels of his coming, but the gay-hued birds that flitted about in the sunshine of the open space took fright at the apparition and rose in a clamoring cloud. The man scowled and glanced quickly back the way he had come, as if fearing their flight had betrayed his position to some one unseen. Then he started across the glade, placing his feet with care. Tall and muscular of frame, he moved with the supple certitude of a panther.

He was naked except for a rag twisted about his loins, and his limbs were criss-crossed with scratches from briars, and caked with dried mud. A brown-crusted bandage was knotted about his thickly-muscled left arm. Under his matted black mane, his face was drawn and gaunt, and his eyes burned like the eyes of a wounded panther. He limped slightly as he followed the dim path that led across the open space.

Half-way across the glade he stopped short and wheeled, facing back the way he had come, as a long-drawn call quavered out across the forest. It sounded like the howl of a wolf. But he knew it was no wolf.

Rage burned redly in his bloodshot eyes as he turned once more and hurried along the path, which, as it left the glade, ran along the edge of a dense thicket that rose in a solid clump of greenery among the trees and bushes. A massive log, deeply embedded in the grassy earth, paralleled the fringe of the thicket, lying between it and the path. When the man came to this log he halted again and looked back across the glade. To the average eye there were no signs to show that he had passed; but there was evidence of that passing visible to his wilderness-sharpened eyes, and therefore to the equally keen eyes of those who pursued him. He snarled silently, the red rage growing in his eyes—the berserk fury of a hunted beast which is ready to turn at bay—and drew war-axe and hunting knife from the girdle which upheld his loin-clout.

He walked down the trail with comparative carelessness, here and there crushing a grass-blade beneath his foot. Then, when he had reached the further end of the great log, he sprang upon it, turned and ran lightly back along it. The bark had long been worn away by the elements. He left no sign to show the sharpest forest-eyes that he had doubled on his trail. When he reached the densest point of the thicket he faded into it like a shadow, with scarcely the quiver of a leaf to mark his passing.

The minutes dragged. The red squirrels chattered again on the branches—then flattened their bodies and were suddenly mute. Again the glade was invaded. As silently as the first man had appeared, three other men materialized out of the eastern edge of the clearing. They were darkskinned men, naked but for beaded buckskin loin-cloths and moccasins, and they were hideously painted.

They had scanned the glade carefully before showing themselves in the open, for they moved out of the bushes without hesitation, in close single-file, treading softly and bending down to stare at the path. They were following the trail of the white man, but it was no easy task even for these human bloodhounds. They moved slowly across the glade, and then one stiffened, grunted and pointed with a flint-tipped spear at a crushed grass-blade where the path entered the forest again. All halted instantly and their beady black eyes quested the forest walls. But their quarry was well hidden. They saw nothing to tell them that the man they hunted hid within a few yards of them. Presently they moved on again, more rapidly now, following the faint marks that seemed to indicate their prey was growing careless through weakness or desperation.

They had just passed the spot where the thicket crowded closest to the ancient trail when the white man bounded into the path behind them and plunged his knife between the shoulders of the last man. The attack was so quick and unexpected the Indian had no chance to save himself. The blade was in his heart before he knew he was in peril. The other two whirled with the instant, steel-trap quickness of savages, but even as his knife sank home, the white man struck a tremendous blow with the war-axe in his right hand. The second Indian caught the blow just as he was turning, and it split his skull.

The remaining Indian came savagely to the attack. He was stabbing at the white man's breast even as the killer wrenched his axe from the dead man's head. The white man hurled the limp body against the savage and followed it with an attack as furious and desperate as the lunge of a wounded tiger. The Indian, staggering under the impact of the corpse against him, made no attempt to parry the dripping axe. The instinct to slay submerging even the instinct to live, he drove his spear ferociously at his enemy's broad breast. The white man had the advantage of a quicker mind, and a weapon in each hand. The hatchet, checking its downward sweep, struck the spear aside, and the knife in the brawny left hand ripped upward into the painted belly.

A frightful howl burst from the Indian's lips as he crumpled, disembowelled—a cry not of fear or pain, but of baffled, bestial fury, the death-screech of a panther. It was answered by a while chorus of yells some distance east of the glade. The white man started convulsively, wheeled, crouching like a wild thing at bay, lips asnarl. Blood trickled down his forearm from under the bandage.

With an incoherent imprecation he turned and fled westward. He did not pick his way now, but ran with all the speed of his long legs. Behind him for a space the woods were silent, than a demoniacal howling burst out on the spot he had just quitted. His pursuers had found the bodies of his victims. He had no breath for cursing the blood drops that kept spilling to the ground from his freshly-opened wound, leaving a trail a child could follow. He had thought that possibly these three Indians were all that still pursued him of the war-party which had followed him for so far. But he might have known these human wolves never quit a blood-trail.

The woods were silent again, and that meant they were racing after him, marking his path by the betraying blood drops he could not check. A wind out of the west blew against his face, laden with salty dampness. Dully he was surprized. If he was that close to the sea the long chase had been even longer than he had realized. But it was nearly over. Even his wolfish vitality was ebbing under the terrific strain. He gasped for breath and there was a sharp pain in his side. His legs trembled with weariness and the lame one ached like the cut of a knife in the tendons each time he set the foot to earth. He had followed the instincts of the wilderness which bred him, straining every nerve and sinew, exhausting every subtlety and artifice to survive. Now in his extremity he was obeying another instinct, looking for a place to turn at bay and sell his life at a bloody price.

He did not leave the trail for the tangled depths on either hand. He knew that it was futile to hope to evade his pursuers now. He ran on down the trail while the blood pounded louder and louder in his ears and each breath he drew was a racking, dry-lipped gulp. Behind him a mad baying broke out, token that they were close on his heels and expected to overhaul their prey swiftly. They would come as fleet as starving wolves now, howling at every leap.

Abruptly he burst from the denseness of the trees and saw, ahead of him, the ground pitching upward, and the ancient trail winding up rocky ledges between jagged boulders. All swam before him in a dizzy red mist, but it was a hill he had come to, a rugged crag rising sheer from the forest about its foot. And the dim trail wound up to a broad ledge near the summit.

That ledge would be as good a place as any to die. He limped up the trail, going on hands and knees in the steeper places, his knife between his teeth. He had not yet reached the jutting ledge when some forty painted savages broke from among the trees.

Their screams rose to a devil's crescendo as they raced toward the foot of the crag, loosing arrows as they came. The shafts showered about the man who doggedly climbed upward, and one stuck in the calf of his leg. Without pausing in his climb, he tore it out and threw it aside, heedless of the less accurate missiles which splintered on the rocks about him. Grimly he hauled himself over the rim of the ledge, and turned about, drawing his hatchet and shifting knife to hand. He lay glaring down at his pursuers over the rim, only his shock of hair and his blazing eyes visible. His great chest heaved as he drank in the air in great shuddering gasps, and he clenched his teeth against a tendency toward nausea.

The warriors came on, leaping agilely over the rocks at the foot of the hill, some changing bows for war-axes. The first to reach the crag was a brawny chief with an eaglefeather in his braided hair. He halted briefly, one foot on the sloping trail, arrow notched and drawn half-way back, head thrown back and lips parted for a yell. But the shaft was never loosed. He froze into statuesque immobility, and the bloodlust in his black eyes gave way to a glare of startled recognition. With a whoop he recoiled, throwing his arms wide to check the rush of his howling braves. The man crouching on the ledge above them understood their tongue, but he was too high above them to catch the significance of the staccato phrases snapped at the warriors by the eagle-feathered chief.

But all ceased their yelping and stood mutely staring up—not at the man on the ledge, but at the hill itself. Then without further hesitation, they unstrung their bows and thrust them into buckskin cases beside their quivers; turned their backs and trotted across the open space, to melt into the forest without a backward look.

The white man glared after them in amazement, recognizing the finality expressed in the departure. He knew they would not come back. They were heading for their village, a hundred miles to the east.

But it was inexplicable. What was there about his refuge that would cause a red war-party to abandon a chase it had followed so long with all the passion of hungry wolves? There was a red score between him and them. He had been their prisoner, and he had escaped, and in that escape a famous war-chief had died. That was why the braves had followed him so relentlessly, over broad rivers and mountains and through long leagues of gloomy forest, the hunting grounds of hostile tribes. And now the survivors of that long chase turned back when their enemy was run to earth and trapped. He shook his head, abandoning the riddle.

He rose gingerly, dizzy from the long grind, and scarcely able to realize that it was over. His limbs were stiff, his wounds ached. He spat dryly and cursed, rubbing his burning, bloodshot eyes with the back of his thick wrist. He blinked and took stock of his surroundings. Below him the green wilderness waved and billowed away and away in a solid mass, and above its western rim rose a steel-blue haze he knew hung over the ocean. The wind stirred his black mane, and the salt tang of the atmosphere revived him. He expanded his enormous chest and drank it in.

Then he turned stiffly and painfully about, growling at the twinge in his bleeding calf, and investigated the ledge whereon he stood. Behind it rose a sheer rocky cliff to the crest of the crag, some thirty feet above him. A narrow ladder-like stair of hand-holds had been niched into the rock. And a few feet from its foot there was a cleft in the wall, wide enough and tall enough to admit a man.

He limped to the cleft, peered in, and grunted explosively. The sun, hanging high above the western forest, slanted into the cleft, revealing a tunnel-like cavern beyond, and rested a revealing beam on the arch at which this tunnel ended. In that arch was set a heavy iron-bound oaken door!

This was astounding. This country was howling wilderness. The white man knew that for a thousand miles this coast ran bare and uninhabited except for the squalid villages of fish-eating tribes, who were even lower in the scale of life than their forest-dwelling brothers. The white man had thought it probable that he was the first man of his color ever to set foot in that particular region. Yet there stood that mysterious door, mute evidence of European civilization.

Being inexplicable, it was an object of suspicion, and suspiciously he approached it, axe and knife ready. Then as his bloodshot eyes became more accustomed to the soft gloom that lurked on either side of the narrow shaft of sunlight, he noticed something else—thick iron-bound chests ranged along the walls. A blaze of comprehension came into his eyes. He bent over one, but the lid resisted his efforts. He lifted his hatchet to shatter the ancient lock, then changed his mind and limped toward the arched door. His bearing was more confident now, his weapons hung at his sides. He pushed against the ornately-carven door and it swung inward without resistance.

Then his manner changed again, with lightning-like abruptness; he recoiled with a startled curse, knife and hatchet flashing to positions of defense. He poised there like a statue of menace, craning his massive neck to glare through the door. It was darker in the large natural chamber into which he was looking, but a dim glow emanated from a shining heap in the center of the great ebony table about which sat those silent shapes whose appearance had so startled the intruder.

They did not move; they did not turn their heads.

"Are you all drunk?" he demanded harshly.

There was no reply. He was a man not easily abashed, yet now he felt disconcerted.

"You might offer me a glass of that wine you're swigging," he growled. "By Satan, you show poor courtesy to a man who's been one of your own brotherhood. Are you going to—" His voice trailed off into silence, and in silence he stood and stared awhile at those fantastic figures sitting so silently and still about the great ebon table.

"They're not drunk," he muttered presently. "They're not even drinking. What devil's game is this?"

He stepped across the threshold and was instantly fighting for his life against the murderous, unseen fingers that clutched so suddenly at his throat.

Chapter .2.
Men From the Sea.

And on the beach, not many miles from the cavern where silent figures sat, shadows were gathering over the tangled lives of men . . .

Francoise d'Chastillon idly stirred a sea-shell with a daintily slippered toe, comparing its delicate pink edges to the first pink haze of dawn that rose over the misty beaches. It was not dawn now, but the sun was not long up, and the light, pearl-grey clouds which drifted over the waters had not yet been dispelled.

Francoise lifted her splendidly shaped head and stared out over a scene alien and repellent to her, yet drearily familiar in every detail. From her feet the tawny sands ran to meet the softly lapping waves which stretched westward to be lost in the blue haze of the horizon. She was standing on the southern curve of the bay, and south of her the land sloped upward to the low ridge which formed one horn of that bay. From that ridge, she knew, one could look southward across the bare waters—into infinities of distance as absolute as the view to west and north.

Turning landward she absently scanned the fortress which had been her home for the past year. Against the pearl and cerulean sky floated the golden and scarlet banner of her house. She made out the figures of men toiling in the gardens and fields that huddled near the fort, seeming to shrink from the gloomy rampart of the forest which fringed the open belt on the east, stretching north and south as far as she could see. Beyond it, to the east, loomed a great mountain range that shut off the coast from the continent that lay behind it. Francoise feared that mountain-flanked forest, and her fear was shared by every one in the tiny settlement. Death lurked in those whispering depths, death swift and terrible, death slow and hideous, hidden, painted, tireless.

She sighed and moved listlessly toward the water's edge. The dragging days were all one color, and the world of cities and courts and gaiety seemed not only thousands of miles, but long ages away. Again she sought in vain for the reason that had caused a Count of

France to flee with his retainers to this wild coast, exchanging the castle of his ancestors for a hut of logs.

Her eyes softened at the light patter of small bare feet across the sands. A young girl came running over the low sandy ridge, quite naked, her slight body dripping, and her flaxen hair plastered wetly on her small head. Her wistful eyes were wide with excitement.

"Oh, my Lady!" she cried. "My Lady!"

Breathless from her scamper, she made incoherent gestures. Francoise smiled and put an arm about the child. In her lonely life Francoise bestowed the tenderness of a naturally affectionate nature on the pitiful waif she had picked up in the French port from which the long voyage had begun.

"What are you trying to tell me, Tina? Get your breath, child."

"A ship!" cried the girl, pointing southward. "I was swimming in a pool the sea had hollowed in the sand, on the other side of the ridge, and I saw it! A ship sailing up out of the south!"

She tugged at Francoise's hand, her slender body all a-quiver. And Francoise felt her own heart beat faster at the thought of an unknown visitor. They had seen no sail since coming to that barren shore.

Tina flitted ahead of her over the yellow sands. They mounted the low, undulating ridge, and Tina poised there, a slender white figure against the clearing sky, her wet hair blowing about her thin face, a frail arm outstretched.

"Look, my Lady!"

Francoise had already seen it—a white sail, filled with the freshening wind, beating up along the coast, a few miles from the point. Her heart skipped a beat. A small event can loom large in colorless and isolated lives; but Francoise felt a premonition of evil. She felt that it was not by chance that this sail was beating up this lonely coast. The nearest port was Panama, thousands of miles to the south. What brought this stranger to lonely d'Chastillon Bay?

Tina pressed close to her mistress, apprehension pinching her thin features.

"Who can it be, my Lady?" she stammered, the wind whipping color into her pale cheeks. "Is it the man the Count fears?"

Francoise looked down at her, her brow shadowed.

"Why do you say that, child? How do you know my uncle fears anyone?"

"He must," returned Tina naively, "or he would never have come to hide in this lonely spot. Look, my Lady, how fast it comes!"

"We must go and inform my uncle," murmured Francoise. "Get your clothes, Tina. Hurry!"

The child scampered down the low slope to the pool where she had been bathing when she sighted the craft, and snatched up the slippers, stockings and dress she had left lying on the sand. She skipped back up the ridge, hopping grotesquely as she donned them in mid-flight.

Francoise, anxiously watching the approaching sail, caught her hand and they hurried toward the fort. A few moments after they had entered the gate of the log stockade which enclosed the building, the strident blare of a bugle startled the workers in the gardens, and the men just opening the boat-house doors to push the fishing boats down their rollers to the water's edge.

Every man outside the fort dropped whatever he was doing and ran for the stockade, and every head was twisted over its shoulder to gaze fearfully at the dark line of woodland to the east. Not one looked seaward.

They thronged through the gate, shouting questions at the sentries who patrolled the firing-ledges built below the points of the upright logs.

"What is it? Why are we called in? Are the Indians coming?"

For answer one taciturn man-at-arms pointed southward. From his vantage point the sail was now visible. Men climbed on the ledge, staring toward the sea.

On a small lookout tower on the roof of the fort, Count Henri d'Chastillon watched the onsweeping sail as it rounded the point of the southern horn. The Count was a lean man of late middle age. He was dark, somber of countenance. Trunk-hose and doublet were of black silk, the only color about his costume was the jewels that twinkled on his sword hilt, and the wine-colored cloak thrown carelessly over his shoulder. He twisted his thin black mustache nervously and turned gloomy eyes on his major-domo—a leather featured man in steel and satin.

"What do you make of it, Gallot?"

"I have seen that ship before," answered the major domo. "Nay, I think—*look there!*"

A chorus of cries below them echoed his ejaculation; the ship had cleared the point and was slanting inward across the bay. And all saw the flag that suddenly broke forth from the masthead—a black flag, with white skull and cross-bones gleaming in the sun.

"A cursed pirate!" exclaimed Gallot. "Aye, I know that craft! It is Harston's *War-Hawk*. What is he doing on this naked coast?"

"He means us no good," growled the Count. The massive gates had been closed and the captain of his menat-arms, gleaming in steel, was directing his men to their stations, some to the firing-ledge, others to the lower loopholes. He was massing his main strength along the western wall, in the midst of which was the gate.

A hundred men shared Count Henri's exile, soldiers and retainers. There were forty of the soldiers, veteran mercenaries, wearing armor and skilled in the use of sword and arquebus. The others, house-servants and laborers, wore shirts of toughened leather, and were armed mostly with hunting bows, woodsmen's axes and boar-spears. Brawny stalwarts, they took their places scowling at the oncoming vessel, as it swung inshore, its brass work flashing in the sun. They could see steel twinkling along the rail, and hear the shouts of the seamen.

The Count had left the tower, and having donned helmet and cuirass, he betook himself to the palisade. The women of the retainers stood silently in the doorways of their huts, built inside the stockade, and quieted the clamor of their children. Francoise and Tina watched eagerly from an upper window in the fort, and Francoise felt the child's tense little body all aquiver within the crook of her protecting arm.

"They will cast anchor near the boat-house," murmured Francoise. "Yes! There goes their anchor, a hundred yards off-shore. Do not tremble so, child! They can not take the fort. Perhaps they wish only fresh water and meat."

"They are coming ashore in long boats!" exclaimed the child. "Oh, my Lady, I am afraid! How the sun strikes fire from their pikes and cutlasses! Will they eat us?"

Francoise burst into laughter in spite of her apprehension.

"Of course not! Who put that idea into your head?"

"Jacques Piriou told me the English eat women."

"He was teasing you. The English are cruel, but they are no worse than the Frenchmen who call themselves buccaneers. Piriou was one of them."

"He was cruel," muttered the child. "I'm glad the Indians cut his head off."

"Hush, child." Francoise shuddered. "Look, they have reached the shore. They line the beach and one of them is coming toward the fort. That must be Harston."

"Ahoy, the fort there!" came a hail in a voice as gusty as the wind. "I come under a flag of truce!"

The Count's helmeted head appeared over the points of the palisade and surveyed the pirate somberly. Harston had halted just within good ear-shot. He was a big man, bare-headed, his tawny hair blowing in the wind.

"Speak!" commanded Henri. "I have few words for men of your breed!"

Harston laughed with his lips, not with his eyes.

"I never thought to meet you on this naked coast, d'Chastillon," said he. "By Satan, I got the start of my life a little while ago when I saw your scarlet falcon floating over a fortress where I'd thought to see only bare beach. You've found it, of course?"

"Found what?" snapped the Count impatiently.

"Don't try to dissemble with me!" The pirate's stormy nature showed itself momentarily. "I know why you came here; I've come for the same reason. Where's your ship?"

"That's none of your affair, sirrah."

"You have none," confidently asserted the pirate. "I see pieces of a galleon's masts in that stockade. Your ship was wrecked! Otherwise you'd sailed away with your plunder long ago."

"What are you talking about, damn you?" yelled the Count. "Am I a pirate to burn and plunder? Even so, what would I loot on this bare coast?"

"That which you came to find," answered the pirate coolly. "The same thing I'm after. I'm easy to deal with— just give me the loot and I'll go my way and leave you in peace."

"You must be mad," snarled Henri. "I came here to find solitude and seclusion, which I enjoyed until you crawled out of the sea, you yellow-headed dog. Begone! I did not ask for a parley, and I weary of this babble."

"When I go I'll leave that hovel in ashes!" roared the pirate in a transport of rage. "For the last time—will you give me the loot in return for your lives? I have you hemmed in here, and a hundred men ready to cut your throats."

For answer the Count made a quick gesture with his hand below the points of the palisade. Instantly a matchlock boomed through a loophole and a lock of yellow hair jumped from Harston's head. The pirate yelled vengefully and ran toward the beach, with bullets knocking up the sand behind him. His men roared and came on like a wave, blades gleaming in the sun.

"Curse you, dog!" raved the Count, felling the offending marksman with an iron-clad fist. "Why did you miss? Ready, men—here they come!"

But Harston had reached his men, checked their headlong rush. The pirates spread out in a long line that overlapped the extremities of the western wall, and advanced warily, firing as they came. The heavy bullets smashed into the stockade, and the defenders returned the fire methodically. The women had herded the children into their huts and now stoically awaited whatever fate the gods had in store for them.

The pirates maintained their wide-spread formation, creeping along and taking advantage of every natural depression and bit of vegetation—which was not much, for the ground had been cleared on all sides of the fort against the threat of Indian raids.

A few bodies lay prone on the sandy earth. But the pirates were quick as cats, always shifting their positions and presenting a constantly moving target, hard to hit with the clumsy matchlocks. Their constant raking fire was a continual menace to the men in the stockade. Still, it was evident that as long as the battle remained an exchange of shots, the advantage must remain with the sheltered Frenchmen.

But down at the boat-house on the shore, men were at work with axes. The Count cursed sulfurously when he saw the havoc they were making among his boats, built laboriously of planks sawn out of solid logs.

"They're making a mantlet, curse them!" he raged. "A sally now, before they complete it—while they're scattered—"

"We'd be no match for them in hand-to-hand fighting," answered Gallot. "We must keep behind our walls."

"Well enough," growled Henri. "If we can keep them outside!"

Presently the intention of the pirates became apparent to all, as a group of some thirty men advanced, pushing before them a great shield made out of the planks from the boats, and the timbers of the boat-house. They had mounted the mantlet on the wheels of an ox-cart they had found, great solid disks of oak, and as they rolled it ponderously before them the defenders had only glimpses of their moving feet.

"Shoot!" yelled Henri, livid. "Stop them before they reach the gate!"

Bullets smashed into the heavy planks, arrows feathered the thick wood harmlessly. A derisive yell answered the volley. The rest of the pirates were closing in, and their bullets were beginning to find the loop-holes. A soldier fell from the ledge, his skull shattered.

"Shoot at their feet!" screamed Henri, and then: "Forty men at the gate with pikes and axes! The rest hold the wall!"

Bullets ripped into the sand beneath the moving breastwork and some found their mark. But, with a deepthroated shout, the mantlet was pushed to the wall, and an iron-tipped boom, thrust through an aperture in the center of the shield, began to thunder on the gate, driven by muscle-knotted arms. The massive gate groaned and staggered, while from the stockade arrows and bullets poured in a steady hail, and some struck home. But the wild men of the sea were afire with fighting lust. With deep shouts they swung the ram, and from all sides the others closed in, braving the weakened fire from the walls.

The Count drew his sword and ran to the gate, cursing like a madman, and a clump of desperate men-atarms closed in behind him, gripping their pikes. In another moment the gate would cave in and they must stop the gap with their living bodies.

Then a new note entered the clamor of the melee. It was a trumpet, blaring stridently from the ship. On the cross-trees a figure waved his arms and gesticulated wildly.

The sound registered on Harston's ears, even as he lent his strength to the swinging ram. Bracing his legs to halt the ram on its backward swing, his great thews standing out as he resisted the surge of the other arms, he turned his head, and listened. Sweat dripped from his face.

"Wait!" he roared. "Wait, damn you! *Listen!*"

In the silence that followed that bull's bellow, the blare of the trumpet was plainly heard, and a voice that yelled something which was unintelligible to the people inside the stockade.

But Harston understood, for his voice was lifted again in profane command. The ram was released, and the mantlet began to recede from the gate.

"Look!" cried Tina at her window. "They are running to the beach! They have abandoned the shield! They are leaping into the boats and rowing for the ship! Oh, my Lady, have we won?"

"I think not!" Francoise was staring seaward. "Look!"

She threw aside the curtains and leaned from the window. Her clear young voice rose above the din, turning men's heads in the direction she pointed. They yelled in amazement as they saw another ship swinging majestically around the southern point. Even as they looked, she broke out the lilies of France.

The pirates were swarming up the sides of their ship, heaving up the anchor. Before the stranger had sailed halfway across the bay, the *War-Hawk* was vanishing around the point of the northern horn.

Chapter .3.
The Coming of the Black Man.

"Out, quick!" snapped the Count, tearing at the bars of the gate. "Destroy that mantlet before these strangers can land!"

"But yonder ship is French!" expostulated Gallot.

"Do as I order!" roared Henri. "My enemies are not all foreigners! Out, dogs, and make kindling of that mantlet!"

Thirty axemen raced down to the beach. They sensed the possibility of peril in the oncoming ship, and there was panic in their haste. The splintering of timbers under their axes came to the ears of the people in the fort, and then the men were racing back across the sands again, as the French ship dropped anchor where the *War-Hawk* had lain.

"Why does the Count close the gate?" wondered Tina. "Is he afraid that the man he fears might be on that ship?"

"What do you mean, Tina?" Francoise demanded uneasily. The Count had never offered a reason for this self-imposed exile. He was not the sort of a man that runs from an enemy, though he had many. But this conviction of Tina's was disquieting, almost uncanny.

The child seemed not to have heard her question.

"The axemen are back in the stockade," she said. "The gate is closed again. The men keep their places on the wall. If that ship was chasing Harston, why did it not pursue him? Look, a man is coming ashore. I see a man in the bow, wrapped in a dark cloak."

The boat grounded, and this man came pacing leisurely up the sands, followed by three others. He was a tall, wiry man, clad in black silk and polished steel.

"Halt!" roared the Count. "I'll parley with your leader, alone!"

The tall stranger removed his morion and made a sweeping bow. His companions halted, drawing their wide cloaks about them, and behind them the sailors leaned on their oars and stared at the palisade.

When he came within easy call of the gate: "Why, surely," said he, "there should be no suspicion between gentlemen in these naked seas!" He spoke French without an accent.

The Count stared at him suspiciously. The stranger was dark, with a lean, predatory face, and a thin black mustache. A bunch of lace was gathered at his throat, and there was lace on his wrists.

"I know you," said Henri slowly. "You are Guillaume Villiers."

Again the stranger bowed. "And none could fail to recognize the red falcon of the d'Chastillons."

"It seems this coast has become the rendezvous of all the rogues of the Spanish Main," growled Henri. "What do you want?"

"Come, come, sir!" remonstrated Villiers. "This is a churlish greeting to one who has just rendered you a service. Was not that English dog, Harston, thundering at your gate? And did he not take to his sea-heels when he saw me round the point?"

"True," conceded the Count grudgingly. "Though there is little to choose between pirates."

Villiers laughed without resentment and twirled his mustache.

"You are blunt, my lord. I am no pirate. I hold my commission from the governor of Tortuga, to fight the Spaniards. Harston is a sea-thief who holds no commission from any king. I desire only leave to anchor in your bay, to let my men hunt for meat and water in your woods, and, perhaps, myself to drink a glass of wine at your board."

"Very well," growled Henri. "But understand this, Villiers: no man of your crew comes within this stockade. If one approaches closer than a hundred feet, he will presently find a bullet through his gizzard. And I charge you do no harm to my gardens, or the cattle in the pens. Three steers you may have for fresh meat, but no more."

"I guarantee the good conduct of my men," Villiers assured him. "May they come ashore?"

Henri grudgingly signified his consent, and Villiers bowed, a thought sardonically, and retired with a tread as measured and stately as if he trod the polished floor of Versailles palace, where, indeed, unless rumor lied, he had once been a familiar figure.

"Let no man leave the stockade," Henri ordered Gallot. "His driving Harston from our gate is no guarantee that he would not cut our throats. Many bloody rogues bear the king's commission."

Gallot nodded. The buccaneers were supposed to prey only on the Spaniards; but Villiers had a sinister reputation.

So no one stirred from the palisade while the buccaneers came ashore, sun-burnt men with scarfs bound about their heads and gold hoops in their ears. They camped on the beach, more than a hundred of them, and Villiers posted lookouts on both points. The three beeves designated by Henri, shouting from the wall, were driven forth and slaughtered. Fires were kindled on the strand, and a wattled barrel of wine was brought ashore and broached.

Other kegs were filled with water from the spring that rose a short distance south of the fort, and men began to straggle toward the woods. Seeing this, Henri shouted to Villiers: "Don't let your men go into the forest. Take another steer from the pens if you haven't enough meat. If they go tramping into the woods, they may fall foul of the Indians.

"We beat off an attack shortly after we landed, and since then six of my men have been murdered in the forest, at one time or another. There's peace between us just now, but it hangs by a thread."

Villiers shot a startled glance at the lowering woods, then he bowed and said: "I thank you for the warning, my lord!" He shouted for his men to come back, in a rasping voice that contrasted strangely with his courtly accents when addressing the Count.

If Villiers could have penetrated the leafy mask he would have been more apprehensive, could he have seen the sinister figure that lurked there, watching the strangers with resentful black eyes—an unpainted Indian warrior, naked but for a doeskin breech-clout; a hawk feather drooped over his left ear.

As evening drew on, a thin skim of grey crawled up from the sea-rim and overcast the sky. The sun sank in a wallow of crimson, touching the tips of the black waves with blood. Fog crawled out of the sea and lapped at the feet of the forest, curling about the stockade in smoky wisps. The fires on the beach shone dull crimson through the mist, and the singing of the buccaneers seemed deadened and far away. They had brought old sail-canvas from the ship and made them shelters along the strand, where beef was still roasting, and the wine was doled out sparingly.

The great gate was barred. Soldiers stolidly tramped the ledges of the palisade, pike on shoulder, beads of moisture glistening on their steel caps. They glanced uneasily at the fires on the beach, stared with greater fixity toward the forest, a vague dark line in the fog. The compound lay empty of life. Candles gleamed feebly through the cracks of the huts, light streamed from the windows of the manor building. There was silence except for the tread of the sentries, the drip of the water from the eaves, the distant singing of the buccaneers.

Some faint echo of this singing penetrated into the great hall where Henri sat at wine with his unsolicited guest.

"Your men make merry, sir," grunted the Count.

"They are glad to feel the sand under their feet again," answered Villiers. "It has been a wearisome voyage—yes, a long, stern chase." He lifted his goblet gallantly to the unresponsive girl who sat on his host's right, and drank ceremoniously.

Impassive attendants ranged the walls, soldiers with pikes and helmets, servants in worn satin coats. Henri's household in this wild land was a shadowy reflection of the court he had kept in France.

The manor house, as he insisted on calling it, was a marvel for a savage coast. A hundred men had worked night and day for months building it. The logs that composed the walls of the interior were hidden with heavy silk goldworked tapestries. Ship beams, stained and polished, formed the beams of the lofty ceiling. The floor was covered with rich carpets. The broad stair that led up from the hall was likewise carpeted, and its massive balustrade had once been a galleon's rail.

A fire in the wide stone fireplace dispelled the dampness of the night. Candles in the great silver candelabrum in the center of the broad mahogany board lit the hall, throwing long shadows on the stair. Count Henri sat at the head of that table, presiding over a company composed of his niece, his piratical guest, Gallot, and the captain of the guard.

"You followed Harston?" asked Henri. "You drove him this far afield?"

"I followed Harston," laughed Villiers. "I followed him around the Horn. But he was not fleeing from me. He came seeking something; something I too desire."

"What could tempt a pirate to this naked land?" muttered Henri.

"What could tempt a Count of France?" retorted Villiers.

"The rottenness of a royal court might sicken a man of honor."

"D'Chastillons of honor have endured its rottenness for several generations," said Villiers bluntly. "My lord, indulge my curiosity—why did you sell your lands, load your galleon with the furnishings of your castle and sail over the horizon out of the knowledge of men? And why settle here, when your sword and your name might carve out a place for you in any civilized land?"

Henri toyed with the golden seal-chain about his neck.

"As to why I left France," he said, "that is my own affair. But it was chance that left me stranded here. I had brought all my people ashore, and much of the furnishings you mentioned, intending to build a temporary habitation. But my ship, anchored out there in the bay, was driven against the cliffs of the north point and wrecked by a sudden storm out of the west. That left us no way of escape from this spot."

"Then you would return to France, if you could?"

"Not to France. To China, perhaps—or to India—"

"Do you not find it tedious here, my Lady?" asked Villiers, for the first time addressing himself directly to Francoise.

Hunger to see a new face and hear a new voice had brought the girl to the banquet-hall that night. But now she wished she had remained in her chamber with Tina. There was no mistaking the meaning in the glance Villiers turned on her. His speech was decorous, his expression respectful, but it was only a mask through which gleamed the violent and sinister spirit of the man.

"There is little diversion here," she answered in a low voice.

"If you had a ship," Villiers addressed his host, "you would abandon this settlement?"

"Perhaps," admitted the Count.

"I have a ship," said Villiers. "If we could reach an agreement—"

"Agreement?" Henri stared suspiciously at his guest.

"Share and share alike," said Villiers, laying his hand on the board with the fingers spread wide. The gesture was repulsively reminiscent of a great spider. But the fingers quivered with tension, and the buccaneer's eyes burned with a new light.

"Share what?" Henri stared at him in bewilderment. "The gold I brought with me went down in my ship, and unlike the broken timbers, it did not wash ashore."

"Not that!" Villiers made an impatient gesture. "Let us be frank, my lord. Can you pretend it was chance which caused you to land at this particular spot, with thousands of miles of coast to choose from?"

"There is no need for me to pretend," answered Henri coldly. "My ship's master was one Jacques Piriou, formerly a buccaneer. He had sailed this coast, and he persuaded me to land here, telling me he had a reason he would later disclose. But this reason he never divulged, because the day we landed he disappeared into the woods, and his headless body was found later by a hunting party. Obviously the Indians slew him."

Villiers stared fixedly at the Count for a space.

"Sink me," quoth he at last. "I believe you, my lord. And I'll make you a proposal. I will admit when I anchored out there in the bay I had other plans in mind. Supposing you to have already secured the treasure, I meant to take this fort by strategy and cut all your throats. But circumstances have caused me to change my mind—" he cast a glance at Francoise that brought color into her face, and made her lift her head indignantly.

"I have a ship to carry you out of exile," said the buccaneer. "But first you must help me secure the treasure."

"What treasure, in Saint Denis' name?" demanded the Count angrily. "You are yammering like that dog Harston, now."

"Did you ever hear of Giovanni da Verrazano?"

"The Italian who sailed as a privateer for France, and captured the caravel loaded with Montezuma's treasures which Cortez was sending to Spain?"

"Aye. That was in 1523. The Spaniards claimed to have hanged him in 1527, but they lied. That was the year he sailed over the horizon and vanished from the knowledge of men. But it was not from the Spaniards that he fled.

"Listen! On that caravel he captured in 1523 was the greatest treasure-trove in the world—the jewels of Montezuma! Tales of Aztec gold rang around the world, but Cortez carefully guarded the secret of the gems, for he feared lest the sight should madden his own men to revolt against him. They went aboard ship concealed in a sack of gold dust, and they fell into Verrazano's hands when he took the caravel.

"Like Cortez, da Verrazano kept their possession a secret, save from his officers. He did not share them with his men. He hid them in his cabin, and their glitter got in his blood and drove him mad, as they did with all men who saw them. The secret got out, somehow; perhaps his mates talked. But da Verrazano became obsessed with the fear that other rovers would attack him and loot him of his hoard. Seeking some safe hiding place for the baubles which had come to mean more than his very life, he sailed westward, rounded the Horn, and vanished, nearly a hundred years ago.

"But the tale persists that one man of his crew returned to the Main, only to be captured by the Spaniards. Before he was hanged he told his story and drew a map on parchment, in his own blood, which he smuggled somehow out of his captors' reach. This was the tale he told: da Verrazano sailed northward, until, beyond Darien, beyond the coast of Mexico, he raised a coast where no Christian had ever set foot before.

"In a lonely bay he anchored and went ashore, taking his treasure, and eleven of his most trusted men. Following his orders, the ship sailed northward, to return in a week's time and pick up their captain and his men—for he feared otherwise men he did not trust would spy upon him and learn the hiding place of his trove. In the meantime he meant to hide the treasure in the vicinity of the bay. The ship returned at the appointed time, but there was no trace of da Verrazano and his men, save for the rude dwelling they had built on the beach.

"This had been demolished, and there were tracks of naked feet about it, but no sign to show there had been fighting. Nor was there any trace of the treasure, or any sign to show where it was hidden. The buccaneers plunged into the forest to search for their captain, but were attacked by the savages and driven back to their ship. In despair they heaved anchor and sailed away, but they were wrecked off the coast of Darien, and only that one man survived.

"That is the tale of the Treasure of da Verrazano, which men have sought in vain for nearly a century. I have seen the map that sailor drew before they hanged him. Harston and Piriou were with me. We looked upon it in a hovel in Havana, where we were skulking in disguise. Somebody knocked over the candle, and somebody howled in the dark, and when we got the light on again, the old miser who owned the map was dead with a dirk in his heart, and the map was gone, and the watch was clattering down the street with their pikes to investigate the clamor. We scattered, and each went his own way.

"For years thereafter Harston and I watched one another, each thinking the other had the map. Well, as it turned out, neither had it, but recently word came to me that Harston had sailed for the Pacific, so I followed him. You saw the end of that chase.

"I had but a glimpse at the map as it lay on the old miser's table, and could tell nothing about it. But Harston's actions show that he knows this is the bay where da Verrazano anchored. I believe they hid the treasure somewhere in that forest and returning, were attacked and slain by the savages. The Indians did not get the treasure. Neither Cabrillo nor Drake, nor any man who ever touched this coast ever saw any gold or jewels in the hands of the Indians.

"This is my proposal: let us combine our forces. Harston fled because he feared to be pinned between us, but he will return. But allied, we can laugh at him. We can work out from the fort, leaving enough men here to hold it if he attacks. I believe the treasure is hidden near by. We will find it and sail for some port of Germany or Italy where I can cover my past with gold. I'm sick of this life. I want to go back to Europe and live like a noble, with riches, and slaves, and a castle—and a wife of noble blood."

"Well?" demanded the Count, slit-eyed with suspicion.

"Give me your niece for my wife," demanded the buccaneer bluntly. Francoise cried out sharply and started to her feet. Henri likewise rose, livid. Villiers did not move. His fingers on the table hooked like talons, and his eyes smoldered with passion and a deep menace.

"You dare!" ejaculated Henri.

"You forget you have fallen from your high estate, Count Henri," growled Villiers. "We are not at Versailles, my lord. On this naked coast nobility is measured by the power of men and arms. And there I rank you. Strangers tread d'Chastillon Castle, and the d'Chastillon fortune is at the bottom of the sea. You will die here, an exile, unless I give you the use of my ship.

"You will have no cause to regret the union of our houses. With a new name and a new fortune you will find that Guillaume Villiers can take his place among the nobility of the world, and make a son-in-law of which not even a d'Chastillon need be ashamed."

"You are mad!" exclaimed the Count violently. "You— what is that?"

It was the patter of soft-slippered feet. Tina came hurriedly into the hall, curtsied timidly, and sidled around the table to thrust her small hands into Francoise's fingers. She was panting slightly, her slippers were damp, and her flaxen hair was plastered wetly on her head.

"Tina! Where have you been? I thought you were in your chamber!"

"I was," answered the child breathlessly, "but I missed my coral necklace you gave me—" She held it up, a trivial trinket, but prized beyond all her other possessions because it had been Francoise's first gift to her. "I was afraid you wouldn't let me go if you knew—a soldier's wife helped me out of the stockade and back again. I found my necklace by the pool where I bathed this morning. Please punish me if I have done wrong."

"Tina!" groaned Francoise, clasping the child to her. "I'm not going to punish you. But you should not have gone outside the stockade. Let me take you to your chamber and change these damp clothes—"

"Yes, my Lady," murmured Tina, "but first let me tell you about the black man—"

"*What?*" It was a cry that burst from Count Henri's lips. His goblet clattered to the floor as he caught the table with both hands. If a thunderbolt had struck him, his bearing could not have been more horrifyingly altered. His face was livid, his eyes starting from his head.

"What did you say?" he panted. "What did you say, wench?"

"A black man, my lord," she stammered, while all stared at Henri in amazement. "When I went down to the pool to get my necklace, I saw him. I was afraid and hid behind a ridge of sand. He came from the sea in an open boat. He drew the boat up on the sands below the south point, and strode toward the forest, looking like a giant in the fog, a great, tall black man—"

Henri reeled as if he had received a mortal blow. He clutched at his throat, snapping the golden chain in his violence. With the face of a madman he lurched about the table and tore the child screaming from Francoise's arms.

"You lie!" he panted. "You lie to torment me! Say that you lie before I tear the skin from your back!"

"Uncle!" cried Francoise, trying to free Tina from his grasp. "Are you mad? What are you about?"

With a snarl he tore her hand from his arm and spun her staggering into the arms of Gallot who received her with a leer he did not conceal.

"Mercy, my lord!" sobbed Tina. "I did not lie!"

"I say you lied!" roared Henri. "Jacques!"

A stolid serving man seized the shivering youngster and tore the garments from her back with one brutal wrench. Wheeling, he drew her slender arms over his shoulders, lifting her feet clear of the floor.

"Uncle!" shrieked Francoise, writhing vainly in Gallot's grasp. "You are mad! You can not—oh, you can not—!" The cry choked in her throat as Henri caught up a jewel-hilted riding whip and brought it down across the child's frail body with a savagery that left a red weal across her naked shoulders.

Francoise went sick with the anguish in Tina's shriek. The world had suddenly gone mad. As if in a nightmare she saw the stolid faces of the retainers, reflecting neither pity nor sympathy. Villiers' sneering face was part of the nightmare. Nothing in that crimson haze was real except Tina's naked white shoulders, crisscrossed with red welts; no sound real except the child's sharp cries of agony, and the panting gasps of Henri as he lashed away with the staring eyes of a madman, shrieking: "You lie! Admit your guilt, or I will flay you! *He* could not have followed me here—"

"Mercy, mercy, my lord!" screamed the child, writhing vainly on the brawny servant's back. "I saw him! I do not lie! Please! Please!"

"You fool! *You fool!*" screamed Francoise, almost beside herself. "Do you not see she is telling the truth? Oh, you beast! Beast! Beast!"

Suddenly some shred of sanity seemed to return to Henri's brain. Dropping the whip he reeled back and fell up against the table, clutching blindly at its edge. He shook as if with an ague. His hair was plastered across his brow in dank strands, and sweat dripped from his livid countenance which was like a carven mask of Fear. Tina, released by Jacques, slipped to the floor in a whimpering heap. Francoise tore free from Gallot, rushed to her, sobbing, and fell on her knees, gathering the pitiful waif into her arms. She lifted a terrible face to her uncle, to pour upon him the full vials of her wrath—but he was not looking at her. In a daze of incredulity, she heard him say: "I accept your offer, Villiers. In God's name, let us find your treasure and begone from this accursed coast!"

At this the fire of her fury sank to sick ashes. In stunned silence she lifted the sobbing child in her arms and carried her up the stair. A backward glance showed Henri crouching rather than sitting at the table, gulping wine from a goblet he gripped in both shaking hands, while Villiers towered over him like a somber predatory bird—puzzled at the turn of events, but quick to take advantage of the shocking change that had come over the Count. He was talking in a low, decisive voice, and Henri nodded mute agreement, like one who scarcely heeds what is being said. Gallot stood back in the shadows, chin pinched between forefinger and thumb, and the retainers along the walls glanced furtively at each other, bewildered by their lord's collapse.

Up in her chamber Francoise laid the half-fainting girl on the bed and set herself to wash and apply soothing ointments to the weals and cuts on her tender skin. Tina gave herself up in complete submission to her mistress's hands, moaning faintly. Francoise felt as if her world had fallen about her ears. She was sick and bewildered, overwrought, her nerves quivering from the brutal shock of what she had witnessed. Fear and hate of her uncle grew in her soul. She had never loved him; he was harsh and without affection, grasping and avid. But she had considered him just and courageous. Revulsion shook her at the memory of his staring eyes and bloodless face. It was some terrible fear which had roused this frenzy; and because of this fear Henri had brutalized the only creature she had to love; because of that fear he was selling her, his niece, to an infamous outlaw. What was behind this madness?

The child muttered in semi-delirium.

"Indeed I did not lie, my Lady! I saw him—a black man, wrapped in a black cloak! My blood ran cold when I saw him. Why did the Count whip me for seeing him?"

"Hush, Tina," soothed Francoise. "Lie quiet, child."

The door opened behind her and she whirled, snatching up a jeweled dagger. Henri stood in the door, and her flesh crawled at the sight of him. He looked years older; his face was grey and drawn, his eyes made her shiver. She had never been close to him; now she felt as though a gulf separated them. He was not her uncle who stood there, but a stranger come to menace her.

She lifted the dagger.

"If you touch her again," she whispered from dry lips, "I swear I will sink this blade in your breast."

He did not heed her threat.

"I have posted a strong guard about the manor," he said. "Villiers brings his men into the stockade tomorrow. He will not sail until he has found the treasure. When he finds it we sail."

"And you will sell me to him?" she whispered. "In God's name—"

He fixed upon her a gloomy gaze from which all considerations but his own self-interest had been crowded out. She shrank before it, seeing in it the frantic cruelty that possessed the man in his mysterious fear.

"You will do as I command," he said presently, with no more human feeling in his voice than there is in the ring of flint on steel. And turning, he left the chamber. Blinded by a sudden rush of horror, Francoise fell fainting beside the couch where Tina lay.

Chapter .4.
A Black Drum Droning.

Francoise never knew how long she lay crushed and senseless. She was first aware of Tina's arms about her and the sobbing of the child in her ear. Mechanically she straightened herself and drew the girl into her arms. She sat there, dry-eyed, staring unseeingly at the flickering candle. There was no sound in the castle. The singing of the buccaneers on the strand had ceased. Dully she reviewed her problem.

The story of the mysterious black man had driven Henri mad. It was to escape this man that he meant to abandon the settlement and flee with Villiers. That much was obvious. Equally obvious was the fact that he was ready to sacrifice her for that opportunity to escape. In the blackness which surrounded her, she saw no glint of light. The serving men were dull or callous brutes, their women stupid and apathetic. They would neither dare nor care to help her. She was utterly helpless.

Tina lifted her tear-stained face as if listening to the prompting of some inner voice. The child's understanding of Francoise's inmost thoughts was almost uncanny, as was her recognition of the inexorable drive of Fate and the only alternative left them.

"We must go, my Lady!" she whispered. "Villiers shall not have you. Let us go far away into the forest. We shall go until we can go no further, and then we shall lie down and die together."

The tragic strength that is the last refuge of the weak entered Francoise's soul. It was the only escape from the shadows that had been closing in upon her since that day when they fled from France.

"We shall go, child."

She rose and was fumbling for a cloak, when an exclamation from Tina brought her about. The child was on her feet, a finger pressed to her lips, her eyes wide and bright with sudden terror.

"What is it, Tina?" Francoise whispered, seized by a nameless dread.

"Someone outside in the hall," whispered Tina, clutching her arm convulsively. "He stopped at our door, and then went on down the hall."

"Your ears are keener than mine," murmured Francoise. "But there's nothing strange in that. It was the Count, perchance, or Gallot."

She moved to open the door, but Tina threw her arms about her neck, and Francoise could feel the wild beating of her heart.

"Do not open the door, my Lady! I am afraid! Some evil thing is near!"

Impressed, Francoise reached a hand toward the metal disk that masked a tiny peep-hole in the door.

"He is coming back!" shivered the girl. "I hear him."

Francoise heard something too—a stealthy pad which she realized, with a chill of fear, was not the step of anyone she knew. Nor was it the tread of Villiers, or any booted man. But who could it be? None slept upstairs besides herself, Tina, the Count, and Gallot.

With a quick motion she extinguished the candle so it would not shine through the hole in the door, and pushed aside the metal disk. Staring through she sensed rather than saw a dim bulk moving past her door, but she could make nothing of its shape except that it was manlike. But a blind unreasoning terror froze her tongue to her palate.

The figure passed on to the stairhead, where it was limned momentarily against the faint glow that came up from below—a vague, monstrous image, black against the red—then it was gone down the stair. She crouched in the darkness, awaiting some outcry to announce that the soldiers on guard had sighted the intruder. But the fort remained silent; somewhere a wind wailed shrilly. That was all.

Francoise's hands were moist with perspiration as she groped to relight the candle. She did not know just what there had been about that black figure etched against the red glow of the fireplace below that had roused such horror in her soul. But she knew she had seen something sinister and grisly beyond comprehension, and that the sight had robbed her of all her new-found resolution. She was demoralized.

The candle flared up, limning Tina's white face in the glow.

"It was the black man!" whispered Tina. "I know! My blood turned cold just as it did when I saw him on the beach! Shall we go and tell the Count?"

Francoise shook her head. She did not wish to repeat the scene that had ensued upon Tina's first mention of the black invader. At any event, she dared not venture out into that darkened hallway. She knew men were patrolling the stockade, and were stationed outside the manor house. How the stranger had got into the fort she could not guess. It smacked of the diabolical. But she was possessed of an inexplicable intuition that the creature was no longer within the fortress; that he had departed as mysteriously as he had come.

"We dare not go into the forest!" shuddered Tina. "He will be lurking there—"

Francoise did not ask the girl how she knew the black man would be in the forest; it was the logical hiding place for any evil thing, man or devil. And she knew Tina was right. They dared not leave the fort now. Her determination which had not faltered at the prospect of certain death, gave way at the thought of traversing those gloomy woods with that black shambling creature at large among them. Helplessly she sat down and sank her face in her hands.

Tina slept, presently, on the couch, whimpering occasionally in her sleep. Tears sparkled on her long lashes. She moved her smarting body restlessly. Toward dawn, Francoise was aware that the atmosphere had become stifling. She heard a low rumble of thunder off to seaward. Extinguishing the candle, which had burned to its socket, she went to a window whence she could see both the ocean and a belt of the forest.

The fog had disappeared, but out to sea a dusky mass was rising from the horizon. From it lightning flickered and the low thunder growled. An answering rumble came from the black woods. Startled, she turned and stared at the forest. A rhythmic pulsing reached her ears—a droning reverberation that was not the thumping of an Indian drum.

"The drum!" sobbed Tina, spasmodically opening and closing her fingers in her sleep. "The black man—beating on a black drum—in the black woods! Oh, save us!"

Francoise shuddered. Along the eastern horizon ran a thin white line that presaged dawn. But that black cloud on the western rim expanded swiftly. She watched in surprize, for storms were practically unknown on that coast at that time of year, and she had never seen such a cloud.

It came pouring up over the world-rim in great boiling masses of fire-veined blackness. It rolled and billowed with the wind in its belly. Its thundering made the air vibrate. And another sound mingled awesomely with the thunder—the voice of the wind, that raced before its coming. The inky horizon was torn and convulsed in the lightning flashes; afar to sea she saw the white-capped waves racing before the wind. She heard its droning roar, rising in volume as it swept shoreward. But as yet no wind stirred on the land. The air was hot, breathless. Somewhere below her a shutter slammed, and a woman's voice was lifted, shrill with alarm. But the manor still slumbered.

She still heard that mysterious drum droning, and her flesh crawled. The forest was a black rampart her sight could not penetrate, but she visualized a hideous black figure squatting under black branches and smiting incessantly on a drum gripped between its knees. *But why?*

She shook off the ghoulish conviction and looked seaward as a blaze of lightning split the sky. Outlined against the glare she saw the masts of Villiers' ship, the tents on the beach, the sandy ridges of the south point and the rocky cliffs of the north point. It all stood out vividly etched. Louder and louder rose the roar of the wind, and now the manor was awake. Feet came pounding up the stair, and Villiers' voice yelled, edged with fright.

Doors slammed and Henri answered him, shouting to make himself heard.

"Why didn't you warn me of a storm from the west?" howled the buccaneer. "If the anchors don't hold she'll drive on the rocks!"

"A storm never came from the west before, at this time of year!" shrieked Henri, rushing from his chamber in his night shirt, his face livid and his hair standing on end. "This is the work of—" His words were drowned as he raced up the ladder that led to the lookout tower, followed by the swearing buccaneer.

Francoise crouched at her window, awed and deafened. The wind drowned all other sound—all except that maddening droning which rose now like a chant of triumph. It roared inshore, driving before it a foaming league-long crest of white—and then all hell was loosed on that coast. Rain swept the beaches in driving torrents. The wind hit like a thunder-clap, making the timbers of the fort quiver. The surf roared over the sands, drowning the coals of the seamen's fires. In the lightning glare Francoise saw, through the curtain of the slashing rain, the tents of the buccaneers ripped to ribbons and washed away, saw the men themselves staggering toward the fort, beaten almost to the sands by the fury of torrent and blast.

And limned against the blue glare she saw Villiers' ship, ripped loose from her moorings, driven headlong against the jagged cliffs that jutted up to receive her.

Chapter .5.
A Man From the Wilderness.

The storm had spent its fury, and the sun shone in a clear blue rain-washed sky. At a small stream which wound among trees and bushes to join the sea, an Englishman bent to lave his hands and face. He performed his ablutions after the manner of his race, grunting and splashing like a buffalo. In the midst of these splashings he lifted his head suddenly, his tawny hair dripping and water running in rivulets over his brawny shoulders. All in one motion he was on his feet and facing inland, sword in hand.

A man as big as himself was striding toward him over the sands, a cutlass in his hand and unmistakable purpose in his approach.

The pirate paled, as recognition blazed in his eyes.

"Satan!" he ejaculated unbelievingly. "*You!*"

Oaths streamed from his lips as he heaved up his cutlass. The birds rose in flaming showers from the trees, frightened at the clang of steel. Blue sparks flew from the hacking blades, and the sand ground under the stamping boot heels. Then the clangor ended in a chopping crunch, and one man went to his knees with a choking gasp. The hilt escaped his hand, and he slid to the reddened sand. With a dying effort he fumbled at his girdle and drew something from it, tried to lift it to his mouth, and then stiffened convulsively and went limp.

The conqueror bent and tore the stiffening fingers from the object they crumpled in their desperate grasp.

VILLIERS and d'Chastillon stood on the beach, staring at the spars, pieces of masts and broken timbers their men were gathering. So savagely had the storm hammered Villiers' ship against the low cliffs that most of the salvage was match-wood. A short distance behind them stood Francoise, with one arm about Tina. The girl was pale and listless, apathetic to whatever Fate held in store for her. She listened to the conversation without interest. She was crushed by the realization that she was but a pawn in the game, however it was to be played out.

Villiers cursed venomously, but Henri seemed dazed.

"This is not the time of year for storms," he muttered. "It was not chance that brought that storm out of the deep to splinter the ship in which I meant to escape. Escape? Nay, we are all trapped rats."

"I don't know what you're talking about," snarled Villiers. "I've been unable to get any sense out of you since that flaxen-haired hussy upset you so last night with her wild tale of black men coming out of the sea. But I know that I'm not going to spend my life on this cursed coast. Ten of my men drowned with the ship, but I've got a hundred more. You've got nearly as many. There are tools in your fort and plenty of trees in yonder forest. We'll build some kind of a craft that will carry us until we can take a ship from the Spaniards."

"It will take months," muttered Henri.

"Well, is there any better way in which we could employ our time? We're here—and we'll get away only by our own efforts. I hope that storm smashed Harston to bits! While we're building our craft we'll hunt for da Verrazano's treasure."

"We will never complete your ship," said Henri somberly.

"You fear the Indians? We have men enough to defy them."

"I do not speak of red men. I speak of a black man."

Villiers turned on him angrily. "Will you talk sense? Who is this accursed black man?"

"Accursed indeed," said Henri, staring seaward. "Through fear of him I fled from France, hoping to drown my trail in the western ocean. But he has smelled me out in spite of all."

"If such a man came ashore he must be hiding in the woods," growled Villiers. "We'll rake the forest and hunt him out."

Henri laughed harshly.

"Grope in the dark for a cobra with your naked hand!"

Villiers cast him an uncertain look, obviously doubting his sanity.

"Who is this man? Have done with ambiguity."

"A devil spawned on that coast of hell, the Slave Coast—"

"Sail ho!" bawled the lookout on the north point.

Villiers wheeled and his voice slashed the wind.

"Do you know her?"

"Aye!" the reply came back faintly. "It's the *War-Hawk*!"

"Harston!" raged Villiers. "The devil takes care of his own! How could he ride out that blow?" His voice rose to a yell that carried up and down the strand. "Back to the fort, you dogs!"

Before the *War-Hawk*, somewhat battered in appearance, nosed around the point, the beach was bare of human life, the palisade bristling with helmets and scarfbound heads. Villiers ground his teeth as a long-boat swung into the beach and Harston strode toward the fort alone.

"Ahoy the fort!" The Englishman's bull bellow carried clearly in the still morning. "I want to parley! The last time I advanced under a flag of truce I was fired upon! I want a promise that it won't happen again."

"All right, I'll give you my promise!" called Villiers sardonically.

"Damn your promise, you French dog! I want d'Chastillon's word."

A measure of dignity remained to the Count. There was an edge of authority to his voice as he answered: "Advance, but keep your men back. You will not be fired upon."

"That's enough for me," said Harston instantly. "Whatever a d'Chastillon's sins, once his word is given, you can trust him."

He strode forward and halted under the gate, laughing at the hate-darkened visage Villiers thrust over at him.

"Well, Guillaume," he taunted, "you are a ship shorter than when last I saw you! But you French never were sailors."

"How did you save your ship, you Bristol gutterscum?" snarled the buccaneer.

"There's a cove some miles to the north protected by a high-ridged arm of land that broke the force of the gale," answered Harston. "I lay behind it. My anchors dragged, but they held me off the shore."

Villiers scowled at Henri, who said nothing. The Count had not known of that cove. He had done little exploring of his domain, fear of the Indians keeping him and his men near the fort.

"I come to make a trade," said Harston easily.

"We've naught to trade with you save sword-strokes," growled Villiers.

"I think otherwise," grinned Harston, thin-lipped. "You tipped your hand when you murdered Richardson, my first mate, and robbed him. Until this morning I supposed that d'Chastillon had da Verrazano's treasure. But if either of you had it, you wouldn't have gone to the trouble of following me and killing my mate to get the map."

"The map?" ejaculated Villiers, stiffening.

"Oh, don't dissemble!" Harston laughed, but anger blazed blue in his eyes. "I know you have it. Indians don't wear boots!"

"But—" began Henri, nonplussed, but fell silent as Villiers nudged him.

"What have you to trade?" Villiers demanded of Harston.

"Let me come into the fort," suggested the pirate. "We can talk there."

"Your men will stay where they are," warned Villiers.

"Aye. But don't think you'll seize me and hold me for a hostage!" He laughed grimly. "I want d'Chastillon's word that I'll be allowed to leave the fort alive and unhurt within the hour, whether we come to terms or not."

"You have my pledge," answered the Count.

"All right, then. Open that gate."

The gate opened and closed, the leaders vanished from sight, and the common men of both parties resumed their silent surveillance of each other.

On the broad stair above the hall, Francoise and Tina crouched, ignored by the men below. Henri, Gallot, Villiers and Harston sat about the broad table. Except for them the hall was empty.

Harston gulped wine and set the empty goblet on the table. The frankness suggested by his bluff countenance was belied by the lights of cruelty and treachery in his wide eyes. But he spoke bluntly enough.

"We all want the treasure da Verrazano hid somewhere near this bay," he said. "Each has something the others need. D'Chastillon has laborers, supplies, a stockade to shelter us from the savages. You, Villiers, have my map. I have a ship."

"If you've had that map all these years," said Villiers, "why haven't you come after the loot sooner?"

"I didn't have it. It was Piriou who knifed the old miser in the dark and stole the map. But he had neither ship nor crew, and it took him more than a year to get them. When he did come after the loot, the Indians prevented his landing, and his men mutinied and made him sail back to the Main. One of them stole the map, and later sold it to me."

"That was why Piriou recognized the bay," muttered Henri.

"Did that dog lead you here? I might have guessed it. Where is he?"

"Slain by Indians, evidently while searching for the treasure."

"Good!" approved Harston heartily. "Well, I don't know how you knew my mate was carrying the map. I trusted him, and the men trusted him more than they did me, so I let him keep it. But this morning he wandered inland, got separated from the rest, and we found him sworded to death near the beach, and the map gone. The men accused me of killing him, but we found the tracks left by the man who killed him, and I showed the fools my feet wouldn't fit them. There wasn't a boot in the crew that made that sort of track. Indians don't wear boots. So it had to be a Frenchman.

"You've got the map, but you haven't got the treasure. If you had it, you wouldn't have let me in the fort. I've got you penned up here. You can't get out to look for the loot, and no ship to carry it away, anyhow.

"Here's my proposal: Villiers, give me the map. And you, Count, give me fresh meat and supplies. My men are nigh to scurvy after the long voyage. In return I'll take you three men, the Lady Francoise and her girl, and set you ashore at some port of the Atlantic where you can take ship to France. And to clinch the bargain, I'll give each of you a handsome share in the treasure."

The buccaneer tugged his mustache meditatively. He knew that Harston would not keep any such pact, if made. Nor did Villiers even consider agreeing to the proposal. But to refuse bluntly would be to force the issue into a clash of arms, and Villiers was not ready for this. He wanted the WarHawk as avidly as he desired the jewels of Montezuma.

"What's to prevent us from holding you captive and forcing your men to give us your ship in exchange for you?" he asked.

Harston laughed at him.

"Do you think I'm a fool? My men have orders to heave up the anchors and sail hence at the first hint of treachery. They wouldn't give you the ship, if you skinned me alive on the beach. Besides, I have Henri's word."

"My word is not wind," said Henri somberly. "Have done with threats, Villiers."

The buccaneer did not reply, his mind being wholly absorbed in the problem of getting possession of Harston's ship; of continuing the parley without betraying the fact that he did not have the map. He wondered who in Satan's name *did* have the accursed map.

"Let me take my men away with me on your ship," he said. "I can not desert my faithful followers—"

Harston snorted.

"Why don't you ask for my cutlass to cut my throat with? Desert your faithful—bah! You'd desert your brother to the devil if it meant money in your pocket. No! You're not going to bring enough men aboard to mutiny and take my ship."

"Give us a day to think it over," urged Villiers, fighting for time.

Harston's heavy fist banged on the table, making the wine dance in the glasses.

"No, by Satan! Give me my answer now!"

Villiers was on his feet, his black rage submerging his craftiness.

"You English dog! I'll give you your answer—in your guts!"

He tore aside his cloak, caught at his sword hilt. Harston heaved up with a roar, his chair crashing backward to the floor. Henri sprang up, spreading his arms between them as they faced each other across the board.

"Gentlemen, have done! Villiers, he has my pledge—"

"The foul fiend gnaw your pledge!" snarled Villiers.

"Stand from between us, my lord," growled the pirate, his voice thick with the killing lust. "I release you from your word until I have slain this dog!"

"Well spoken, Harston!" It was a deep, powerful voice behind them, vibrant with grim amusement. All wheeled and glared open-mouthed. Up on the stair Francoise started up with an involuntary exclamation.

A man strode out from the hangings that masked a chamber door, and advanced toward the table without haste or hesitation. Instantly he dominated the group, and all felt the situation subtly charged with a new, dynamic atmosphere.

The stranger was as tall as either of the freebooters, and more powerfully built than either, yet for all his size he moved with a pantherish suppleness in his flaring-topped boots. His thighs were cased in close-fitting breeches of white silk, his wide-skirted sky-blue coat open to reveal an open-necked white silken shirt beneath, and the scarlet sash that girdled his waist. There were silver acorn-shaped buttons on the coat, and it was adorned with gilt-worked cuffs and pocket-flaps, and a satin collar. A broad brimmed, plumed hat was on the stranger's head, and a heavy cutlass hung at his hip.

"Vulmea!" ejaculated Harston, and the others caught their breath.

"Who else?" The giant strode up to the table, laughing sardonically at their amazement.

"What—what do you here?" stuttered Gallot.

"I climbed the palisade on the east side while you fools were arguing at the gate," Vulmea answered. His Irish accent was faint, but not to be mistaken. "Every man in the fort was craning his neck westward. I entered the house while Harston was being let in at the gate. I've been in that chamber there ever since, eavesdropping."

"I thought you were drowned," said Villiers slowly. "Three years ago the shattered hull of your ship was sighted off the coast of Amichel, and you were seen no more on the Main."

"But I live, as you see," retorted Vulmea.

Up on the stair Tina was staring through the balustrades with all her eyes, clutching Francoise in her excitement.

"Vulmea! It is Black Vulmea, my Lady! Look! Look!"

Francoise was looking. It was like encountering a legendary character in the flesh. Who of all the sea-folk had not heard the tales and ballads celebrating the wild deeds of Black Vulmea, once a scourge of the Spanish Main? The man could not be ignored. Irresistibly he had stalked into the scene, to form another, dominant element in the tangled plot.

Henri was recovering from the shock of finding a stranger in his hall. "What do you want?" he demanded. "Did you come from the sea?"

"I came from the woods," answered the Irishman. "And I gather there is some dissension over a map!"

"That's none of your affair," growled Harston.

"Is this it?" Grinning wickedly, Vulmea drew from his pocket a crumpled object—a square of parchment, marked with crimson lines.

Harston started violently, paling.

"My map!" he ejaculated. "Where did you get it?"

"From Richardson, after I killed him!" was the grim answer.

"You dog!" raved Harston, turning on Villiers. "You never had the map! You lied—"

"I never said I had it," snarled the Frenchman. "You deceived yourself. Don't be a fool. Vulmea is alone. If he had a crew he'd have cut our throats already. We'll take the map from him—"

"You'll never touch it!" Vulmea laughed fiercely.

Both men sprang at him, cursing. Stepping back he crumpled the parchment and cast it into the glowing coals of the fireplace. With a bellow Harston lunged past him, to be met with a buffet under the ear that stretched him half-senseless on the floor. Villiers whipped out his sword, but before he could thrust Vulmea's cutlass beat it out of his hand.

Villiers staggered against the table, with hell in his eyes. Harston lurched to his feet, blood dripping from his ear. Vulmea leaned over the table, his outstretched blade just touching Count Henri's breast.

"Don't call for your soldiers, Count," said the Irishman softly. "Not a sound out of you, either, dog-face!" His name for Gallot, who showed no intention of disobeying. "The map's burned to ashes, and it'll do no good to spill blood. Sit down, all of you."

Harston hesitated, then shrugged his shoulders and sank sullenly into a chair. The others followed suit. Vulmea stood, towering over the table, while his enemies watched him with bitter eyes of hate.

"You were bargaining," he said. "That's all I've come to do."

"And what have you to trade?" sneered Villiers.

"*The jewels of Montezuma!*"

"What?" All four men were on their feet, leaning toward him.

"Sit down!" he roared, banging his broad blade on the table. They sank back, tense and white with excitement. He grinned hardly.

"Yes! I found it before I got the map. That's why I burned the map. I don't need it. And now nobody will ever find it, unless I show him where it is."

They stared at him with murder in their eyes, and Villiers said: "You're lying. You've told us one lie already. You say you came from the woods, yet all men know this country is a wilderness, inhabited only by savages."

"And I've been living for three years with those same savages," retorted Vulmea. "When a gale wrecked my ship near the mouth of the Rio Grande, I swam ashore and fled inland and northward, to escape the Spaniards. I fell in with a wandering tribe of Indians who were drifting westward to escape a stronger tribe, and nothing better offering itself, I lived with them and shared their wanderings until a month ago.

"By this time our rovings had brought us so far westward I believed I could reach the Pacific Coast, so I set forth alone. But a hundred miles to the east I encountered a hostile tribe of red men, who would have burned me alive, if I hadn't killed their war-chief and three or four others and broken away one night.

"They chased me to within a few miles of this coast, where I finally shook them off. And by Satan, the place where I took refuge turned out to be the treasure-trove of da Verrazano! I found it all: chests of garments and weapons— that's where I clothed and armed myself—heaps of gold and silver, and in the midst of all the jewels of Montezuma gleaming like frozen starlight! And da Verrazano and his eleven buccaneers sitting about an ebon table as they've sat for nearly a hundred years!"

"What?"

"Aye! They died in the midst of their treasure! Their bodies have shriveled but not rotted. They sit there with their wine glasses in their stiff hands, just as they have sat for nearly a century!"

"That's an unchancy thing!" muttered Harston uneasily, but Villiers snarled: "What boots it? It's the loot we want. Go on, Vulmea."

Vulmea seated himself and filled a goblet before he resumed: "I lay up and rested a few days, made snares to catch rabbits, and let my wounds heal. I saw smoke against the western sky, but thought it some Indian village on the beach. I lay close, but the loot's hidden in a place the redskins shun. If any spied on me, they didn't show themselves.

"Last night I started for the beach, meaning to strike it some miles north of the spot where I'd seen the smoke. I was close to the shore when the storm hit. I took shelter under a big rock, and when it had blown itself out, I climbed a tree to look for Indians. Then I saw your ship at anchor, Harston, and your men coming in to shore. I was making my way toward your camp on the beach when I met Richardson. I killed him because of an old quarrel. I wouldn't have known he had a map if he hadn't tried to eat it before he died.

"I recognized it, of course, and was considering what use I could make of it, when the rest of you dogs came up and found the body. I was lying in a thicket close by while you were arguing with your men about the killing. I judged the time wasn't ripe for me to show myself then!"

He laughed at the rage displayed in Harston's face.

"Well, while I lay there listening to your talk, I got a drift of the situation and learned, from the things you let fall, that d'Chastillon and Villiers were a few miles south on the beach. So when I heard you say that Villiers must have done the killing and taken the map, and that you meant to parley with him, seeking an opportunity to murder him and get it back—"

"Dog!" snarled Villiers.

Harston was livid, but he laughed mirthlessly.

"Do you think I'd deal fair with a dog like you? Go on, Vulmea."

The Irishman grinned. It was evident that he was deliberately fanning the fires of hate between the two men.

"Nothing much, then. I came straight through the woods while you were beating along the coast, and raised the fort before you did. And there's the tale. I have the treasure, Harston has a ship, Henri has supplies. By Satan, Villiers, I don't see where you fit in, but to avoid strife I'll include you. My proposal is simple enough.

"We'll split the loot four ways. Harston and I will sail away with our shares aboard the *War-Hawk*. You and d'Chastillon take yours and remain lords of the wilderness, or build a ship out of logs, as you wish."

Henri blenched and Villiers swore, while Harston grinned quietly.

"Are you fool enough to go aboard the *War-Hawk* with Harston?" snarled Villiers. "He'll cut your throat before you're out of sight of land!"

"This is like the problem of the sheep, the wolf and the cabbage," laughed Vulmea. "How to get them across the river without their devouring each other!"

"And that appeals to your Celtic sense of humor," complained Villiers.

"I will not stay here!" cried Henri. "Treasure or no, I must go!"

Vulmea gave him a slit-eyed glance of speculation.

"Well, then," said he, "let Harston sail away with Villiers, yourself, and such members of your household as you may select, leaving me in command of the fort and the rest of your men, and all of Villiers'. I'll build a boat that will get me into Spanish waters."

Villiers looked slightly sick.

"I am to have the choice of remaining here in exile, or abandoning my crew and going alone on the *War-Hawk* to have my throat cut?"

Vulmea's gusty laughter boomed through the hall, and he smote Villiers jovially on the back, ignoring the black murder in the buccaneer's glare.

"That's it, Guillaume!" quoth he. "Stay here while Dick and I sail away, or sail away with Dick, leaving your men with me."

"I'd rather have Villiers," said Harston frankly. "You'd turn my own men against me, Vulmea, and cut my throat before I rounded the Horn."

Sweat dripped from Villiers' livid face.

"Neither I, the Count, nor his niece will ever reach France alive if we ship with that devil," said he. "You are both in my power now. My men surround this hall. What's to prevent me cutting you both down?"

"Nothing," admitted Vulmea cheerfully. "Except that if you do Harston's men will sail away with the ship; and that with me dead you'll never find the treasure; and that I'll split your skull if you summon your men."

Vulmea laughed as he spoke, but even Francoise sensed that he meant what he said. His naked cutlass lay across his knees, and Villiers' sword was under the table, out of reach.

"Aye!" said Harston with an oath. "You'd find the two of us no easy prey. I'm agreeable to Vulmea's offer. What do you say, my lord?"

"I must leave this coast!" whispered Henri, staring blankly. "I must hasten. I must go far—go quickly!"

Harston frowned, puzzled at the Count's strange manner, and turned to Villiers, grinning wickedly: "And you Guillaume?"

"What choice have I?" snarled Villiers. "Let me take my three officers and forty men aboard the *War-Hawk*, and the bargain's made."

"The officers and fifteen men!"

"Very well."

"Done!"

There was no shaking of hands to seal the pact. The two captains glared at each other like hungry wolves. The Count plucked his mustache with a trembling hand, rapt in his own somber thoughts. Vulmea drank wine and grinned on the assemblage, but it was the grin of a stalking tiger. Francoise sensed the murderous purposes that reigned there, the treacherous intent that dominated each man's mind. Not one had any intention of keeping his part of the pact, Henri possibly excluded. Each of the freebooters intended to possess both the ship and the entire treasure. Neither would be satisfied with less. But what was going on in each crafty mind? Francoise felt oppressed by the atmosphere of hatred and treachery. The Irishman, for all his savage frankness, was no less subtle than the others—and even fiercer. His gigantic shoulders and massive limbs seemed too big even for the great hall. There was an iron vitality about the man that overshadowed even the hard vigor of the other freebooters.

"Lead us to the treasure!" Villiers demanded.

"Wait a bit," returned Vulmea. "We must keep our power evenly balanced, so one can't take advantage of the others. This is what we'll do: Harston's men will come ashore, all but half a dozen or so, and camp on the beach. Villiers' men will come out of the fort and likewise camp on the beach, within easy sight of them. Then each crew can keep a check on the other, to see that nobody slips after us who go after the treasure. Those left aboard the WarHawk will take her out into the bay out of reach of either party. Henri's men will stay in the fort, but leave the gate open. Will you come with us, Count?"

"Go into that forest?" Henri shuddered, and drew his cloak about his shoulders. "Not for all the gold of Mexico!"

"All right. We'll take fifteen men from each crew and start as soon as possible."

Francoise saw Villiers and Harston shoot furtive glances at each other, then lower their gaze quickly as they lifted their wine glasses to hide the murky intent in their eyes. Francoise saw the fatal weakness in Vulmea's plan, and wondered how he could have overlooked it. She knew he would never come out of that forest alive. Once the treasure was in their grasp, the others would form a rogue's alliance long enough to rid themselves of the man both hated. She shuddered, staring morbidly at the man she knew was doomed; strange to see that powerful fighting man sitting there, laughing and swilling wine, in full prime and power, and to know that he was already doomed to a bloody death.

The whole situation was pregnant with bloody portents. Villiers would trick and kill Harston if he could, and she knew that the Englishman had already marked Villiers for death, and doubtless, also, her uncle and herself. If Villiers won the final battle of cruel wits, their lives were safe—but looking at the buccaneer as he sat there chewing his mustache, with all the stark evil of his nature showing naked in his dark face, she could not decide which was more abhorrent—death or Villiers.

"How far is it?" demanded Harston.

"If we start within the hour we can be back before midnight," answered Vulmea.

He emptied his glass, rose, hitched at his girdle and looked at Henri.

"D'Chastillon," he said, "are you mad, to kill an Indian hunter?"

"What do you mean?" demanded Henri, starting.

"You mean to say you don't know that your men killed an Indian in the woods last night?"

"None of my men was in the woods last night," declared the Count.

"Well, somebody was," grunted Vulmea, fumbling in a pocket. "I saw his head nailed to a tree near the edge of the forest. He wasn't painted for war. I didn't find any boot-tracks, from which I judged it'd been nailed up there before the storm. But there were plenty of moccasin tracks on the wet ground. Indians had seen that head. They were men of some other tribe, or they'd have taken it down. If they happen to be at peace with the tribe the dead man belonged to, they'll make tracks to his village and tell his people."

"Perhaps they killed him," suggested Henri.

"No, they didn't. But they know who did, for the same reason that I know. This chain was knotted about the stump of the severed neck. You must have been utterly mad, to identify your handiwork like that."

He drew forth something and tossed it on the table before the Count, who lurched up choking, as his hand flew to his throat. It was the gold seal-chain he habitually wore about his neck.

Vulmea glanced questioningly at the others, and Villiers made a quick gesture to indicate the Count was not quite right in the head. Vulmea sheathed his cutlass and donned his plumed hat.

"All right; let's go."

The captains gulped down their wine and rose, hitching at their sword-belts. Villiers laid a hand on Henri's arm and shook him slightly. The Count started and stared about him, then followed the others out, dazedly, the chain dangling from his fingers. But not all left the hall.

Francoise and Tina, forgotten on the stair as they peeped between the balustrades, saw Gallot loiter behind until the heavy door closed behind the others. Then he hurried to the fireplace and raked carefully at the smoldering coals. He sank to his knees and peered closely at something for a long space. Then he rose and stole out of the hall by another door.

"What did he find in the fire?" whispered Tina.

Francoise shook her head, then, obeying the promptings of her curiosity, rose and went down to the empty hall. An instant later she was kneeling where the major domo had knelt, and she saw what he had seen.

It was the charred remnant of the map Vulmea had thrown into the fire. It was ready to crumble at a touch, but faint lines and bits of writing were still discernible upon it. She could not read the writing, but she could trace the outlines of what seemed to be the picture of a hill or crag, surrounded by marks evidently representing dense trees. From Gallot's actions she believed he recognized it as portraying some topographical feature familiar to him. She knew the major domo had penetrated further inland than any other man of the settlement.

Chapter .6.
"The Plunder of the Dead."

Francoise came down the stair and paused at the sight of Count Henri seated at the table, turning the broken chain about in his hands. The fortress stood strangely quiet in the noonday heat. Voices of people within the stockade sounded subdued, muffled. The same drowsy stillness reigned on the beach outside where the rival crews lay in armed suspicion, separated by a few hundred yards of bare sand. Far out in the bay the *War-Hawk* lay with a handful of men aboard her, ready to snatch her out of reach at the slightest indication of treachery. The ship was Harston's trump card, his best guarantee against the trickery of his associates.

Vulmea had plotted shrewdly to eliminate the chances of an ambush in the forest by either party, but as far as Francoise could see he had failed utterly to safeguard himself against the treachery of his companions. He had disappeared into the woods, leading the two captains and their thirty men, and the girl was positive she would never see him alive again.

Presently she spoke, and her voice was strained and harsh.

"When they have the treasure they will kill Vulmea. What then? Are we to go aboard the ship? Can we trust Harston?"

Henri shook his head absently.

"Villiers whispered his plan to me. He will see that night overtakes the treasure-party so they are forced to camp in the forest. He will find a way to kill the Englishmen in their sleep. Then he and his men will come stealthily on to the beach. Just before dawn I will send some of my fishermen secretly from the fort to swim out and seize the ship. Neither Harston nor Vulmea thought of that. Villiers will come out of the forest, and with our united forces we will destroy the pirates camped on the beach. Then we will sail in the *War-Hawk* with all the treasure."

"And what of me?" she asked with dry lips.

"I have promised you to Villiers," he answered harshly, and without the slightest touch of sympathy. "But for my promise he would not take us off."

He lifted the chain so it caught the gleam of the sun, slanting through a window. "I must have dropped it on the sand," he muttered. "*He* found it—"

"You did not drop it on the strand," said Francoise, in a voice as devoid of mercy as his own; her soul seemed turned to stone. "You tore it from your throat last night when you flogged Tina. I saw it gleaming on the floor before I left the hall."

He looked up, his face grey with a terrible fear.

She laughed bitterly, sensing the mute question in his dilated eyes.

"Yes! The black man! He was here! He must have found the chain on the floor. I saw him, padding along the upper hallway."

He sank back in his chair, the chain slipping from his nerveless hands.

"In the manor!" he whispered. "In spite of guards and bolted doors! I can no more guard against him than I can escape him! Then it was no dream—that clawing at my door last night! At my door!"

he shrieked, tearing at the lace upon his collar as though it strangled him. "God curse him!"

The paroxysm passed, leaving him faint and trembling.

"I understand," he panted. "The bolts on my chamber door balked even him. So he destroyed the ship upon which I might have escaped him, and he slew that wretched savage and left my chain upon him, to bring down the vengeance of his people on me. They have seen that chain upon my neck many a time."

"Who is this black man?" asked Francoise, fear crawling along her spine.

"A juju-man of the Slave Coast," he whispered, staring at her with weird eyes that seemed to look through her and far beyond to some dim doom.

"I built my wealth on human flesh. When I was younger my ships plied between the Slave Coast and the West Indies, supplying black men to the Spanish plantations. My partner was a black wizard of a coast-tribe. He captured the slaves with his warriors, and I delivered them to the Indies. I was evil in those days, but he was ten times more evil. If ever a man sold his soul to the Devil, he was that man. Even now in nightmares I am haunted by the sights I saw in his village when the moon hung red in the jungle trees, and the drums bellowed, and human victims screamed on the altars of his heathen gods.

"In the end I tricked him out of his share of the trade, and sold him to the Spaniards who chained him to a galley's oar. He swore an awful vengeance upon me, but I laughed, for I believed not even he could escape the fate to which I had delivered him.

"As the years passed, however, I could not forget him, and would wake sometimes in fright, his threat ringing in my ears. I told myself that he was dead, long ago, under the lashes of the Spaniards. Then one day there came to me word that a strange black man, with the scars of the galley-chains on his wrists, had come to France and was seeking me.

"He knew me by another name, in the old days, but I knew he would trace me out. In haste I sold my lands and put to sea, as you know. With a whole world between us, I thought I would be safe. But he has tracked me down and he is lurking out there, like a coiled cobra."

"What do you mean, 'He destroyed the ship'?" asked Francoise uneasily.

"The wizards of the Slave Coast have the power of raising tempests!" whispered the Count, from grey lips. "Witchcraft!"

Francoise shuddered. That sudden tempest, she knew, had been but a freak of chance; no man could summon a storm at will. And a savage raised in the blackness of a West Coast jungle might be able to enter a fortress guarded by armed men, when there was a mist to blur their sight. This grim stranger was only a man of flesh and blood. But she shivered, remembering a drum that droned exultantly above the whine of the storm—

Henri's weird eyes lit palely as he gazed beyond the tapestried walls to far, invisible horizons.

"I'll trick him yet," he whispered. "Let him delay to strike this night—dawn will find me with a ship under my heels and again I'll cast an ocean between me and his vengeance."

"HELL'S fire!"

Vulmea stopped short. Behind him the seamen halted, in two compact clumps. They were following an old Indian path which led due east, and the beach was no longer visible.

"What are you stopping for?" demanded Harston suspiciously.

Somebody's on the trail ahead of us," growled Vulmea. "Somebody in boots. His spoor's not more than an hour old. Did either of you swine send a man ahead of us for any reason?"

Both captains loudly disclaimed any such act, glaring at each other with mutual disbelief. Vulmea shook his head disgustedly and strode on, and the seamen rolled after him. Men of the sea, accustomed to the wide expanses of blue water, they were ill at ease with the green mysterious walls of trees and vines hemming them in. The path wound and twisted until most of them lost all sense of direction.

"Damned peculiar things going on around here," growled Vulmea. "If Henri didn't hang up that Indian's head, who did? They'll believe he did, anyway. That's an insult. When his tribe learns about it, there'll be hell to pay. I hope we're out of these woods before they take the warpath."

When the trail veered northward Vulmea left it, and began threading his way through the dense trees in a southeasterly direction. Harston glanced uneasily at Villiers. This might force a change in their plans. Within a few hundred feet from the path both were hopelessly lost.

Suspicions of many kinds were gnawing both men when they suddenly emerged from the thick woods and saw just ahead of them a gaunt crag that jutted up from the forest floor. A dim path leading out of the woods from the east ran among a cluster of boulders and wound up the crag on a ladder of stony shelves to a flat ledge near the summit.

"That trail is the one I followed, running from the Indians," said Vulmea, halting. "It leads up to a cave behind that ledge. In that cave are the bodies of da Verrazano and his men, and the treasure. But a word before we go up after it: if you kill me here, you'll never find your way back to the trail. I know how helpless you all are in the deep woods. Of course the beach lies due west, but if you have to make your way through the tangled woods, burdened with the plunder, it'll take you days instead of hours. I don't think these woods will be very safe for white men when the Indians learn about that head in the tree."

He laughed at the ghastly, mirthless smiles with which they greeted his recognition of their secret intentions. And he also comprehended the thought that sprang in the mind of each: let the Irishman secure the loot for them, and lead them back to the trail before they killed him.

"Three of us are enough to lug the loot down from the cave," he said.

Harston laughed sardonically.

"Do you think I'm fool enough to go up there alone with you and Villiers? My boatswain comes with me!" He designated a brawny, hard-faced giant, naked to his belt, with gold hoops in his ears, and a crimson scarf knotted about his head.

"And my executioner comes with me!" growled Villiers. He beckoned a lean sea-thief with a face like a parchmentcovered skull, who carried a great scimitar naked over his bony shoulder.

Vulmea shrugged his shoulders. "Very well. Follow me."

They were close on his heels as he strode up the winding path. They crowded him close as he passed through the cleft in the wall behind the ledge, and their breath sucked in greedily as he called their attention to the iron-bound chests on either side of the short tunnel.

"A rich cargo there," he said carelessly. "Garments, weapons, ornaments. But the real treasure lies beyond that door."

He pushed it partly open and drew aside to let his companions look through.

They looked into a wide cavern, lit vaguely by a blue glow that shimmered through a smoky mist-like haze. A great ebon table stood in the midst of the cavern, and in a carved chair with a high back and broad arms sat a giant figure, fabulous and fantastic—there sat Giovanni da Verrazano, his great head sunk on his bosom, one shriveled hand still gripping a jeweled goblet; da Verrazano, in his plumed hat, his gilt-embroidered coat with jeweled buttons that winked in the blue flame, his flaring boots and goldworked baldric that upheld a jewel-hilted sword in a golden sheath.

And ranging the board, each with his chin resting on his lace-bedecked breast, sat the eleven buccaneers. The blue fire played weirdly on them, as it played like a nimbus of frozen fire about the heap of curiously-cut gems which shone in the center of the table—the jewels of the Montezumas! The stones whose value was greater than the value of all the rest of the known gems in the world put together!

The faces of the pirates showed pallid in the blue glow.

"Go in and take them," invited Vulmea, and Harston and Villiers crowded past him, jostling one another in their haste. Their followers were treading on their heels. Villiers kicked the door wide open—and halted with one foot on the threshold at the sight of a figure on the floor, previously hidden by the partly-closed door. It was a man, prone and contorted, head drawn back between his shoulders, white face twisted in a grin of mortal agony, clawed fingers gripping his own throat.

"Gallot!" ejaculated Villiers. "What—!" With sudden suspicion he thrust his head into the bluish mist that filled the inner cavern. And he choked and screamed: "There is death in the smoke!"

Even as he screamed, Vulmea hurled his weight against the four men bunched in the doorway, sending them staggering—but not headlong into the cavern as he had planned. They were recoiling at the sight of the dead man and the realization of the trap, and his violent impact, while it threw them off their feet, yet failed of the result he desired. Harston and Villiers sprawled half over the threshold on their knees, the boatswain tumbling over their legs, and the executioner caromed against the wall. Before Vulmea could follow up his intention of kicking the fallen men into the cavern and holding the door against them until the poisonous mist did its deadly work, he had to turn and defend himself against the frothing onslaught of the executioner.

The Frenchman missed a tremendous swipe with his headsman's sword as the Irishman ducked, and the great blade banged against the stone wall, scattering blue sparks. The next instant his skull-faced head rolled on the cavern floor under the bite of Vulmea's cutlass.

In the split seconds this action had consumed, the boatswain regained his feet and fell on the Irishman, raining blows with a cutlass. Blade met blade with a ring of steel that was deafening in the narrow tunnel. The two captains rolled back across the threshold, gagging and purple in the face, too near strangled to shout, and Vulmea redoubled his efforts, striving to dispose of his antagonist so he could cut down his rivals before they could recover from the effects of the poison. The boatswain was driven backward, dripping blood at each step, and he began desperately to bellow for his mates. But before Vulmea could deal the final stroke, the two chiefs, gasping but murderous, came at him with swords in their hands, croaking for their men.

Vulmea bounded back and leaped out onto the ledge, fearing to be trapped by the men coming in response to their captains' yells.

These were not coming as fast as he expected, however. They heard the muffled shouts issuing from the cavern, but no man dared start up the path for fear of a sword in the back. Each band faced the other tensely, grasping weapons but incapable of decision, and when they saw Vulmea bound out on the ledge, they merely gaped. While they stood with their matches smoldering he ran up the ladder of handholds niched in the rock and threw himself prone on the summit of the crag, out of their sight.

The captains stormed out on the ledge and their men, seeing their leaders were not at sword-strokes, ceased menacing each other and gaped in greater bewilderment.

"Dog!" screamed Villiers. "You planned to poison us! Traitor!"

Vulmea mocked them from above.

"What did you expect? You two were planning to cut my throat as soon as I got the plunder for you. If it hadn't been for that fool Gallot I'd have trapped the four of you and explained to your men how you rushed in heedless to your doom!"

"And you'd have taken my ship and all the loot!" frothed Harston.

"Aye! And the pick of both crews! It was Gallot's footprints I saw on the trail. I wonder how the fool learned of this cave."

"If we hadn't seen his body we'd have walked into that death-trap," muttered Villiers, his dark face still ashy. "That blue smoke was like unseen fingers crushing my throat."

"Well, what are you going to do?" their tormentor yelled sardonically.

"What *are* we going to do?" asked Villiers of Harston.

"You can't get the jewels," Vulmea assured them with satisfaction from his aerie. "That mist will strangle you. It nearly got me, when I stepped in there. Listen and I'll tell you a tale the Indians tell in their lodges when the fires burn low! Once, long ago, twelve strange men came out of the sea and found a cave and heaped it with gold and gems. But while they sat drinking and singing, the earth shook and smoke came out of the earth and strangled them. Thereafter the tribes all shunned the spot as haunted and accursed by evil spirits.

"When I crawled in there to escape the Indians, I realized that the old legend was true, and referred to da Verrazano. An earthquake must have cracked the rock floor of the cavern they'd fortified, and he and his buccaneers were overcome as they sat at wine by the poisonous fumes of gases welling up from some vent in the earth. Death guards their loot!"

Harston peered into the tunnel mouth.

"The mist is drifting out into the tunnel," he growled, "but it dissipates itself in the open air. Damn Vulmea! Let's climb up after him."

"Do you think any man on earth could climb those hand-holds against his sword?" snarled Villiers. "We'll have the men up here, and set some to watch and shoot him if he shows himself. He had some plan of getting those jewels, and if he could get them, so can we. We'll tie a hook to a rope, cast it about the leg of that table and drag it, jewels and all, out onto the ledge."

"Well thought, Guillaume!" came down Vulmea's mocking voice. "Just what I had in mind. But how will you find your way back to the path? It'll be dark before you reach the beach, if you have to feel your way through the woods, and I'll follow you and kill you one by one in the dark."

"It's no empty boast," muttered Harston. "He is like an Indian for stealth. If he hunts us back through the forest, few of us will live to see the beach."

"Then we'll kill him here," gritted Villiers. "Some of us will shoot at him while the rest climb the crag. Listen! Why does he laugh?"

"To hear dead men making plots!" came Vulmea's grimly amused voice.

"Heed him not," scowled Villiers, and lifting his voice, he shouted for the men below to join him and Harston on the ledge.

As the sailors started up the slanting trail, there sounded a hum like that of an angry bee, ending in a sharp thud. A buccaneer gasped and sank to his knees, clutching the shaft that quivered in his breast. A yell of alarm went up from his companions.

"What's the matter?" yelled Harston.

"Indians!" bawled a pirate, and went down with an arrow in his neck.

"Take cover, you fools!" shrieked Villiers. From his vantage point he glimpsed painted figures moving in the bushes. One of the men on the winding path fell back dying. The rest scrambled hastily down among the rocks about the foot of the crag. Arrows flickered from the bushes, splintering on the boulders. The men on the ledge lay prone.

"We're trapped!" Harston's face was pale. Bold enough with a deck under his feet, this silent, savage warfare shook his nerves.

"Vulmea said they feared this crag," said Villiers. "When night falls the men must climb up here. The Indians won't rush us on the ledge."

"That's true!" mocked Vulmea. "They won't climb the crag. They'll merely surround it and keep you here until you starve."

"Make a truce with him," muttered Harston. "If any man can get us out of this, he can. Time enough to cut his throat later." Lifting his voice he called: "Vulmea, let's forget our feud. You're in this as much as we are."

"How do you figure that?" retorted the Irishman. "When it's dark I can climb down the other side of this crag and crawl through the line the Indians have thrown around this hill. They'll never see me. I can return to the fort and report you all slain by the savages—which will shortly be the truth!"

Harston and Villiers stared at each other in pallid silence.

"But I'm not going to do that!" Vulmea roared. "Not because I have any love for you dogs, but because a white man doesn't leave white men, even his enemies, to be butchered by red savages."

The Irishman's tousled black head appeared over the crest of the crag.

"Listen! There's only a small band down there. I saw them sneaking through the brush when I laughed, awhile ago. I believe a big war-party is heading in our direction, and those are a group of fleet-footed young braves sent ahead of it to cut us off from the beach.

"They're all on the west side of the crag. I'm going down on the east side and work around behind them. Meanwhile, you crawl down the path and join your men among the rocks. When you hear me yell, rush the trees."

"What of the treasure?"

"To hell with it! We'll be lucky if we get out of here with our scalps."

The black-maned head vanished. They listened for sounds to indicate that Vulmea had crawled to the almost sheer eastern wall and was working his way down, but they heard nothing. Nor did any sound come from the forest. No more arrows broke against the rocks where the sailors were hidden, but all knew that fierce black eyes were watching with murderous patience. Gingerly Harston, Villiers and the boatswain started down the winding path. They were halfway down when the shafts began to whisper around them. The boatswain groaned and toppled down the slope, shot through the heart. Arrows splintered on the wall about the captains as they tumbled in frantic haste down the steep trail. They reached the foot in a scrambling rush and lay panting among the rocks.

"Is this more of Vulmea's trickery?" wondered Villiers profanely.

"We can trust him in this matter," asserted Harston. "There's a racial principle involved here. He'll help us against the Indians, even though he plans to murder us himself. *Hark!*"

A blood-freezing yell knifed the silence. It came from the woods to the west, and simultaneously an object arched out of the trees, struck the ground and rolled bouncingly toward the rocks—a severed human head, the hideously painted face frozen in a death-snarl.

"Vulmea's signal!" roared Harston, and the desperate pirates rose like a wave from the rocks and rushed headlong toward the woods.

Arrows whirred out of the bushes, but their flight was hurried and erratic. Only three men fell. Then the wild men of the sea plunged through the fringe of foliage and fell on the naked painted figures that rose out of the gloom before them. There was a murderous instant of panting, hand to hand ferocity, cutlasses beating down war-axes, booted feet trampling naked bodies, and then bare feet were rattling through the bushes in headlong flight as the survivors of that brief carnage quit the field, leaving seven still, painted figures stretched on the bloodstained leaves that littered the earth. Further back in the thickets sounded a thrashing and heaving, and then it ceased and Vulmea strode into view, his hat gone, his coat torn, his cutlass dripping in his hand.

"What now?" panted Villiers. He knew the charge had succeeded only because Vulmea's unexpected attack on the rear of the Indians had demoralized the painted men, and prevented them from melting back before the rush.

"Come on!"

They let their dead lie where they had fallen, and crowded close at his heels as he trotted through the trees. Alone they would have sweated and blundered among the thickets for hours before they found the trail that led to the beach—if they had ever found it. Vulmea led them as unerringly as if he had been following an open road, and the rovers shouted with hysterical relief as they burst suddenly upon the trail that ran westward.

"Fool!" Vulmea clapped a hand on the shoulder of a pirate who started to break into a run, and hurled him back among his companions. "You'd burst your heart within a thousand yards. We're miles from the beach. Take an easy gait. We may have to sprint the last mile. Save some of your wind for it. Come on, now."

He set off down the trail at a steady jog-trot, and the seamen followed him, suiting their pace to his.

THE sun was touching the waves of the western ocean. Tina stood at the window from which Francoise had watched the storm.

"The sunset turns the ocean to blood," she said. "The ship's sail is a white fleck on the crimson waters. The woods are already darkening."

"What of the seamen on the beach?" asked Francoise languidly. She reclined on a couch, her eyes closed, her hands clasped behind her head.

"Both camps are preparing their supper," answered Tina. "They are gathering driftwood and building fires. I can hear them shouting to one another—*what's that?*"

The sudden tenseness in the girl's tone brought Francoise upright on her couch. Tina gripped the window sill and her face was white.

"Listen! A howling, far off, like many wolves!"

"Wolves?" Francoise sprang up, fear clutching her heart. "Wolves do not hunt in packs at this time of the year!"

"Look!" shrilled the girl. "Men are running out of the forest!"

In an instant Francoise was beside her, staring wideeyed at the figures, small in the distance, streaming out of the woods.

"The sailors!" she gasped. "Empty handed! I see Villiers—Harston—"

"Where is Vulmea?" whispered the girl.

Francoise shook her head.

"Listen! Oh, listen!" whimpered the child, clinging to her.

All in the fort could hear it now—a vast ululation of mad bloodlust, rising from the depths of the dark forest.

That sound spurred on the panting men reeling toward the stockade.

"They're almost at our heels!" gasped Harston, his face a drawn mask of muscular exhaustion. "My ship—"

"She's too far out for us to reach," panted Villiers. "Make for the fort. See, the men camped on the beach have seen us!" He waved his arms in breathless pantomime, but the men on the strand had already recognized the significance of that wild howling in the forest. They abandoned their fires and cooking-pots and fled for the stockade gate. They were pouring through it as the fugitives from the forest rounded the south angle and reeled into the gate, half dead from exhaustion. The gate was slammed with frenzied haste, and men swarmed up the firing ledge.

Francoise confronted Villiers.

"Where is Black Vulmea?"

The buccaneer jerked a thumb toward the blackening woods. His chest heaved, and sweat poured down his face. "Their scouts were at our heels before we gained the beach. He paused to slay a few and give us time to get away."

He staggered away to take his place on the wall, whither Harston had already mounted. Henri stood there, a somber, cloak-wrapped figure, aloof and silent. He was like a man bewitched.

"Look!" yelped a pirate above the howling of the yet unseen horde.

A man emerged from the forest and raced fleetly toward the fort.

"Vulmea!"

Villiers grinned wolfishly.

"We're safe in the stockade. We know where the treasure is. No reason why we shouldn't put a bullet through him now."

"Wait!" Harston caught his arm. "We'll need his sword! Look!"

Behind the fleeing Irishman a wild horde burst from the forest, howling as they ran—naked savages, hundreds and hundreds of them. Their arrows rained about the fugitive. A few strides more and Vulmea reached the eastern wall of the stockade, bounded high, seized the points of the palisades and heaved himself up and over, his cutlass in his teeth. Arrows thudded venomously into the logs where his body had just been. His resplendent coat was gone, his white silk shirt torn and bloodstained.

"Stop them!" he roared as his feet hit the ground inside. "If they get on the wall we're done for!"

Seamen, soldiers and henchmen responded instantly and a storm of bullets tore into the oncoming horde.

Vulmea saw Francoise, with Tina clinging to her hand, and his language was picturesque.

"Get into the manor," he commanded in conclusion. "Their arrows will arch over the wall—what did I tell you?" A shaft cut into the earth at Francoise's feet and quivered like a serpent-head. Vulmea caught up a musket and leaped to the firing-ledge. "Some of you dogs prepare torches!" he roared, above the rising clamor of battle. "We can't fight them in the dark!"

The sun had sunk in a welter of blood; out in the bay the men about the ship had cut the anchor chain and the *War-Hawk* was rapidly receding on the crimson horizon.

Chapter .7.
Men of the Woods.

Night had fallen, but torches streamed across the strand, casting the mad scene into lurid revealment. Naked men in paint swarmed the beach; like waves they came against the palisade, bared teeth and blazing eyes gleaming in the glare of the torches thrust over the wall.

From up and down the coast the tribes had gathered to rid their country of the white-skinned invaders, and they surged against the stockade, driving a storm of arrows before them, fighting into the hail of bullets and shafts that tore into their masses. Sometimes they came so close to the wall they were hewing at the gate with their war-axes and thrusting their spears through the loopholes. But each time the tide ebbed back, leaving its drift of dead. In this kind of fighting the pirates were at their stoutest. Their matchlocks tore holes in the charging horde, their cutlasses hewed the wild men from the palisades.

Yet again and again the men of the woods returned to the onslaught with all the stubborn ferocity that had been roused in their fierce hearts.

"They are like mad dogs!" gasped Villiers, hacking downward at the dark hands that grasped at the palisade points, the dark faces that snarled up at him.

"If we can hold the fort till dawn they'll lose heart," grunted Vulmea, splitting a feathered skull. "They won't maintain a long siege. Look, they're falling back again."

The charge rolled back and the men on the wall shook the sweat out of their eyes, counted their dead, and took a fresh grasp on the blood-slippery hilts of their swords. Like blood-hungry wolves, grudgingly driven from a cornered prey, the Indians slunk back beyond the ring of torch-light. Only the bodies of the slain lay before the palisades.

"Have they gone?" Harston shook back his wet, tawny locks. The cutlass in his fist was notched and red, his brawny bare arm was splashed with blood.

"They're still out there." Vulmea nodded toward the outer darkness which ringed the circle of torches. He glimpsed movements in the shadows, glitter of eyes and the dull sheen of spears.

"They've drawn off for a bit, though," he said. "Put sentries on the wall and let the rest drink and eat. It's past midnight. We've been fighting steadily for hours."

The captains clambered down, calling their men from the walls. A sentry was posted in the middle of each wall, east, west, north and south, and a clump of soldiers was left at the gate. The Indians, to reach the wall, would have to charge across a wide, torch-lit space, and the defenders could resume their places long before the rush could reach the stockade.

"Where's d'Chastillon?" demanded Vulmea, gnawing a huge beef-bone as he stood beside the fire the men had built in the center of the compound. Englishmen and Frenchmen mingled together, wolfing the meat and wine the women brought them, and allowing their wounds to be bandaged.

"He was fighting on the wall beside me an hour ago," grunted Harston, "when suddenly he stopped short and glared out into the darkness as if he saw a ghost. 'Look!' he croaked. 'The black devil! I see him, out there in the night!' Well, I could swear I saw a strange figure moving among the shadows that was too dark even for an Indian. But it was just a glimpse and it was gone. But Henri jumped down from the wall and staggered into the manor like a man with a mortal wound. I haven't seen him since."

"He probably saw a forest-devil," said Vulmea tranquilly. "The Indians say this coast is lousy with them. What I'm more afraid of is fire-arrows. They're likely to start shooting them at any time. What's that? It sounded like a cry for help!"

WHEN the lull came in the fighting, Francoise and Tina had crept to their window, from which they had been driven by the danger of flying arrows. They watched the men gather about the fire.

"There are not enough sentries on the stockade," said Tina.

In spite of her nausea at the sight of the corpses sprawled about the palisades, Francoise was moved to laugh.

"Do you think you know more about war than the men?" she chided gently.

"There should be more men on the walls," insisted the child, shivering. "Suppose the black man came back! One man to a side is not enough. The black man could creep beneath the wall and shoot him with a poisoned dart before he could cry out. He is like a shadow, and hard to see by torchlight."

Francoise shuddered at the thought.

"I am afraid," murmured Tina. "I hope Villiers and Harston are killed."

"And not Vulmea?" asked Francoise curiously.

"Black Vulmea would not harm a woman," said the child confidently.

"You are wise beyond your years, Tina," murmured Francoise.

"Look!" Tina stiffened. "The sentry is gone from the south wall! I saw him on the ledge a moment ago. Now he has vanished."

From their window the palisade points of the south wall were just visible over the slanting roofs of a row of huts which paralleled that wall almost its entire length. A sort of open-topped corridor, three or four yards wide, was formed by the stockade-wall and the back of the huts, which were built in a solid row. These huts were occupied by the retainers.

"Where could the sentry have gone?" whispered Tina uneasily.

Francoise was watching one end of the hut-row which was not far from a side door of the manor. She could have sworn she saw a shadowy figure glide from behind the huts and disappear at the door. Was that the vanished sentry? Why had he left the wall, and why should he steal so subtly into the manor? She did not believe it was the sentry she had seen, and a nameless fear congealed her blood.

"Where is the Count, Tina?" she asked.

"In the great hall, my Lady. He sits alone at the table, wrapped in his cloak and drinking wine, with a face grey as death."

"Go and tell him what we have seen. I will keep watch from this window, lest the Indians climb the unguarded wall."

Tina scampered away. Francoise heard her slippered feet pattering along the corridor, receding down the stair. Then suddenly, terribly, there rang out a scream of such poignant fear that Francoise's heart almost stopped with the shock of it. She was out of the chamber and flying down the corridor before she was aware that her limbs were in motion. She ran down the stair—and halted as if turned to stone.

She did not scream as Tina had screamed. She was incapable of sound or motion. She saw Tina, was aware of the reality of small hands grasping her frantically. But these were the only realities in a scene of nightmare, and brainshattering horror.

Out in the stockade Harston had shaken his head at Vulmea's question.

"I heard nothing."

"I did!" Vulmea's wild instincts were roused. "It came from the south wall, behind those huts!"

Drawing his cutlass he strode toward the palisades. From the compound the south wall and the sentry posted there were not visible, being hidden behind the huts. Harston followed, impressed by Vulmea's manner.

At the mouth of the open lane between the huts and the wall Vulmea halted, swearing. The space was dimly lighted by torches flaring at either corner of the stockade. And midway of that natural corridor a crumpled shape sprawled on the ground.

"The sentry!"

"Hawksby!" swore Harston, running forward and dropping on one knee beside the figure. "By Satan, his throat's cut from ear to ear!"

Vulmea swept the alley with a quick glance, finding it empty save for himself, Harston and the dead man. He peered through a loop-hole. No living man moved within the ring of torchlight outside the fort.

"Who could have done this?" he wondered.

"Villiers!" Harston sprang up, spitting fury like a wildcat. "He has set his dogs to stabbing my men in the back! He plans to destroy me by treachery!"

"Wait, Dick!" Vulmea caught his arm. He had glimpsed the tufted end of a dart jutting from the dead pirate's neck. "I don't believe Villiers—"

But the maddened pirate jerked away and rushed around the end of the hut row, breathing blasphemies. Vulmea ran after him, swearing. Harston made straight toward the fire by which Villiers' tall form was visible as the buccaneer chief quaffed a jack of ale.

His amazement was supreme when the jack was dashed violently from his hand, spattering his breastplate with foam, and he was jerked around to confront the convulsed face of the Englishman.

"You murdering dog!" roared Harston. "Will you slay my men behind my back while they fight for your filthy hide as well as for mine?"

On all sides men ceased eating and drinking to gape in amazement.

"What do you mean?" sputtered Villiers.

"You've set your men to murdering mine at their posts!" bellowed Harston.

"You lie!" Smoldering hate burst into sudden flame.

With a howl Harston heaved up his cutlass and cut at the Frenchman's head. Villiers caught the blow on his armored left arm and sparks flew as he staggered back, ripping out his own sword.

In an instant the captains were fighting like madmen, their blades flaming and flashing in the firelight. Their crews reacted instantly and blindly. A deep roar went up as Englishmen and Frenchmen drew their swords and fell upon one another. The pirates left on the walls abandoned their posts and leaped down into the stockade, blades in hand. In an instant the compound was swarming with battling groups of men. The soldiers at the gate turned and stared down in amazement, forgetful of the enemy lurking outside.

It had all happened so quickly—smoldering passions exploding into sudden battle—that men were fighting all over the compound before Vulmea could reach the maddened captains. Ignoring the swords that flashed about his ears, he tore them apart with such violence that they staggered backward and Villiers tripped and fell headlong.

"You cursed fools, will you throw away all our lives?"

Harston was frothing, and Villiers was bawling for assistance. A buccaneer ran at Vulmea and cut at him from behind. The Irishman half turned and caught his arm, checking the stroke in midair.

"Look, you fools!" he roared, pointing with his sword.

Something in his tone caught the attention of the battle-crazed mob. Men froze in their places, with lifted swords, Villiers on one knee, and twisted their heads to stare. Vulmea was pointing at a soldier on the wall. The man was reeling, clawing the air, choking as he tried to shout. Suddenly he pitched to the ground and all saw the shaft standing up between his shoulders.

A yell of alarm rose from the compound. On the heels of the shout came a clamor of blood-freezing screams, the shattering impact of axes on the gate. Flaming arrows arched over the wall and stuck in logs, and thin wisps of blue smoke curled upward. Then from behind the huts along the south wall dark figures came gliding.

"The Indians are in!" roared Vulmea.

Bedlam followed his yell. The freebooters ceased their feud, some turned to meet the savages already within the stockade, some to spring to the wall. The painted men were pouring from behind the huts and their axes clashed against the cutlasses of the sailors.

Villiers was struggling to his feet when a painted savage rushed upon him from behind and brained him with a war-axe.

Vulmea led the Frenchmen against the Indians inside the stockade, and Harston, with most of his men, climbed on the firing-ledge, slashing at the dark figures already swarming up on the wall. The savages, who had crept up unobserved while the defenders of the fort were fighting among themselves, were attacking from all sides. Henri's soldiers were clustered at the gate, trying to hold it against a howling swarm of blood-mad demons.

More and more savages scaled the undefended south wall and streamed from behind the huts. Harston and his men were beaten back from the north and west walls and in an instant the compound was swarming with naked warriors who came over the palisades in a wave. They dragged down the defenders like wolves dragging down a stag; the battle resolved into swirling whirlpools of painted figures surging about small clumps of desperate white men. Blood-smeared braves dived into the huts and the shrieks that rose as women and children died beneath the red axes rose above the roar of the battle. The soldiers abandoned the gate when they heard those cries, and in an instant the savages had burst it in and were pouring into the stockade at that point also. Huts began to go up in flames.

"Make for the manor!" roared Vulmea, and a dozen men surged in behind him as he hewed a red way through the snarling pack.

Harston was at his side, wielding his red cutlass like a cleaver.

"We can't hold the manor," grunted the Englishman.

"Why not?" Vulmea was too busy with his crimson work to spare a glance.

"Because—uh!" A knife in a dark hand sank deep in the pirate's back. "Devil eat you, dog!" Harston turned and split the savage's head, then reeled and fell to his knees, blood starting from his lips.

"The manor's burning!" he croaked, and slumped over in the dust.

Vulmea glared about him. The men who had followed him were all down in their blood. An Indian gasping out his life under his feet was the last of the group which had barred his way. All about him battle swirled and surged, but for the moment he stood alone. A few strides and he could leap to the wall, swing over and be gone through the night. But he remembered the helpless girls in the manor—from which, now, smoke was rolling in billowing masses. He ran toward the manor.

A feathered chief wheeled from the door, lifting a waraxe, and behind the Irishman groups of fleet-footed braves were converging upon him. He did not check his stride. His downward sweeping cutlass met and deflected the axe and crushed the skull of the wielder, and an instant later he was through the door and had slammed and bolted it against the axes that splintered into the wood.

The great hall was full of drifting wisps of smoke through which he groped, half blinded. Somewhere a woman was sobbing hysterically. He emerged from a whorl of smoke and stopped dead in his tracks.

The hall was dim and shadowy with the drifting smoke; the silver candelabrum was overturned, the candles extinguished. The only illumination was a lurid glow from the great fireplace and the flames which licked from burning floor to smoking roof beams. And against that lurid glare Vulmea saw a human form swinging slowly at the end of a rope. The dead face turned toward him as the body swung, and it was distorted beyond recognition. But Vulmea knew it was Count Henri d'Chastillon, hanged to his own roof beam.

He saw Francoise and Tina, clutched in each others' arms, crouching at the foot of the stair. And he saw something else, dimly through the smoke—a giant black man, looming against the red glare like a black devil stalking out of hell. The scarred, twisted face, dim in the smoke, was fiendish, the eyes burned red as the reflection of flame on black waters. At the stark evil of that face even the fierce pirate felt a chill along his spine. And then the shadow of death fell across him as he saw the long bamboo tube in the black man's hand.

Slowly, gloatingly the black man lifted it to his lips, and Vulmea knew winged death would strike him before he could reach the killer with his sword. His desperate eyes fell on a massive silver bench, ornately carven, once part of the splendor of Chateau d'Chastillon. It stood at his feet. With desperate quickness he grasped it and heaved it above his head.

"Take this to hell with you!" he roared in a voice like a clap of wind, and hurled the bench with all the power of his iron muscles, even as the dart leaped from the lifted bamboo. In midair it splintered on the hurtling bench, and full on the broad black breast crashed a hundred pounds of silver. The impact shattered bones and carried the black man off his feet—hurled him backward into the open fireplace. A horrible scream shook the hall. The mantel cracked and stones fell from the great chimney, half hiding the black writhing limbs. Burning beams crashed down from the roof and thundered on the stones, and the whole heap was enveloped by a roaring burst of flames.

Fire was licking at the stair when Vulmea reached it. He caught up Tina under one arm and dragged Francoise to her feet. Through the crackle and snap of the flames sounded the splintering of the door under the war-axes.

He glared about, sighted a door at the other end of the hall, and hurried through it, half carrying, half dragging his dazed charges. As they came into the chamber beyond, a reverberation behind them told them that the roof was falling in the hall. Through a strangling cloud of smoke Vulmea saw an open, outer door on the other side of the chamber. As he lugged his charges through it, he saw that the lock had been forced.

"The black man came in by this door!" Francoise sobbed hysterically. "I saw him—but I did not know—"

They emerged into the fire-lit compound, a few yards from the hut-row that lined the south wall. A warrior was skulking toward the door, eyes red in the firelight, axe lifted. Turning the girl on his arm away from the blow, Vulmea drove his cutlass through the Indian's breast, and ran toward the south wall.

The enclosure was full of smoke clouds that hid half the red work going on there, but the fugitives had been seen. Naked figures, black against the red glare, pranced out of the smoke, brandishing axes. They were only a few yards behind him when Vulmea ducked into the space between the huts and the wall. At the other end of the lane he saw other warriors running to cut him off. He tossed Francoise bodily to the firing-ledge and leaped after her. Swinging her over the palisades he dropped her to the sand outside and dropped Tina after her. A thrown axe crashed into a log by his shoulder, and then he too was over the wall and gathering up his helpless charges. When the Indians reached the wall the space before the palisades was empty of any living humans.

DAWN was tingeing the dim waters with an old rose hue. Far out across the tinted waters a fleck of white grew out of the mist—a sail that seemed to hang suspended in the pearly sky. On a bushy headland Black Vulmea held a ragged cloak over a fire of green wood. As he manipulated the cloak, puffs of smoke rose upward.

Francoise sat near him, one arm about Tina.

"Do you think they'll see it and understand?"

"They'll see it, right enough," he assured her. "They've been hanging off and on this coast all night, hoping to sight some survivors. They're scared stiff. There's only a dozen of them, and not one can navigate well enough to reach the Horn, much less round it. They'll understand my signal; it's a trick the lads of the Brotherhood learned from the Indians. They know I can navigate, and they'll be glad enough to pick us up. Aye, and to give me command of the ship. I'm the only captain left."

"But suppose the Indians see the smoke?" She shuddered, glancing back over the misty sands and bushes to where, miles to the north, a column of smoke stood up in the still air.

"Not likely. After I hid you in the woods last night I sneaked back and saw them dragging barrels of wine out of the storehouses. Most of them were reeling already. They'll be lying around dog-drunk by this time. If I had a hundred men I could wipe out the whole horde. Look! The WarHawk's coming around and heading for the shore. They've seen the signal."

He stamped out the fire and handed the cloak back to Francoise, who watched him in wonder. The night of fire and blood, and the flight through the black woods afterward, had not shaken his nerves. His tranquil manner was genuine. Francoise did not fear him; she felt safer with him than she had felt since she landed on that wild coast. The man had his own code of honor, and it was not to be despised.

"Who was that black man?" he asked suddenly.

She shivered. "A man the Count sold as a galley-slave long ago. Somehow he escaped and tracked us down. My uncle believed him to be a wizard."

"He might have been," muttered Vulmea. "I've seen some queer things on the Slave Coast. But no matter. We have other things to think of. What will you do when you get back to France?"

She shook her head helplessly. "I do not know. I have neither money nor friends. Perhaps it would have been better had one of those arrows struck my heart."

"Do not say that, my Lady!" begged Tina. "I will work for us both!"

Vulmea drew a small leather bag from inside his girdle.

"I didn't get Montezuma's jewels," he rumbled, "but here are some baubles I found in the chest where I got these clothes." He spilled a handful of flaming rubies into his palm. "They're worth a fortune, themselves."

He dumped them back into the bag and handed it to her.

"But I can't take these—" she began.

"Of course you'll take them! I might as well leave you for the Indians to scalp as to take you back to France to starve."

"But what of you?"

Vulmea grinned and nodded toward the swiftly approaching *War-Hawk.*

"A ship and a crew are all I want. As soon as I set foot on that deck I'll have a ship, and as soon as I raise the coast of Darien I'll have a crew. I'll take a galley and free its slaves, or raid some Spanish plantation on the coast. There are plenty of stout French and British lads toiling as slaves to the Dons, and waiting the chance to escape and join some captain of the Brotherhood. And, as soon as I get back on the Main, and put you and the girl on some honest ship bound for France, I'll show the Spaniards that Black Vulmea still lives! Nay, nay, no thanks! What are a handful of gems to me, when all the loot of the western world is waiting for me to grab?"

Flint's Passing

Bring aft the rum! Life's measure's overfull
And down the sides the splashing liquor slops
To mingle in the unknown seas of Doubt.
Bring aft the rum! The tide is going out;
The breeze has lain, the tattered mainsail drops
Against the mast. And on the battered hull
I hear the drowsy slap of lazy waves.
And through the port I see the sandy beach,
And sullen trees beyond, a swampland dank.
I've known the isles the furtherest tide surge laves —
Now like a stranded hulk I come to die
Beside a shore mud-foul and forest-rank.
Bring aft the rum! And set it just in reach.
I've sailed the seven seas, long, bloody years.
I've seen men die and ships go reeling down —
I might have robbed my fellow man in style
But I was long on force and short on guile —
So 'stead of trade I chose the buccaneers —
Rig aft a plank there, damn you! Sink or drown! —
Life is a vain, illusive, fickle thing —
Now nearly done with me — it could not hold
Allurement to allay my thirst — for rum.
Steps on the main companion? Let them come.
Here is the map; let Silver have the gold.
Gems, wenches, rum — aye, I have shed my fling.
I guzzled Life as I have guzzled rum.
Run up the sails — throw off the anchor chain —
The courses sway, the straining braces thrum,
The breezes lift, the scents of ocean come —
Bring aft the rum! I'll put to sea again.

Black Vulmea's Vengeance

Chapter .1.

Out of the *Cockatoo's* cabin staggered Black Terence Vulmea, pipe in one hand and flagon in the other. He stood with booted legs wide, teetering slightly to the gentle lift of the lofty poop. He was bareheaded and his shirt was open, revealing his broad hairy chest. He emptied the flagon and tossed it over the side with a gusty sigh of satisfaction, then directed his somewhat blurred gaze on the deck below. From poop ladder to forecastle it was littered by sprawling figures. The ship smelt like a brewery. Empty barrels, with their heads stove in, stood or rolled between the prostrate forms. Vulmea was the only man on his feet. From galley boy to first mate the rest of the ship's company lay senseless after a debauch that had lasted a whole night long. There was not even a man at the helm.

But it was lashed securely and in that placid sea no hand was needed on the wheel. The breeze was light but steady. Land was a thin blue line to the east. A stainless blue sky held a sun whose heat had not yet become fierce.

Vulmea blinked indulgently down upon the prone figures of his crew, and glanced idly over the larboard side. He grunted incredulously and batted his eyes. A ship loomed where he had expected to see only naked ocean stretching to the skyline. She was little more than a hundred yards away, and was bearing down swiftly on the *Cockatoo*, obviously with the intention of laying her alongside. She was tall and square rigged, her white canvas flashing dazzlingly in the sun. From the main-truck the flag of England whipped red against the blue. Her bulwarks were lined with tense figures, bristling with boarding pikes and grappling irons, and through her open ports the astounded pirate glimpsed the glow of the burning matches the gunners held ready.

"All hands to battle-quarters!" yelled Vulmea confusedly. Reverberant snores answered the summons. All hands remained as they were.

"Wake up, you lousy dogs!" roared their captain. "Up, curse you! A king's ship is at our throats!"

His only response came in the form of staccato commands from the frigate's deck, barking across the narrowing strip of blue water.

"Damnation!"

Cursing luridly he lurched in a reeling run across the poop to the swivel gun which stood at the head of the larboard ladder. Seizing this he swung it about until its muzzle bore full on the bulwark of the approaching frigate. Objects wavered dizzily before his bloodshot eyes, but he squinted along its barrel as if he were aiming a musket.

"Strike your colors, you damned pirate!" came a hail from the trim figure that trod the warship's poop, sword in hand.

"Go to hell!" roared Vulmea, and knocked the glowing coals of his pipe into the vent of the gun breech. The falcon crashed, smoke puffed out in a white cloud, and the double handful of musket balls with which the gun had been charged mowed a ghastly lane through the boarding party clustered along the frigate's bulwark. Like a clap of thunder came the answering broadside and a storm of metal raked the *Cockatoo's* decks, turning them into a red shambles.

Sails ripped, ropes parted, timbers splintered, and blood and brains mingled with the pools of liquor spilt on the decks. A round shot as big as a man's head smashed into the falcon, ripping it loose from the swivel and dashing it against the man who had fired it. The impact knocked him backward headlong across the poop where his head hit the rail with a crack that was too much even for an Irish skull. Black Vulmea sagged senseless to the boards. He was as deaf to the triumphant shouts and the stamp of victorious feet on his red-streaming decks as were his men who had gone from the sleep of drunkenness to the black sleep of death without knowing what had hit them.

CAPTAIN John Wentyard, of his Majesty's frigate the *Redoubtable*, sipped his wine delicately and set down the glass with a gesture that in another man would have smacked of affectation. Wentyard was a tall man, with a narrow, pale face, colorless eyes, and a prominent nose. His costume was almost sober in comparison with the glitter of his officers who sat in respectful silence about the mahogany table in the main cabin.

"Bring in the prisoner," he ordered, and there was a glint of satisfaction in his cold eyes.

They brought in Black Vulmea, between four brawny sailors, his hands manacled before him and a chain on his ankles that was just long enough to allow him to walk without tripping. Blood was clotted in the pirate's thick black hair. His shirt was in tatters, revealing a torso bronzed by the sun and rippling with great muscles. Through the stern windows, he could see the topmasts of the *Cockatoo*, just sinking out of sight. That close-range broadside had robbed the frigate of a prize. His conquerors were before him and there was no mercy in their stares, but Vulmea did not seem at all abashed or intimidated. He met the stern eyes of the officers with a level gaze that reflected only a sardonic amusement. Wentyard frowned. He preferred for his captives to cringe before him. It made him feel more like Justice personified, looking unemotionally down from a great height on the sufferings of the evil.

"You are Black Vulmea, the notorious pirate?"

"I'm Vulmea," was the laconic answer.

"I suppose you will say, as do all these rogues," sneered Wentyard, "that you hold a commission from the Governor of Tortuga? These privateer commissions from the French mean nothing to his Majesty. You—"

"Save your breath, fisheyes!" Vulmea grinned hardly. "I hold no commission from anybody. I'm not one of your accursed swashbucklers who hide behind the name of buccaneer. I'm a pirate, and I've plundered English ships as well as Spanish—and be damned to you, heron-beak!"

The officers gasped at this effrontery, and Wentyard smiled a ghastly, mirthless smile, white with the anger he held in rein.

"You know that I have the authority to hang you out of hand?" he reminded the other.

"I know," answered the pirate softly. "It won't be the first time you've hanged me, John Wentyard."

"What?" The Englishman stared.

A flame grew in Vulmea's blue eyes and his voice changed subtly in tone and inflection; the brogue thickened almost imperceptibly.

"On the Galway coast it was, years ago, captain. You were a young officer then, scarce more than a boy—but with all your present characteristics already fully developed. There were some wholesale evictions, with the military to see the job was done, and the Irish were mad enough to make a fight of it—poor, ragged, half-starved peasants, fighting with sticks against full-armed English soldiers and sailors. After the massacre there were the usual hangings, and there was a boy crept into a thicket to watch—a lad of ten, who didn't even know what it was all about. You spied him, John Wentyard, and had your dogs drag him forth and string him up alongside the kicking bodies of the others. 'He's Irish,' you said as they heaved him aloft. 'Little snakes grow into big ones.' I was that boy. I've looked forward to this meeting, you English dog!"

Vulmea still smiled, but the veins knotted in his temples and the great muscles stood out distinctly on his manacled arms. Ironed and guarded though the pirate was, Wentyard involuntarily drew back, daunted by the stark and naked hate that blazed from those savage eyes.

"How did you escape your just deserts?" he asked coldly, recovering his poise.

Vulmea laughed shortly.

"Some of the peasants escaped the massacre and were hiding in the thickets. As soon as you left they came out, and not being civilized, cultured Englishmen, but only poor, savage Irishry, they cut me down along with the others, and found there was still a bit of life in me. We Gaels are hard to kill, as you Britons have learned to your cost."

"You fell into our hands easily enough this time," observed Wentyard.

Vulmea grinned. His eyes were grimly amused now, but the glint of murderous hate still lurked in their deeps.

"Who'd have thought to meet a king's ship in these western seas? It's been weeks since we sighted a sail of any kind, save for the carrack we took yesterday, with a cargo of wine bound for Panama from Valparaiso. It's not the time of year for rich prizes. When the lads wanted a drinking bout, who was I to deny them? We drew out of the lanes the Spaniards mostly follow, and thought we had the ocean to ourselves. I'd been sleeping in my cabin for some hours before I came on deck to smoke a pipe or so, and saw you about to board us without firing a shot."

"You killed seven of my men," harshly accused Wentyard.

"And you killed all of mine," retorted Vulmea. "Poor devils, they'll wake up in hell without knowing how they got there."

He grinned again, fiercely. His toes dug hard against the floor, unnoticed by the men who gripped him on either side. The blood was rioting through his veins, and the berserk feel of his great strength was upon him. He knew he could, in a sudden, volcanic explosion of power, tear free from the men who held him, clear the space between him and his enemy with one bound, despite his chains, and crush Wentyard's skull with a smashing swing of his manacled fists. That he himself would die an instant later mattered not at all. In that moment he felt neither fears nor regrets—only a reckless, ferocious exultation and a cruel contempt for these stupid Englishmen about him. He laughed in their faces, joying in the knowledge that they did not know why he laughed. So they thought to chain the tiger, did they? Little they guessed of the devastating fury that lurked in his catlike thews.

He began filling his great chest, drawing in his breath slowly, imperceptibly, as his calves knotted and the muscles of his arms grew hard. Then Wentyard spoke again.

"I will not be overstepping my authority if I hang you within the hour. In any event you hang, either from my yardarm or from a gibbet on the Port Royal wharves. But life is sweet, even to rogues like you, who notoriously cling to every moment granted them by outraged society. It would gain you a few more months of life if I were to take you back to Jamaica to be sentenced by the governor. This I might be persuaded to do, on one condition."

"What's that?" Vulmea's tensed muscles did not relax; imperceptibly he began to settle into a semi-crouch.

"That you tell me the whereabouts of the pirate, Van Raven."

In that instant, while his knotted muscles went pliant again, Vulmea unerringly gauged and appraised the man who faced him, and changed his plan. He straightened and smiled.

"And why the Dutchman, Wentyard?" he asked softly. "Why not Tranicos, or Villiers, or McVeigh, or a dozen others more destructive to English trade than Van Raven? Is it because of the treasure he took from the Spanish plate-fleet? Aye, the king would like well to set his hands on that hoard, and there's a rich prize would go to the captain lucky or bold enough to find Van Raven and plunder him. Is that why you came all the way around the Horn, John Wentyard?"

"We are at peace with Spain," answered Wentyard acidly. "As for the purposes of an officer in his Majesty's navy, they are not for such as you to question."

Vulmea laughed at him, the blue flame in his eyes.

"Once I sank a king's cruiser off Hispaniola," he said. "Damn you and your prating of 'His Majesty'! Your English king is no more to me than so much rotten driftwood. Van Raven? He's a bird of passage. Who knows where he sails? But if it's treasure you want, I can show you a hoard that would make the Dutchman's loot look like a peat-pool beside the Caribbean Sea!"

A pale spark seemed to snap from Wentyard's colorless eyes, and his officers leaned forward tensely. Vulmea grinned hardly. He knew the credulity of navy men, which they shared with landsmen and honest mariners, in regard to pirates and plunder. Every seaman not himself a rover believed that every buccaneer had knowledge of vast hidden wealth. The loot the men of the Red Brotherhood took from the Spaniards, rich enough as it was, was magnified a thousand times in the telling, and rumor made every swaggering sea rat the guardian of a treasure trove.

Coolly plumbing the avarice of Wentyard's hard soul, Vulmea said: "Ten days' sail from here there's a nameless bay on the coast of Ecuador. Four years ago Dick Harston, the English pirate and I anchored there, in quest of a hoard of ancient jewels called the Fangs of Satan. An Indian swore he had found them, hidden in a ruined temple in an uninhabited jungle a day's march inland, but superstitious fear of the old gods kept him from helping himself. But he was willing to guide us there.

"We marched inland with both crews, for neither of us trusted the other. To make a long tale short, we found the ruins of an old city, and, beneath an ancient, broken altar, we found the jewels—rubies, diamonds, emeralds, sapphires, bloodstones, big as hen eggs, making a quivering flame of fire about the crumbling old shrine!"

The flame grew in Wentyard's eyes. His white fingers knotted about the slender stem of his wine glass.

"The sight of them was enough to madden a man," Vulmea continued, watching the captain narrowly. "We camped there for the night, and, one way or another, we fell out over the division of the spoil, though there was enough to make every man of us rich for life. We came to blows, though, and whilst we fought among ourselves, there came a scout running with word that a Spanish fleet had come into the bay, driven our ships away, and sent five hundred men ashore to pursue us. By Satan, they were on us before the scout ceased the telling! One of my men snatched the plunder away and hid it in the old temple, and we scattered, each band for itself. There was no time to take the plunder. We barely got away with our naked lives. Eventually I, with most of my crew, made my way back to the coast and was picked up by my ship which came slinking back after escaping from the Spaniards.

"Harston gained his ship with a handful of men, after skirmishing all the way with the Spaniards who chased him instead of us, and later was slain by savages on the coast of California.

"The Dons harried me all the way around the Horn, and I never had an opportunity to go back after the loot—until this voyage. It was there I was going when you overhauled me. The treasure's still there. Promise me my life and I'll take you to it."

"That is impossible," snapped Wentyard. "The best I can promise you is trial before the governor of Jamaica."

"Well," said Vulmea, "maybe the governor might be more lenient than you. And much may happen between here and Jamaica."

Wentyard did not reply, but spread a map on the broad table.

"Where is this bay?"

Vulmea indicated a certain spot on the coast. The sailors released their grip on his arms while he marked it, and Wentyard's head was within reach, but the Irishman's plans were changed, and they included a chance for life—desperate, but nevertheless a chance.

"Very well. Take him below."

Vulmea went out with his guards, and Wentyard sneered coldly.

"A gentleman of his Majesty's navy is not bound by a promise to such a rogue as he. Once the treasure is aboard the *Redoubtable*, gentlemen, I promise you he shall swing from a yardarm."

Ten days later the anchors rattled down in the nameless bay Vulmea had described.

Chapter .2.

It seemed desolate enough to have been the coast of an uninhabited continent. The bay was merely a shallow indentation of the shoreline. Dense jungle crowded the narrow strip of white sand that was the beach. Gay-plumed birds flitted among the broad fronds, and the silence of primordial savagery brooded over all. But a dim trail led back into the twilight vistas of green-walled mystery.

Dawn was a white mist on the water when seventeen men marched down the dim path. One was John Wentyard. On an expedition designed to find treasure, he would trust the command to none but himself. Fifteen were soldiers, armed with hangers and muskets. The seventeenth was Black Vulmea. The Irishman's legs, perforce, were free, and the irons had been removed from his arms. But his wrists were bound before him with cords, and one end of the cord was in the grip of a brawny marine whose other hand held a cutlass ready to chop down the pirate if he made any move to escape.

"Fifteen men are enough," Vulmea had told Wentyard. "Too many! Men go mad easily in the tropics, and the sight of the Fangs of Satan is enough to madden any man, king's man or not. The more that see the jewels, the greater chance of mutiny before you raise the Horn again. You don't need more than three or four. Who are you afraid of? You said England was at peace with Spain, and there are no Spaniards anywhere near this spot, in any event."

"I wasn't thinking of Spaniards," answered Wentyard coldly. "I am providing against any attempt you might make to escape."

"Well," laughed Vulmea, "do you think you need fifteen men for that?"

"I'm taking no chances," was the grim retort. "You are stronger than two or three ordinary men, Vulmea, and full of wiles. My men will march with pieces ready, and if you try to bolt, they will shoot you down like the dog you are—should you, by any chance, avoid being cut down by your guard. Besides, there is always the chance of savages."

The pirate jeered.

"Go beyond the Cordilleras if you seek real savages. There are Indians there who cut off your head and shrink it no bigger than your fist. But they never come on this side of the mountains. As for the race that built the temple, they've all been dead for centuries. Bring your armed escort if you want to. It will be of no use. One strong man can carry away the whole hoard."

"One strong man!" murmured Wentyard, licking his lips as his mind reeled at the thought of the wealth represented by a load of jewels that required the full strength of a strong man to carry. Confused visions of knighthood and admiralty whirled through his head. "What about the path?" he asked suspiciously. "If this coast is uninhabited, how comes it there?"

"It was an old road, centuries ago, probably used by the race that built the city. In some places you can see where it was paved. But Harston and I were the first to use it for centuries. And you can tell it hasn't been used since. You can see where the young growth has sprung up above the scars of the axes we used to clear a way."

Wentyard was forced to agree. So now, before sunrise, the landing party was swinging inland at a steady gait that ate up the miles. The bay and the ship were quickly lost to sight. All morning they tramped along through steaming heat, between green, tangled jungle walls where gay-hued birds flitted silently and monkeys chattered. Thick vines hung low across the trail, impeding their progress, and they were sorely annoyed by gnats and other insects. At noon they paused only long enough to drink some water and eat the ready-cooked food they had brought along. The men were stolid veterans, inured to long marches, and Wentyard would allow them no more rest than was necessary for their brief meal. He was afire with savage eagerness to view the hoard Vulmea had described.

The trail did not twist as much as most jungle paths. It was overgrown with vegetation, but it gave evidence that it had once been a road, well-built and broad. Pieces of paving were still visible here and there. By midafternoon the land began to rise slightly, to be broken by low, jungle-choked hills. They were aware of this only by the rising and dipping of the trail. The dense walls on either hand shut off their view.

Neither Wentyard nor any of his men glimpsed the furtive, shadowy shapes which now glided along through the jungle on either hand. Vulmea was aware of their presence, but he only smiled grimly and said nothing. Carefully and so subtly that his guard did not suspect it, the pirate worked at the cords on his wrists, weakening and straining the strands by continual tugging and twisting. He had been doing this all day, and he could feel them slowly giving way.

The sun hung low in the jungle branches when the pirate halted and pointed to where the old road bent almost at right angles and disappeared into the mouth of a ravine.

"Down that ravine lies the old temple where the jewels are hidden."

"On, then!" snapped Wentyard, fanning himself with his plumed hat. Sweat trickled down his face, wilting the collar of his crimson, gilt-embroidered coat. A frenzy of impatience was on him, his eyes dazzled by the imagined glitter of the gems Vulmea had so vividly described. Avarice makes for credulity, and it never occurred to Wentyard to doubt Vulmea's tale. He saw in the Irishman only a hulking brute eager to buy a few months more of life. Gentlemen of his Majesty's navy were not accustomed to analyzing the characters of pirates. Wentyard's code was painfully simple: a heavy hand and a roughshod directness. He had never bothered to study or try to understand outlaw types.

They entered the mouth of the ravine and marched on between cliffs fringed with overhanging fronds. Wentyard fanned himself with his hat and gnawed his lip with impatience as he stared eagerly about for some sign of the ruins described by his captive. His face was paler than ever, despite the heat which reddened the bluff faces of his men, tramping ponderously after him. Vulmea's brown face showed no undue moisture. He did not tramp; he moved with the sure, supple tread of a panther, and without a suggestion of a seaman's lurching roll. His eyes ranged the walls above them and when a frond swayed without a breath of wind to move it, he did not miss it.

The ravine was some fifty feet wide, the floor carpeted by a low, thick growth of vegetation. The jungle ran densely along the rims of the walls, which were some forty feet high. They were sheer for the most part, but here and there natural ramps ran down into the gulch, half covered with tangled vines. A few hundred yards ahead of them they saw that the ravine bent out of sight around a rocky shoulder. From the opposite wall there jutted a corresponding crag. The outlines of these boulders were blurred by moss and creepers, but they seemed too symmetrical to be the work of nature alone.

Vulmea stopped, near one of the natural ramps that sloped down from the rim. His captors looked at him questioningly.

"Why are you stopping?" demanded Wentyard fretfully. His foot struck something in the rank grass and he kicked it aside. It rolled free and grinned up at him—a rotting human skull. He saw glints of white in the green all about him—skulls and bones almost covered by the dense vegetation.

"Is this where you piratical dogs slew each other?" he demanded crossly. "What are you waiting on? What are you listening for?"

Vulmea relaxed his tense attitude and smiled indulgently.

"That used to be a gateway there ahead of us," he said. "Those rocks on each side are really gate pillars. This ravine was a roadway, leading to the city when people lived there. It's the only approach to it, for it's surrounded by sheer cliffs on all sides." He laughed harshly. "This is like the road to Hell, John Wentyard: easy to go down—not so easy to go up again."

"What are you maundering about?" snarled Wentyard, clapping his hat viciously on his head. "You Irish are all babblers and mooncalves! Get on with—"

From the jungle beyond the mouth of the ravine came a sharp twang. Something whined venomously down the gulch, ending its flight with a vicious thud. One of the soldiers gulped and started convulsively. His musket clattered to the earth and he reeled, clawing at his throat from which protruded a long shaft, vibrating like a serpent's head. Suddenly he pitched to the ground and lay twitching.

"Indians!" yelped Wentyard, and turned furiously on his prisoner. "Dog! Look at that! You said there were no savages hereabouts!"

Vulmea laughed scornfully.

"Do you call them savages? Bah! Poor-spirited dogs that skulk in the jungle, too fearful to show themselves on the coast. Don't you see them slinking among the trees? Best give them a volley before they grow too bold."

Wentyard snarled at him, but the Englishman knew the value of a display of firearms when dealing with natives, and he had a glimpse of brown figures moving among the green foliage. He barked an order and fourteen muskets crashed, and the bullets rattled among the leaves. A few severed fronds drifted down; that was all. But even as the smoke puffed out in a cloud, Vulmea snapped the frayed cords on his wrists, knocked his guard staggering with a buffet under the ear, snatched his cutlass and was gone, running like a cat up the steep wall of the ravine. The soldiers with their empty muskets gaped helplessly after him, and Wentyard's pistol banged futilely, an instant too late. From the green fringe above them came a mocking laugh.

"Fools! You stand in the door of Hell!"

"Dog!" yelled Wentyard, beside himself, but with his greed still uppermost in his befuddled mind. "We'll find the treasure without your help!"

"You can't find something that doesn't exist," retorted the unseen pirate. "There never were any jewels. It was a lie to draw you into a trap. Dick Harston never came here. I came here, and the Indians butchered all my crew in that ravine, as those skulls in the grass there testify."

"Liar!" was all Wentyard could find tongue for. "Lying dog! You told us there were no Indians hereabouts!"

"I told you the headhunters never came over the mountains," retorted Vulmea. "They don't, either. I told you the people who built the city were all dead. That's so, too. I didn't tell you that a tribe of brown devils live in the jungle near here. They never go down to the coast, and they don't like for white men to come into the jungle. I think they were the people who wiped out the race that built the city, long ago. Anyway, they wiped out my men, and the only reason I got away was because I'd lived with the red men of North America and learned their woodscraft. You're in a trap you won't get out of, Wentyard!"

"Climb that wall and take him!" ordered Wentyard, and half a dozen men slung their muskets on their backs and began clumsily to essay the rugged ramp up which the pirate had run with such catlike ease.

"Better trim sail and stand by to repel boarders," Vulmea advised him from above. "There are hundreds of red devils out there—and no tame dogs to run at the crack of a caliver, either."

"And you'd betray white men to savages!" raged Wentyard.

"It goes against my principles," the Irishman admitted, "but it was my only chance for life. I'm sorry for your men. That's why I advised you to bring only a handful. I wanted to spare as many as possible. There are enough Indians out there in the jungle to eat your whole ship's company. As for you, you filthy dog, what you did in Ireland forfeited any consideration you might expect as a white man. I gambled on my neck and took my chances with all of you. It might have been me that arrow hit."

The voice ceased abruptly, and just as Wentyard was wondering if there were no Indians on the wall above them, the foliage was violently agitated, there sounded a wild yell, and down came a naked brown body, all asprawl, limbs revolving in the air. It crashed on the floor of the ravine and lay motionless—the figure of a brawny warrior, naked but for a loincloth of bark. The dead man was deep chested, broad shouldered and muscular, with features not unintelligent, but hard and brutal. He had been slashed across the neck.

The bushes waved briefly, and then again, further along the rim, which agitation Wentyard believed marked the flight of the Irishman along the ravine wall, pursued by the companions of the dead warrior, who must have stolen up on Vulmea while the pirate was shouting his taunts.

The chase was made in deadly silence, but down in the ravine conditions were anything but silent. At the sight of the falling body a blood-curdling ululation burst forth from the jungle outside the mouth of the ravine, and a storm of arrows came whistling down it. Another man fell, and three more were wounded, and Wentyard called down the men who were laboriously struggling up the vine-matted ramp. He fell back down the ravine, almost to the bend where the ancient gateposts jutted, and beyond that point he feared to go. He felt sure that the ravine beyond the Gateway was filled with lurking savages. They would not have hemmed him in on all sides and then left open an avenue of escape.

At the spot where he halted there was a cluster of broken rocks that looked as though they might have once formed the walls of a building of some sort. Among them Wentyard made his stand. He ordered his men to lie prone, their musket barrels resting on the rocks. One man he detailed to watch for savages creeping up the ravine from behind them, the others watched the green wall visible beyond the path that ran into the mouth of the ravine. Fear chilled Wentyard's heart. The sun was already lost behind the trees and the shadows were lengthening. In the brief dusk of the tropic twilight, how could a white man's eye pick out a swift, flitting brown body, or a musket ball find its mark? And when darkness fell—Wentyard shivered despite the heat.

Arrows kept singing down the ravine, but they fell short or splintered on the rocks. But now bowmen hidden on the walls drove down their shafts, and from their vantage point the stones afforded little protection. The screams of men skewered to the ground rose harrowingly. Wentyard saw his command melting away under his eyes. The only thing that kept them from being instantly exterminated was the steady fire he had them keep up at the foliage on the cliffs. They seldom saw their foes; they only saw the fronds shake, had an occasional glimpse of a brown arm. But the heavy balls, ripping through the broad leaves, made the hidden archers wary, and the shafts came at intervals instead of in volleys. Once a piercing death yell announced that a blind ball had gone home, and the English raised a croaking cheer.

Perhaps it was this which brought the infuriated warriors out of the jungle. Perhaps, like the white men, they disliked fighting in the dark, and wanted to conclude the slaughter before night fell. Perhaps they were ashamed longer to lurk hidden from a handful of men.

At any rate, they came out of the jungle beyond the trail suddenly, and by the scores, not scrawny primitives, but brawny, hard-muscled warriors, confident of their strength and physically a match for even the sinewy Englishmen. They came in a wave of brown bodies that suddenly flooded the ravine, and others leaped down the walls, swinging from the lianas. They were hundreds against the handful of Englishmen left. These rose from the rocks without orders, meeting death with the bulldog stubbornness of their breed. They fired a volley full into that tide of snarling faces that surged upon them, and then drew hangers and clubbed empty muskets. There was no time to reload. Their blast tore lanes in the onsweeping human torrent, but it did not falter; it came on and engulfed the white men in a snarling, slashing, smiting whirlpool.

Hangers whirred and bit through flesh and bone, clubbed muskets rose and fell, spattering brains. But copper-headed axes flashed dully in the twilight, war clubs made a red ruin of the skulls they kissed, and there were a score of red arms to drag down each struggling white man. The ravine was choked with a milling, eddying mass, revolving about a fast-dwindling cluster of desperate, white-skinned figures.

Not until his last man fell did Wentyard break away, blood smeared on his arms, dripping from his sword. He was hemmed in by a surging ring of ferocious figures, but he had one loaded pistol left. He fired it full in a painted face surmounted by a feathered crest and saw it vanish in red ruin. He clubbed a shaven head with the empty barrel, and rushed through the gap made by the falling bodies. A wild figure leaped at him, swinging a war club, but the sword was quicker. Wentyard tore the blade free as the savage fell. Dusk was ebbing swiftly into darkness, and the figures swirling about him were becoming indistinct, vague of outline. Twilight waned quickly out of the ravine and darkness had settled there before it veiled the jungle outside. It was the darkness that saved Wentyard, confusing his attackers. As the sworded Indian fell he found himself free, though men were rushing on him from behind, with clubs lifted.

Blindly he fled down the ravine. It lay empty before him. Fear lent wings to his feet. He raced through the stone-abutted Gateway. Beyond it he saw the ravine widen out; stone walls rose ahead of him, almost hidden by vines and creepers, pierced with blank windows and doorways. His flesh crawled with the momentary expectation of a thrust in the back. His heart was pounding so loudly, the blood hammering so agonizingly in his temples, that he could not tell whether or not bare feet were thudding close behind him.

His hat and coat were gone, his shirt torn and bloodstained, though somehow he had come through that desperate melee unwounded. Before him he saw a vine-tangled wall, and an empty doorway. He ran reelingly into the door and turned, falling to his knee from sheer exhaustion. He shook the sweat from his eyes, panting gaspingly as he fumbled to reload his pistols. The ravine was a dim alleyway before him, running to the rock-buttressed bend. Moment by moment he expected to see it thronged with fierce faces, with swarming figures. But it lay empty and fierce cries of the victorious warriors drew no nearer. For some reason they had not followed him through the Gateway.

Terror that they were creeping on him from behind brought him to his feet, pistols cocked, staring this way and that.

He was in a room whose stone walls seemed ready to crumble. It was roofless, and grass grew between the broken stones of the floor. Through the gaping roof he could see the stars just blinking out, and the frond-fringed rim of the cliff. Through a door opposite the one by which he crouched he had a vague glimpse of other vegetation-choked, roofless chambers beyond.

Silence brooded over the ruins, and now silence had fallen beyond the bend of the ravine. He fixed his eyes on the blur that was the Gateway, and waited. It stood empty. Yet he knew that the Indians were aware of his flight. Why did they not rush in and cut his throat? Were they afraid of his pistols? They had shown no fear of his soldiers' muskets. Had they gone away, for some inexplicable reason? Were those shadowy chambers behind him filled with lurking warriors? If so, why in God's name were they waiting?

He rose and went to the opposite door, craned his neck warily through it, and after some hesitation, entered the adjoining chamber. It had no outlet into the open. All its doors led into other chambers, equally ruinous, with broken roofs, cracked floors and crumbling walls. Three or four he traversed, his tread, as he crushed down the vegetation growing among the broken stones, seeming intolerably loud in the stillness. Abandoning his explorations—or the labyrinth seemed endless—he returned to the room that opened toward the ravine. No sound came up the gulch, but it was so dark under the cliff that men could have entered the Gateway and been crouching near him, without his being able to see them.

At last he could endure the suspense no longer. Walking as quietly as he was able, he left the ruins and approached the Gateway, now a well of blackness. A few moments later he was hugging the left-hand abutment and straining his eyes to see into the ravine beyond. It was too dark to see anything more than the stars blinking over the rims of the walls. He took a cautious step beyond the Gateway—it was the swift swish of feet through the vegetation on the floor that saved his life. He sensed rather than saw a black shape loom out of the darkness, and he fired blindly and pointblank. The flash lighted a ferocious face, falling backward, and beyond it the Englishman dimly glimpsed other figures, solid ranks of them, surging inexorably toward him.

With a choked cry he hurled himself back around the gate pillar, stumbled and fell and lay dumb and quaking, clenching his teeth against the sharp agony he expected in the shape of a spear thrust. None came. No figure came lunging after him. Incredulously he gathered himself to his feet, his pistols shaking in his hands. They were waiting, beyond that bend, but they would not come through the Gateway, not even to glut their bloodlust. This fact forced itself upon him, with its implication of inexplicable mystery.

Stumblingly he made his way back to the ruins and groped into the black doorway, overcoming an instinctive aversion against entering the roofless chamber. Starlight shone through the broken roof, lightening the gloom a little, but black shadows clustered along the walls and the inner door was an ebon well of mystery. Like most Englishmen of his generation John Wentyard more than half believed in ghosts, and he felt that if ever there was a place fit to be haunted by the phantoms of a lost and forgotten race, it was these sullen ruins.

He glanced fearfully through the broken roof at the dark fringe of overhanging fronds on the cliffs above, hanging motionless in the breathless air, and wondered if moonrise, illuminating his refuge, would bring arrows questing down through the roof. Except for the far lone cry of a night bird, the jungle was silent. There was not so much as the rustle of a leaf. If there were men on the cliffs there was no sign to show it. He was aware of hunger and an increasing thirst; rage gnawed at him, and a fear that was already tinged with panic.

He crouched at the doorway, pistols in his hands, naked sword at his knee, and after a while the moon rose, touching the overhanging fronds with silver long before it untangled itself from the trees and rose high enough to pour its light over the cliffs. Its light invaded the ruins, but no arrows came from the cliff, nor was there any sound from beyond the Gateway. Wentyard thrust his head through the door and surveyed his retreat.

The ravine, after it passed between the ancient gate pillars, opened into a broad bowl, walled by cliffs, and unbroken except for the mouth of the gulch. Wentyard saw the rim as a continuous, roughly circular line, now edged with the fire of moonlight. The ruins in which he had taken refuge almost filled this bowl, being built against the cliffs on one side. Decay and smothering vines had almost obliterated the original architectural plan. He saw the structure as a maze of roofless chambers, the outer doors opening upon the broad space left between it and the opposite wall of the cliff. This space was covered with low, dense vegetation, which also choked some of the chambers. Wentyard saw no way of escape. The cliffs were not like the walls of the ravine. They were of solid rock and sheer, even jutting outward a little at the rim. No vines trailed down them. They did not rise many yards above the broken roofs of the ruins, but they were as far out of his reach as if they had towered a thousand feet. He was caught like a rat in a trap. The only way out was up the ravine, where the blood-lusting warriors waited with grim patience. He remembered Vulmea's mocking warning: "—Like the road to Hell: easy to go down; not so easy to go up again!" Passionately he hoped that the Indians had caught the Irishman and slain him slowly and painfully. He could have watched Vulmea flayed alive with the most intense satisfaction.

Presently, despite hunger and thirst and fear, he fell asleep, to dream of ancient temples where drums muttered and strange figures in parrot-feather mantles moved through the smoke of sacrificial fires; and he dreamed at last of a silent, hideous shape which came to the inner door of his roofless chamber and regarded him with cold, inhuman eyes.

It was from this dream that he awakened, bathed in cold sweat, to start up with an incoherent cry, clutching his pistols. Then, fully awake, he stood in the middle of the chamber, trying to gather his scattered wits. Memory of the dream was vague but terrifying. Had he actually seen a shadow sway in the doorway and vanish as he awoke, or had it been only part of his nightmare? The red, lopsided moon was poised on the western rim of the cliffs, and that side of the bowl was in thick shadow, but still an illusive light found its way into the ruins. Wentyard peered through the inner doorway, pistols cocked. Light floated rather than streamed down from above, and showed him an empty chamber beyond. The vegetation on the floor was crushed down, but he remembered having walked back and forth across it several times.

Cursing his nervous imagination he returned to the outer doorway. He told himself that he chose that place the better to guard against an attack from the ravine, but the real reason was that he could not bring himself to select a spot deeper in the gloomy interior of the ancient ruins.

He sat down cross-legged just inside the doorway, his back against the wall, his pistols beside him and his sword across his knees. His eyes burned and his lips felt baked with the thirst that tortured him. The sight of the heavy globules of dew that hung on the grass almost maddened him, but he did not seek to quench his thirst by that means, believing as he did that it was rank poison. He drew his belt closer, against his hunger, and told himself that he would not sleep. But he did sleep, in spite of everything.

Chapter .3.

It was a frightful scream close at hand that awakened Wentyard. He was on his feet before he was fully awake, glaring wildly about him. The moon had set and the interior of the chamber was dark as Egypt, in which the outer doorway was but a somewhat lighter blur. But outside of it there sounded a blood-chilling gurgling, the heaving and flopping of a heavy body. Then silence.

It had been a human being that had screamed. Wentyard groped for his pistols, found his sword instead, and hurried forth, his taut nerves thrumming. The starlight in the bowl, dim as it was, was less Stygian than the absolute blackness of the ruins. But he did not see the figure stretched in the grass until he stumbled over it. That was all he saw, then—just that dim form stretched on the ground before the doorway. The foliage hanging over the cliff rustled a little in the faint breeze. That was all. Shadows hung thick under the wall and about the ruins. A score of men might have been lurking near him, unseen. But there was no sound.

After a while Wentyard knelt beside the figure, straining his eyes in the starlight. He grunted softly. The dead man was not an Indian, but a black man, a brawny ebon giant, clad, like the red men, in a bark loin clout, with a crest of parrot feathers on his kinky head. A murderous copper-headed axe lay near his hand, and a great gash showed in his muscular breast, a lesser wound under his shoulder blade. He had been stabbed so savagely that the blade had transfixed him and come out through his back.

Wentyard swore at the accumulated mystery of it. The presence of the black man was not inexplicable. Negro slaves, fleeing from Spanish masters, frequently took to the jungle and lived with the natives. This black evidently did not share in whatever superstition or caution kept the Indians outside the bowl; he had come in alone to butcher the victim they had at bay. But the mystery of his death remained. The blow that had impaled him had been driven with more than ordinary strength. There was a sinister suggestion about the episode, though the mysterious killer had saved Wentyard from being brained in his sleep—it was as if some mysterious being, having claimed the Englishman for its own, refused to be robbed of its prey. Wentyard shivered, shaking off the thought.

Then he realized that he was armed only with his sword. He had rushed out of the ruins half asleep, leaving his pistols behind him, after a brief fumbling that failed to find them in the darkness. He turned and hurried back into the chamber and began to grope on the floor, first irritably, then with growing horror. *The pistols were gone.*

At this realization panic overwhelmed Wentyard. He found himself out in the starlight again without knowing just how he had got there. He was sweating, trembling in every limb, biting his tongue to keep from screaming in hysterical horror.

Frantically he fought for control. It was not imagination, then, which peopled those ghastly ruins with furtive, sinister shapes that glided from room to shadowy room on noiseless feet, and spied upon him while he slept. *Something* besides himself had been in that room—something that had stolen his pistols either while he was fumbling over the dead Negro outside, or—grisly thought!—while he slept. He believed the latter had been the case. He had heard no sound in the ruins while he was outside. But why had it not taken his sword as well? Was it the Indians, after all, playing a horrible game with him? Was it their eyes he seemed to feel burning upon him from the shadows? But he did not believe it was the Indians. They would have no reason to kill their black ally.

Wentyard felt that he was near the end of his rope. He was nearly frantic with thirst and hunger, and he shrank from the contemplation of another day of heat in that waterless bowl. He went toward the ravine mouth, grasping his sword in desperation, telling himself that it was better to be speared quick than haunted to an unknown doom by unseen phantoms, or perish of thirst. But the blind instinct to live drove him back from the rock-buttressed Gateway. He could not bring himself to exchange an uncertain fate for certain death. Faint noises beyond the bend told him that men, many men, were waiting there, and retreated, cursing weakly.

In a futile gust of passion he dragged the black man's body to the Gateway and thrust it through. At least he would not have it for a companion to poison the air when it rotted in the heat.

He sat down about halfway between the ruins and the ravine mouth, hugging his sword and straining his eyes into the shadowy starlight, and felt that he was being watched from the ruins; he sensed a Presence there, inscrutable, inhuman, waiting—waiting—

He was still sitting there when dawn flooded jungle and cliffs with grey light, and a brown warrior, appearing in the Gateway, bent his bow and sent an arrow at the figure hunkered in the open space. The shaft cut into the grass near Wentyard's foot, and the white man sprang up stiffly and ran into the doorway of the ruins. The warrior did not shoot again. As if frightened by his own temerity, he turned and hurried back through the Gateway and vanished from sight.

Wentyard spat dryly and swore. Daylight dispelled some of the phantom terrors of the night, and he was suffering so much from thirst that his fear was temporarily submerged. He was determined to explore the ruins by each crevice and cranny and bring to bay whatever was lurking among them. At least he would have daylight by which to face it.

To this end he turned toward the inner door, and then he stopped in his tracks, his heart in his throat. In the inner doorway stood a great gourd, newly cut and hollowed, and filled with water; beside it was a stack of fruit, and in another calabash there was meat, still smoking faintly. With a stride he reached the door and glared through. Only an empty chamber met his eyes.

Sight of water and scent of food drove from his mind all thoughts of anything except his physical needs. He seized the water gourd and drank gulpingly, the precious liquid splashing on his breast. The water was fresh and sweet, and no wine had ever given him such delirious satisfaction. The meat he found was still warm. What it was he neither knew nor cared. He ate ravenously, grasping the joints in his fingers and tearing away the flesh with his teeth. It had evidently been roasted over an open fire, and without salt or seasoning, but it tasted like the meat of the gods to the ravenous man. He did not seek to explain the miracle, nor to wonder if the food were poisoned. The inscrutable haunter of the ruins which had saved his life that night, and which had stolen his pistols, apparently meant to preserve him for the time being, at least, and Wentyard accepted the gifts without question.

And having eaten he lay down and slept. He did not believe the Indians would invade the ruins; he did not care much if they did, and speared him in his sleep. He believed that the unknown being which haunted the rooms could slay him any time it wished. It had been close to him again and again and had not struck. It had showed no signs of hostility so far, except to steal his pistols. To go searching for it might drive it into hostility.

Wentyard, despite his slaked thirst and full belly, was at the point where he had a desperate indifference to consequences. His world seemed to have crumbled about him. He had led his men into a trap to see them butchered; he had seen his prisoner escape; he was caught like a caged rat himself; the wealth he had lusted after and dreamed about had been proved a lie. Worn out with vain ragings against his fate, he slept.

The sun was high when he awoke and sat up with a startled oath. Black Vulmea stood looking down at him.

"Damn!" Wentyard sprang up, snatching at his sword. His mind was a riot of maddening emotions, but physically he was a new man, and nerved to a rage that was tinged with near-insanity.

"You dog!" he raved. "So the Indians didn't catch you on the cliffs!"

"Those red dogs?" Vulmea laughed. ""They didn't follow me past the Gateway. They don't come on the cliffs overlooking these ruins. They've got a cordon of men strung through the jungle, surrounding this place, but I can get through any time I want to. I cooked your breakfast—and mine—right under their noses, and they never saw me."

"*My breakfast!*" Wentyard glared wildly. "You mean it was you brought water and food for me?"

"Who else?"

"But—but why?" Wentyard was floundering in a maze of bewilderment.

Vulmea laughed, but he laughed only with his lips. His eyes were burning. "Well, at first I thought it would satisfy me if I saw you get an arrow through your guts. Then when you broke away and got in here, I said, 'Better still! They'll keep the swine there until he starves, and I'll lurk about and watch him die slowly.' I knew they wouldn't come in after you. When they ambushed me and my crew in the ravine, I cut my way through them and got in here, just as you did, and they didn't follow me in. But I got out of here the first night. I made sure you wouldn't get out the way I did that time, and then settled myself to watch you die. I could come or go as I pleased after nightfall, and you'd never see or hear me."

"But in that case, I don't see why—"

"You probably wouldn't understand!" snarled Vulmea. "But just watching you starve wasn't enough. I wanted to kill you myself—I wanted to see your blood gush, and watch your eyes glaze!" The Irishman's voice thickened with his passion, and his great hands clenched until the knuckles showed white. "And I didn't want to kill a man half dead with want. So I went back up into the jungle on the cliffs and got water and fruit, and knocked a monkey off a limb with a stone, and roasted him. I brought you a good meal and set it there in the door while you were sitting outside the ruins. You couldn't see me from where you were sitting, and of course you didn't hear anything. You English are all dull-eared."

"And it was you who stole my pistols last night!" muttered Wentyard, staring at the butts jutting from Vulmea's Spanish girdle.

"Aye! I took them from the floor beside you while you slept. I learned stealth from the Indians of North America. I didn't want you to shoot me when I came to pay my debt. While I was getting them I heard somebody sneaking up outside, and saw a black man coming toward the doorway. I didn't want him to be robbing me of my revenge, so I stuck my cutlass through him. You awakened when he howled, and ran out, as you'll remember, but I stepped back around the corner and in at another door. I didn't want to meet you except in broad open daylight and you in fighting trim."

"Then it was you who spied on me from the inner door," muttered Wentyard. "You whose shadow I saw just before the moon sank behind the cliffs."

"Not I!" Vulmea's denial was genuine. "I didn't come down into the ruins until after moonset, when I came to steal your pistols. Then I went back up on the cliffs, and came again just before dawn to leave your food."

"But enough of this talk!" he roared gustily, whipping out his cutlass. "I'm mad with thinking of the Galway coast and dead men kicking in a row, and a rope that strangled me! I've tricked you, trapped you, and now I'm going to kill you!"

Wentyard's face was a ghastly mask of hate, livid, with bared teeth and glaring eyes.

"Dog!" with a screech he lunged, trying to catch Vulmea off-guard.

But the cutlass met and deflected the straight blade, and Wentyard bounded back just in time to avoid the decapitating sweep of the pirate's steel. Vulmea laughed fiercely and came on like a storm, and Wentyard met him with a drowning man's desperation.

Like most officers of the British navy, Wentyard was proficient in the use of the long straight sword he carried. He was almost as tall as Vulmea, and though he looked slender beside the powerful figure of the pirate, he believed that his skill would offset the sheer strength of the Irishman.

He was disillusioned within the first few moments of the fight. Vulmea was neither slow nor clumsy. He was as quick as a wounded panther, and his swordplay was no less crafty than Wentyard's. It only seemed so, because of the pirate's furious style of attack, showering blow on blow with what looked like sheer recklessness. But the very ferocity of his attack was his best defense, for it gave his opponent no time to launch a counterattack.

The power of his blows, beating down on Wentyard's blade, rocked and shook the Englishman to his heels, numbing his wrist and arm with their impact. Blind fury, humiliation, naked fright combined to rob the captain of his poise and cunning. A stamp of feet, a louder clash of steel, and Wentyard's blade whirred into a corner. The Englishman reeled back, his face livid, his eyes like those of a madman.

"Pick up your sword!" Vulmea was panting, not so much from exertion as from rage. Wentyard did not seem to hear him.

"Bah!" Vulmea threw aside his cutlass in a spasm of disgust. "Can't you even fight? I'll kill you with my bare hands!"

He slapped Wentyard viciously first on one side of the face and then on the other. The Englishman screamed wordlessly and launched himself at the pirate's throat, and Vulmea checked him with a buffet in the face and knocked him sprawling with a savage smash under the heart. Wentyard got to his knees and shook the blood from his face, while Vulmea stood over him, his brows black and his great fists knotted.

"Get up!" muttered the Irishman thickly. "Get up, you hangman of peasants and children!"

Wentyard did not heed him. He was groping inside his shirt, from which he drew out something he stared at with painful intensity.

"Get up, damn you, before I set my boot heels on your face—"

Vulmea broke off, glaring incredulously. Wentyard, crouching over the object he had drawn from his shirt, was weeping in great, racking sobs.

"What the hell!" Vulmea jerked it away from him, consumed by wonder to learn what could bring tears from John Wentyard. It was a skillfully painted miniature. The blow he had struck Wentyard had cracked it, but not enough to obliterate the soft gentle faces of a pretty young woman and child which smiled up at the scowling Irishman.

"Well, I'm damned!" Vulmea stared from the broken portrait in his hand to the man crouching miserably on the floor. "Your wife and daughter?"

Wentyard, his bloody face sunk in his hands, nodded mutely. He had endured much within the last night and day. The breaking of the portrait he always carried over his heart was the last straw; it seemed like an attack on the one soft spot in his hard soul, and it left him dazed and demoralized.

Vulmea scowled ferociously, but it somehow seemed forced.

"I didn't know you had a wife and child," he said almost defensively.

"The lass is but five years old," gulped Wentyard. "I haven't seen them in nearly a year. My God, what's to become of them now? A navy captain's pay is none so great. I've never been able to save anything. It was for them I sailed in search of Van Raven and his treasure. I hoped to get a prize that would take care of them if aught happened to me. Kill me!" he cried shrilly, his voice cracking at the highest pitch. "Kill me and be done with it, before I lose my manhood with thinking of them, and beg for my life like a craven dog!"

But Vulmea stood looking down at him with a frown. Varying expressions crossed his dark face, and suddenly he thrust the portrait back in the Englishman's hand.

"You're too poor a creature for me to soil my hands with!" he sneered, and turning on his heel, strode through the inner door.

Wentyard stared dully after him, then, still on his knees, began to caress the broken picture, whimpering softly like an animal in pain as if the breaks in the ivory were wounds in his own flesh. Men break suddenly and unexpectedly in the tropics, and Wentyard's collapse was appalling.

He did not look up when the swift stamp of boots announced Vulmea's sudden return, without the pirate's usual stealth. A savage clutch on his shoulder raised him to stare stupidly into the Irishman's convulsed face.

"You're an infernal dog!" snarled Vulmea, in a fury that differed strangely from his former murderous hate. He broke into lurid imprecations, cursing Wentyard with all the proficiency he had acquired during his years at sea. "I ought to split your skull," he wound up. "For years I've dreamed of it, especially when I was drunk. I'm a cursed fool not to stretch you dead on the floor. I don't owe you any consideration, blast you! Your wife and daughter don't mean anything to me. But I'm a fool, like all the Irish, a blasted, chicken-hearted, sentimental fool, and I can't be the cause of a helpless woman and her colleen starving. Get up and quit sniveling!"

Wentyard looked up at him stupidly.

"You—you came back to help me?"

"I might as well stab you as leave you here to starve!" roared the pirate, sheathing his sword. "Get up and stick your skewer back in its scabbard. Who'd have ever thought that a scrawn like you would have womenfolk like those innocents? Hell's fire! You ought to be shot! Pick up your sword. You may need it before we get away. But remember, I don't trust you any further than I can throw a whale by the tail, and I'm keeping your pistols. If you try to stab me when I'm not looking I'll break your head with my cutlass hilt."

Wentyard, like a man in a daze, replaced the painting carefully in his bosom and mechanically picked up his sword and sheathed it. His numbed wits began to thaw out, and he tried to pull himself together.

"What are we to do now?" he asked.

"Shut up!" growled the pirate. "I'm going to save you for the sake of the lady and the lass, but I don't have to talk to you!" With rare consistency he then continued: "We'll leave this trap the same way I came and went.

"Listen: four years ago I came here with a hundred men. I'd heard rumors of a ruined city up here, and I thought there might be loot hidden in it. I followed the old road from the beach, and those brown dogs let me and my men get in the ravine before they started butchering us. There must have been five or six hundred of them. They raked us from the walls, and then charged us—some came down the ravine and others jumped down the walls behind us and cut us off. I was the only one who got away, and I managed to cut my way through them, and ran into this bowl. They didn't follow me in, but stayed outside the Gateway to see that I didn't get out.

"But I found another way—a slab had fallen away from the wall of a room that was built against the cliff, and a stairway was cut in the rock. I followed it and came out of a sort of trap door up on the cliffs. A slab of rock was over it, but I don't think the Indians knew anything about it anyway, because they never go up on the cliffs that overhang the basin. They never come in here from the ravine, either. There's something here they're afraid of—ghosts, most likely.

"The cliffs slope down into the jungle on the outer sides, and the slopes and the crest are covered with trees and thickets. They had a cordon of men strung around the foot of the slopes, but I got through at night easily enough, made my way to the coast and sailed away with the handful of men I'd left aboard my ship.

"When you captured me the other day, I was going to kill you with my manacles, but you started talking about treasure, and a thought sprang in my mind to steer you into a trap that I might possibly get out of. I remembered this place, and I mixed a lot of truth in with some lies. The Fangs of Satan are no myth; they are a hoard of jewels hidden somewhere on this coast, but this isn't the place. There's no plunder about here.

"The Indians have a ring of men strung around this place, as they did before. I can get through, but it isn't going to be so easy getting you through. You English are like buffaloes when you start through the brush. We'll start just after dark and try to get through before the moon rises.

"Come on; I'll show you the stair."

Wentyard followed him through a series of crumbling, vine-tangled chambers, until he halted before a doorway that gaped in the wall that was built against the cliff. A thick slab leaned against the wall which obviously served as a door. The Englishman saw a flight of narrow steps, carved in the solid rock, leading upward through a shaft tunneled in the cliff.

"I meant to block the upper mouth by heaping big rocks on the slab that covers it," said Vulmea. "That was when I was going to let you starve. I knew you might find the stair. I doubt if the Indians know anything about it, as they never come in here or go up on the cliffs. But they know a man might be able to get out over the cliffs some way, so they've thrown that cordon around the slopes.

"That nigger I killed was a different proposition. A slave ship was wrecked off this coast a year ago, and the blacks escaped and took to the jungle. There's a regular mob of them living somewhere near here. This particular black man wasn't afraid to come into the ruins. If there are more of his kind out there with the Indians, they may try again tonight. But I believe he was the only one, or he wouldn't have come alone."

"Why don't we go up the cliff now and hide among the trees?" asked Wentyard.

"Because we might be seen by the men watching below the slopes, and they'd guess that we were going to make a break tonight, and redouble their vigilance. After awhile I'll go and get some more food. They won't see me."

The men returned to the chamber where Wentyard had slept. Vulmea grew taciturn, and Wentyard made no attempt at conversation. They sat in silence while the afternoon dragged by. An hour or so before sundown Vulmea rose with a curt word, went up the stair and emerged on the cliffs. Among the trees he brought down a monkey with a dexterously thrown stone, skinned it, and brought it back into the ruins along with a calabash of water from a spring on the hillside. For all his woodscraft he was not aware that he was being watched; he did not see the fierce black face that glared at him from a thicket that stood where the cliffs began to slope down into the jungle below.

Later, when he and Wentyard were roasting the meat over a fire built in the ruins, he raised his head and listened intently.

"What do you hear?" asked Wentyard.

"A drum," grunted the Irishman.

"I hear it," said Wentyard after a moment. "Nothing unusual about that."

"It doesn't sound like an Indian drum," answered Vulmea. "Sounds more like an African drum."

Wentyard nodded agreement; his ship had lain off the mangrove swamps of the Slave Coast, and he had heard such drums rumbling to one another through the steaming night. There was a subtle difference in the rhythm and timbre that distinguished it from an Indian drum.

Evening came on and ripened slowly to dusk. The drum ceased to throb. Back in the low hills, beyond the ring of cliffs, a fire glinted under the dusky trees, casting brown and black faces into sharp relief.

An Indian whose ornaments and bearing marked him as a chief squatted on his hams, his immobile face turned toward the ebony giant who stood facing him. This man was nearly a head taller than any other man there, his proportions overshadowing both the Indians squatting about the fire and the black warriors who stood in a close group behind him. A jaguar-skin mantle was cast carelessly over his brawny shoulders, and copper bracelets ornamented his thickly muscled arms. There was an ivory ring on his head, and parrot feathers stood up from his kinky hair. A shield of hardwood and toughened bull hide was on his left arm, and in his right hand he gripped a great spear whose hammered iron head was as broad as a man's hand.

"I came swiftly when I heard the drum," he said gutturally, in the bastard-Spanish that served as a common speech for the savages of both colors. "I knew it was N'Onga who called me. N'Onga had gone from my camp to fetch Ajumba, who was lingering with your tribe. N'Onga told me by the drum talk that a white man was at bay, and Ajumba was dead. I came in haste. Now you tell me that you dare not enter the Old City."

"I have told you a devil dwells there," answered the Indian doggedly. "He has chosen the white man for his own. He will be angry if you try to take him away from him. It is death to enter his kingdom."

The black chief lifted his great spear and shook it defiantly.

"I was a slave to the Spaniards long enough to know that the only devil is a white man! I do not fear your devil. In my land his brothers are big as he, and I have slain one with a spear like this. A day and a night have passed since the white man fled into the Old City. Why has not the devil devoured him, or this other who lingers on the cliffs?"

"The devil is not hungry," muttered the Indian. "He waits until he is hungry. He has eaten recently. When he is hungry again he will take them. I will not go into his lair with my men. You are a stranger in this country. You do not understand these things."

"I understand that Bigomba who was a king in his own country fears nothing, neither man nor demon," retorted the black giant. "You tell me that Ajumba went into the Old City by night, and died. I have seen his body. The devil did not slay him. One of the white men stabbed him. If Ajumba could go into the Old City and not be seized by the devil, then I and my thirty men can go. I know how the big white man comes and goes between the cliffs and the ruins. There is a hole in the rock with a slab for a door over it. N'Onga watched from the bushes high up on the slopes and saw him come forth and later return through it. I have placed men there to watch it. If the white men come again through that hole, my warriors will spear them. If they do not come, we will go in as soon as the moon rises. Your men hold the ravine, and they can not flee that way. We will hunt them like rats through the crumbling houses."

Chapter .4.

"Easy now," muttered Vulmea. "It's as dark as Hell in this shaft."

Dusk had deepened into early darkness. The white men were groping their way up the steps cut in the rock. Looking back and down Wentyard made out the lower mouth of the shaft only as a slightly lighter blur in the blackness. They climbed on, feeling their way, and presently Vulmea halted with a muttered warning. Wentyard, groping, touched his thigh and felt the muscles tensing upon it. He knew that Vulmea had placed his shoulders under the slab that closed the upper entrance, and was heaving it up. He saw a crack appear suddenly in the blackness above him, limning the Irishman's bent head and foreshortened figure.

The stone came clear and starlight gleamed through the aperture, laced by the overhanging branches of the trees. Vulmea let the slab fall on the stone rim, and started to climb out of the shaft. He had emerged head, shoulders and hips when without warning a black form loomed against the stars and a gleam of steel hissed downward at his breast.

Vulmea threw up his cutlass and the spear rang against it, staggering him on the steps with the impact. Snatching a pistol from his belt with his left hand he fired pointblank and the black man groaned and fell, head and arms dangling in the opening. He struck the pirate as he fell, destroying Vulmea's already precarious balance. He toppled backward down the steps, carrying Wentyard with him. A dozen steps down they brought up in a sprawling heap, and staring upward, saw the square well above them fringed with indistinct black blobs they knew were heads outlined against the stars.

"I thought you said the Indians never—" panted Wentyard.

"They're not Indians," growled Vulmea, rising. "They're negroes. Cimarroons! The same dogs who escaped from the slave ship. That drum we heard was one of them calling the others. Look out!"

Spears came whirring down the shaft, splintering on the steps, glancing from the walls. The white men hurled themselves recklessly down the steps at the risk of broken limbs. They tumbled through the lower doorway and Vulmea slammed the heavy slab in place.

"They'll be coming down it next," he snarled. "We've got to heap enough rocks against it to hold it—no, wait a minute! If they've got the guts to come at all, they'll come by the ravine if they can't get in this way, or on ropes hung from the cliffs. This place is easy enough to get into—not so damned easy to get out of. We'll leave the shaft open. If they come this way we can get them in a bunch as they try to come out."

He pulled the slab aside, standing carefully from in front of the door.

"Suppose they come from the ravine and this way, too?"

"They probably will," growled Vulmea, "but maybe they'll come this way first, and maybe if they come down in a bunch we can kill them all. There may not be more than a dozen of them. They'll never persuade the Indians to follow them in."

He set about reloading the pistol he had fired, with quick, sure hands in the dark. It consumed the last grain of powder in the flask. The white men lurked like phantoms of murder about the doorway of the stair, waiting to strike suddenly and deadly. Time dragged. No sound came from above. Wentyard's imagination was at work again, picturing an invasion from the ravine, and dusky figures gliding about them, surrounding the chamber. He spoke of this and Vulmea shook his head.

"When they come I'll hear them; nothing on two legs can get in here without my knowing it."

Suddenly Wentyard was aware of a dim glow pervading the ruins. The moon was rising above the cliffs. Vulmea swore.

"No chance of our getting away tonight. Maybe those black dogs were waiting for the moon to come up. Go into the chamber where you slept and watch the ravine. If you see them sneaking in that way, let me know. I can take care of any that come down the stair."

Wentyard felt his flesh crawl as he made his way through those dim chambers. The moonlight glinted down through vines tangled across the broken roofs, and shadows lay thick across his path. He reached the chamber where he had slept, and where the coals of their fire still glowed dully. He started across toward the outer door when a soft sound brought him whirling around. A cry was wrenched from his throat.

Out of the darkness of a corner rose a swaying shape; a great wedge-shaped head and an arched neck were outlined against the moonlight. In one brain-staggering instant the mystery of the ruins became clear to him; he knew what had watched him with lidless eyes as he lay sleeping, and what had glided away from his door as he awoke—he knew why the Indians would not come into the ruins or mount the cliffs above them. He was face to face with the devil of the deserted city, hungry at last—and that devil was a giant anaconda!

In that moment John Wentyard experienced such fear and loathing horror as ordinarily come to men only in foul nightmares. He could not run, and after that first scream his tongue seemed frozen to his palate. Only when the hideous head darted toward him did he break free from the paralysis that engulfed him and then it was too late.

He struck at it wildly and futilely, and in an instant it had him—lapped and wrapped about with coils which were like huge cables of cold, pliant steel. He shrieked again, fighting madly against the crushing constriction—he heard the swift rush of Vulmea's boots—then the pirate's pistols crashed together and he heard plainly the thud of the bullets into the great snake's body. It jerked convulsively and whipped from about him, hurling him sprawling to the floor, and then it came at Vulmea like the rush of a hurricane through the grass, its forked tongue licking in and out in the moonlight, and the noise of its hissing filling the chamber.

Vulmea avoided the battering-ram stroke of the blunt nose with a sidewise spring that would have shamed a starving jaguar, and his cutlass was a sheen in the moonlight as it hewed deep into the mighty neck. Blood spurted and the great reptile rolled and knotted, sweeping the floor and dislodging stones from the wall with its thrashing tail. Vulmea leaped high, clearing it as it lashed but Wentyard, just climbing to his feet, was struck and knocked sprawling into a corner. Vulmea was springing in again, cutlass lifted, when the monster rolled aside and fled through the inner door, with a loud rushing sound through the thick vegetation.

Vulmea was after it, his berserk fury fully roused. He did not wish the wounded reptile to crawl away and hide, perhaps to return later and take them by surprize. Through chamber after chamber the chase led, in a direction neither of the men had followed in his former explorations, and at last into a room almost choked by tangled vines. Tearing these aside Vulmea stared into a black aperture in the wall, just in time to see the monster vanishing into its depths. Wentyard, trembling in every limb, had followed, and now looked over the pirate's shoulder. A reptilian reek came from the aperture, which they now saw as an arched doorway, partly masked by thick vines. Enough moonlight found its way through the roof to reveal a glimpse of stone steps leading up into darkness.

"I missed this," muttered Vulmea. "When I found the stair I didn't look any further for an exit. Look how the door sill glistens with scales that have been rubbed off that brute's belly. He uses it often. I believe those steps lead to a tunnel that goes clear through the cliffs. There's nothing in this bowl that even a snake could eat or drink. He has to go out into the jungle to get water and food. If he was in the habit of going out by the way of the ravine, there'd be a path worn away through the vegetation, like there is in this room. Besides, the Indians wouldn't stay in the ravine. Unless there's some other exit we haven't found, I believe that he comes and goes this way, and that means it lets into the outer world. It's worth trying, anyway."

"You mean to follow that fiend into that black tunnel?" ejaculated Wentyard aghast.

"Why not? We've got to follow and kill him anyway. If we run into a nest of them—well, we've got to die some time, and if we wait here much longer the Cimarroons will be cutting our throats. This is a chance to get away, I believe. But we won't go in the dark."

Hurrying back to the room where they had cooked the monkey, Vulmea caught up a fagot, wrapped a torn strip of his shirt about one end and set it smouldering in the coals which he blew into a tiny flame. The improvised torch flickered and smoked, but it cast light of a sort. Vulmea strode back to the chamber where the snake had vanished, followed by Wentyard who stayed close within the dancing ring of light, and saw writhing serpents in every vine that swayed overhead.

The torch revealed blood thickly spattered on the stone steps. Squeezing their way between the tangled vines which did not admit a man's body as easily as a serpent's, they mounted the steps warily. Vulmea went first, holding the torch high and ahead of him, his cutlass in his right hand. He had thrown away the useless, empty pistols. They climbed half a dozen steps and came into a tunnel some fifteen feet wide and perhaps ten feet high from the stone floor to the vaulted roof. The serpent reek and the glisten of the floor told of long occupancy by the brute, and the blood drops ran on before them.

The walls, floor and roof of the tunnel were in a much better state of preservation than were the ruins outside, and Wentyard found time to marvel at the ingenuity of the ancient race which had built it.

Meanwhile, in the moonlit chamber they had just quitted, a giant black man appeared as silently as a shadow. His great spear glinted in the moonlight, and the plumes on his head rustled as he turned to look about him. Four warriors followed him.

"They went into that door," said one of these, pointing to the vine-tangled entrance. "I saw their torch vanish into it. But I feared to follow them, alone as I was, and I ran to tell you, Bigomba."

"But what of the screams and the shot we heard just before we descended the shaft?" asked another uneasily.

"I think they met the demon and slew it," answered Bigomba. "Then they went into this door. Perhaps it is a tunnel which leads through the cliffs. One of you go gather the rest of the warriors who are scattered through the rooms searching for the white dogs. Bring them after me. Bring torches with you. As for me, I will follow with the other three, at once. Bigomba sees like a lion in the dark."

As Vulmea and Wentyard advanced through the tunnel Wentyard watched the torch fearfully. It was not very satisfactory, but it gave some light, and he shuddered to think of its going out or burning to a stump and leaving them in darkness. He strained his eyes into the gloom ahead, momentarily expecting to see a vague, hideous figure rear up amidst it. But when Vulmea halted suddenly it was not because of an appearance of the reptile. They had reached a point where a smaller corridor branched off the main tunnel, leading away to the left.

"Which shall we take?"

Vulmea bent over the floor, lowering his torch.

"The blood-drops go to the left," he grunted. "That's the way he went."

"Wait!" Wentyard gripped his arm and pointed along the main tunnel. "Look! There ahead of us! Light!"

Vulmea thrust his torch behind him, for its flickering glare made the shadows seem blacker beyond its feeble radius. Ahead of them, then, he saw something like a floating gray mist, and knew it was moonlight finding its way somehow into the tunnel. Abandoning the hunt for the wounded reptile, the men rushed forward and emerged into a broad square chamber, hewn out of solid rock. But Wentyard swore in bitter disappointment. The moonlight was coming, not from a door opening into the jungle, but from a square shaft in the roof, high above their heads.

An archway opened in each wall, and the one opposite the arch by which they had entered was fitted with a heavy door, corroded and eaten by decay. Against the wall to their right stood a stone image, taller than a man, a carven grotesque, at once manlike and bestial. A stone altar stood before it, its surface channeled and darkly stained. Something on the idol's breast caught the moonlight in a frosty sparkle.

"The devil!" Vulmea sprang forward and wrenched it away. He held it up—a thing like a giant's necklace, made of jointed plates of hammered gold, each as broad as a man's palm and set with curiously-cut jewels.

"I thought I lied when I told you there were gems here," grunted the pirate. "It seems I spoke the truth unwittingly! These are not the Fangs of Satan, but they'll fetch a tidy fortune anywhere in Europe."

"What are you doing?" demanded Wentyard, as the Irishman laid the huge necklace on the altar and lifted his cutlass. Vulmea's reply was a stroke that severed the ornament into equal halves. One half he thrust into Wentyard's astounded hands.

"If we get out of here alive that will provide for the wife and child," he grunted.

"But you—" stammered Wentyard. "You hate me—yet you save my life and then give me this—"

"Shut up!" snarled the pirate. "I'm not giving it to you; I'm giving it to the girl and her baby. Don't you venture to thank me, curse you! I hate you as much as I—"

He stiffened suddenly, wheeling to glare down the tunnel up which they had come. He stamped out the torch and crouched down behind the altar, drawing Wentyard with him.

"Men!" he snarled. "Coming down the tunnel. I heard steel clink on stone. I hope they didn't see the torch. Maybe they didn't. It wasn't much more than a coal in the moonlight."

They strained their eyes down the tunnel. The moon hovered at an angle above the open shaft which allowed some of its light to stream a short way down the tunnel. Vision ceased at the spot where the smaller corridor branched off. Presently four shadows bulked out of the blackness beyond, taking shape gradually like figures emerging from a thick fog. They halted, and the white men saw the largest one—a giant who towered above the others—point silently with his spear, up the tunnel, then down the corridor. Two of the shadowy shapes detached themselves from the group and moved off down the corridor out of sight. The giant and the other man came on up the tunnel.

"The Cimarroons, hunting us," muttered Vulmea. "They're splitting their party to make sure they find us. Lie low; there may be a whole crew right behind them."

They crouched lower behind the altar while the two blacks came up the tunnel, growing more distinct as they advanced. Wentyard's skin crawled at the sight of the broad-bladed spears held ready in their hands. The biggest one moved with the supple tread of a great panther, head thrust forward, spear poised, shield lifted. He was a formidable image of rampant barbarism, and Wentyard wondered if even such a man as Vulmea could stand before him with naked steel and live.

They halted in the doorway, and the white men caught the white flash of their eyes as they glared suspiciously about the chamber. The smaller black seized the giant's arm convulsively and pointed, and Wentyard's heart jumped into his throat. He thought they had been discovered, but the negro was pointing at the idol. The big man grunted contemptuously. However slavishly in awe he might be of the fetishes of his native coast, the gods and demons of other races held no terrors for him.

But he moved forward majestically to investigate, and Wentyard realized that discovery was inevitable.

Vulmea whispered fiercely in his ear: "We've got to get them, quick! Take the brave. I'll take the chief. Now!"

They sprang up together, and the blacks cried out involuntarily, recoiling from the unexpected apparitions. In that instant the white men were upon them.

The shock of their sudden appearance had stunned the smaller black. He was small only in comparison with his gigantic companion. He was as tall as Wentyard and the great muscles knotted under his sleek skin. But he was staggering back, gaping stupidly, spear and shield lowered on limply hanging arms. Only the bite of steel brought him to his senses, and then it was too late. He screamed and lunged madly, but Wentyard's sword had girded deep into his vitals and his lunge was wild. The Englishman sidestepped and thrust again and yet again, under and over the shield, fleshing his blade in groin and throat. The black man swayed in his rush, his arms fell, shield and spear clattered to the floor and he toppled down upon them.

Wentyard turned to stare at the battle waging behind him, where the two giants fought under the square beam of moonlight, black and white, spear and shield against cutlass.

Bigomba, quicker-witted than his follower, had not gone down under the unexpected rush of the white man. He had reacted instantly to his fighting instinct. Instead of retreating he had thrown up his shield to catch the down-swinging cutlass, and had countered with a ferocious lunge that scraped blood from the Irishman's neck as he ducked aside.

Now they fought in grim silence, while Wentyard circled about them, unable to get in a thrust that might not imperil Vulmea. Both moved with the sure-footed quickness of tigers. The black man towered above the white, but even his magnificent proportions could not overshadow the sinewy physique of the pirate. In the moonlight the great muscles of both men knotted, rippled and coiled in response to their herculean exertions. The play was bewildering, almost blinding the eye that tried to follow it.

Again and again the pirate barely avoided the dart of the great spear, and again and again Bigomba caught on his shield a stroke that otherwise would have shorn him asunder. Speed of foot and strength of wrist alone saved Vulmea, for he had no defensive armor. But repeatedly he either dodged or sidestepped the savage thrusts, or beat aside the spear with his blade. And he rained blow on blow with his cutlass, slashing the bull hide to ribbons, until the shield was little more than a wooden framework through which, slipping in a lightning-like thrust, the cutlass drew first blood as it raked through the flesh across the black chief 's ribs.

At that Bigomba roared like a wounded lion, and like a wounded lion he leaped. Hurling the shield at Vulmea's head he threw all his giant body behind the arm that drove the spear at the Irishman's breast. The muscles leaped up in quivering bunches on his arm as he smote, and Wentyard cried out, unable to believe that Vulmea could avoid the lunge. But chain lightning was slow compared to the pirate's shift. He ducked, sidestepped, and as the spear whipped past under his armpit, he dealt a cut that found no shield in the way. The cutlass was a blinding flicker of steel in the moonlight, ending its arc in a butcher shop *crunch*. Bigomba fell as a tree falls and lay still. His head had been all but severed from his body.

Vulmea stepped back, panting. His great chest heaved under the tattered shirt, and sweat dripped from his face. At last he had met a man almost his match, and the strain of that terrible encounter left the tendons of his thighs quivering.

"We've got to get out of here before the rest of them come," he gasped, catching up his half of the idol's necklace. "That smaller corridor must lead to the outside, but those niggers are in it, and we haven't any torch. Let's try this door. Maybe we can get out that way."

The ancient door was a rotten mass of crumbling panels and corroded copper bands. It cracked and splintered under the impact of Vulmea's heavy shoulder, and through the apertures the pirate felt the stir of fresh air, and caught the scent of a damp river-reek. He drew back to smash again at the door, when a chorus of fierce yells brought him about snarling like a trapped wolf. Swift feet pattered up the tunnel, torches waved, and barbaric shouts re-echoed under the vaulted roof. The white men saw a mass of fierce faces and flashing spears, thrown into relief by the flaring torches, surging up the tunnel. The light of their coming streamed before them. They had heard and interpreted the sounds of combat as they hurried up the tunnel, and now they had sighted their enemies, and they burst into a run, howling like wolves.

"Break the door, quick!" cried Wentyard.

"No time now," grunted Vulmea. "They'd be on us before we could get through. We'll make our stand here."

He ran across the chamber to meet them before they could emerge from the comparatively narrow archway, and Wentyard followed him. Despair gripped the Englishman and in a spasm of futile rage he hurled the half-necklace from him. The glint of its jewels was mockery. He fought down the sick memory of those who waited for him in England as he took his place at the door beside the giant pirate.

As they saw their prey at bay the howls of the oncoming blacks grew wilder. Spears were brandished among the torches—then a shriek of different timbre cut the din. The foremost blacks had almost reached the point where the corridor branched off the tunnel—and out of the corridor raced a frantic figure. It was one of the black men who had gone down it exploring. And behind him came a blood-smeared nightmare. The great serpent had turned at bay at last.

It was among the blacks before they knew what was happening. Yells of hate changed to screams of terror, and in an instant all was madness, a clustering tangle of struggling black bodies and limbs, and that great sinuous cablelike trunk writhing and whipping among them, the wedge-shaped head darting and battering. Torches were knocked against the walls, scattering sparks. One man, caught in the squirming coils, was crushed and killed almost instantly, and others were dashed to the floor or hurled with bone-splintering force against the walls by the battering-ram head, or the lashing, beamlike tail. Shot and slashed as it was, wounded mortally, the great snake clung to life with the horrible vitality of its kind, and in the blind fury of its death throes it became an appalling engine of destruction.

Within a matter of moments the blacks who survived had broken away and were fleeing down the tunnel, screaming their fear. Half a dozen limp and broken bodies lay sprawled behind them, and the serpent, unlooping himself from these victims, swept down the tunnel after the living who fled from him. Fugitives and pursuer vanished into the darkness, from which frantic yells came back faintly.

"God!" Wentyard wiped his brow with a trembling hand. "That might have happened to us!"

"Those niggers who went groping down the corridor must have stumbled onto him lying in the dark," muttered Vulmea. "I reckon he got tired of running. Or maybe he knew he had his death wound and turned back to kill somebody before he died. He'll chase those niggers until either he's killed them all, or died himself. They may turn on him and spear him to death when they get into the open. Pick up your part of the necklace. I'm going to try that door again."

Three powerful drives of his shoulder were required before the ancient door finally gave way. Fresh, damp air poured through, though the interior was dark. But Vulmea entered without hesitation, and Wentyard followed him. After a few yards of groping in the dark, the narrow corridor turned sharply to the left, and they emerged into a somewhat wider passage, where a familiar, nauseating reek made Wentyard shudder.

"The snake used this tunnel," said Vulmea. "This must be the corridor that branches off the tunnel on the other side of the idol room. There must be a regular network of subterranean rooms and tunnels under these cliffs. I wonder what we'd find if we explored all of them."

Wentyard fervently disavowed any curiosity in that direction, and an instant later jumped convulsively when Vulmea snapped suddenly: "Look there!"

"Where? How can a man look anywhere in this darkness?"

"Ahead of us, damn it! It's light at the other end of this tunnel!"

"Your eyes are better than mine," muttered Wentyard, but he followed the pirate with new eagerness, and soon he too could see the tiny disk of grey that seemed set in a solid black wall. After that it seemed to the Englishman that they walked for miles. It was not that far in reality, but the disk grew slowly in size and clarity, and Wentyard knew that they had come a long way from the idol room when at last they thrust their heads through a round, vine-crossed opening and saw the stars reflected in the black water of a sullen river flowing beneath them.

"This is the way he came and went, all right," grunted Vulmea.

The tunnel opened in the steep bank and there was a narrow strip of beach below it, probably existent only in dry seasons. They dropped down to it and looked about at the dense jungle walls which hung over the river.

"Where are we?" asked Wentyard helplessly, his sense of direction entirely muddled.

"Beyond the foot of the slopes," answered Vulmea, "and that means we're outside the cordon the Indians have strung around the cliffs. The coast lies in that direction; come on!"

The sun hung high above the western horizon when two men emerged from the jungle that fringed the beach, and saw the tiny bay stretching before them.

Vulmea stopped in the shadow of the trees.

"There's your ship, lying at anchor where we left her. All you've got to do now is hail her for a boat to be sent ashore, and your part of the adventure is over."

Wentyard looked at his companion. The Englishman was bruised, scratched by briars, his clothing hanging in tatters. He could hardly have been recognized as the trim captain of the *Redoubtable*. But the change was not limited to his appearance. It went deeper. He was a different man than the one who marched his prisoner ashore in quest of a mythical hoard of gems.

"What of you? I owe you a debt that I can never—"

"You owe me nothing," Vulmea broke in. "I don't trust you, Wentyard."

The other winced. Vulmea did not know that it was the cruelest thing he could have said. He did not mean it as cruelty. He was simply speaking his mind, and it did not occur to him that it would hurt the Englishman.

"Do you think I could ever harm you now, after this?" exclaimed Wentyard. "Pirate or not, I could never—"

"You're grateful and full of the milk of human kindness now," answered Vulmea, and laughed hardly. "But you might change your mind after you got back on your decks. John Wentyard lost in the jungle is one man; Captain Wentyard aboard his king's warship is another."

"I swear—" began Wentyard desperately, and then stopped, realizing the futility of his protestations. He realized, with an almost physical pain, that a man can never escape the consequences of a wrong, even though the victim may forgive him. His punishment now was an inability to convince Vulmea of his sincerity, and it hurt him far more bitterly than the Irishman could ever realize. But he could not expect Vulmea to trust him, he realized miserably. In that moment he loathed himself for what he had been, and for the smug self-sufficient arrogance which had caused him to ruthlessly trample on all who fell outside the charmed circle of his approval. At that moment there was nothing in the world he desired more than the firm hand-clasp of the man who had fought and wrought so tremendously for him; but he knew he did not deserve it.

"You can't stay here!" he protested weakly.

"The Indians never come to this coast," answered Vulmea. "I'm not afraid of the Cimarroons. Don't worry about me." He laughed again, at what he considered the jest of anyone worrying about his safety. "I've lived in the wilds before now. I'm not the only pirate in these seas. There's a rendezvous you know nothing about. I can reach it easily. I'll be back on the Main with a ship and a crew the next time you hear about me."

And turning supply, he strode into the foliage and vanished, while Wentyard, dangling in his hand a jeweled strip of gold, stared helplessly after him.

A Dying Pirate Speaks of Treasure

Lash me two round shot hard to my ankles;
Over the rail let me slide to the deep;
I'll never see Bristol; the crack of a pistol
Has weighted my eyelids wi' coming o' sleep.

The prize it was ours, its crew all a-lying
Face down in the scuppers and dead on the deck;
When spat! came the ball of the mate who lay dying,
Cheating the gallows, mayhap, o' my neck.

You'll take a new captain and share all the plunder
And sail for Tortuga or ever it's morn,
And maybe you'll drink for him that lies under
The tides that come creeping around from the Horn.

Give you a map o' the treasure I've taken?
Tell where the gems and the doubloons are hid?
Why hiding of treasure's the custom and pleasure
Of Drake and of Morgan, of Flint and of Kidd.

Of the twenty-odd years I've sailed on the ocean,
On the Red Sea Trade with the Main's Brotherhood,
By all the winds shaken, great loot I ha' taken
And mainly considered it splendid and good.

So clap on all sails and steer for the sunset,
If ever my treasure you're wishful to find —
Where white combers thunder you'll find rarer plunder
Than out o' Golconda there ever was mined.

For I've hidden my loot in the winds and the surges,
Where the keel breaks the waves and soft surges croon,
It's the gems o' the skyline where sea and sky merges,
It's the gold o' the sun and the silk o' the moon.

It's the silver o' starlight, the mist o' the morning
All gossamer webs, and the deep coral caves,
The winds and the wonder o' reef-riven thunder,
The emerald sheen o' the snow-crested waves.

The gold that I gathered that mankind had minted,
It slipped through my fingers like sands on the beach;
But the silver o' starlight was ever unstinted,
And the gold o' the sunset was ever in reach.

Oh, the sea is my love, though my fingers be crimson,
The treasure I've hidden, you hunt for in vain;
So sail ye for plunder till Judgment Day's thunder —
But I'll go to my Treasure House under the Main.

Miscellanea

List of Names

(The Treasure of Henry Morgan)

Sir Henry Morgan,
Harry Allgry,
Captain Ned Davies,

Morgan,
Soring,
Nase Liron,
The Panther,
Hawkins
Kirby
Blackbeard
Bonnet
Avary
England
Israel Hands.
O'Hallery.

The Treasure of Henry Morgan

(unfinished)

Chapter .1.

The sun was shining brightly and the birds were chirping as I walked down the streets of Charlestown on a fair day in the early part of the summer of 1718. The town was humming with life and activity, for at that time it was the center of trade of the new world. All trading vessels made port there, sooner or later, and all types of men were to be seen. One type was passing me then: a short, stocky fellow, who walked with the rolling gait of a sailor, eying insolently everyone he met. A gaudy colored kerchief on his head, earrings, a tattooed anchor on his bare, brawny arm, a wide belt full of dirks and pistols, he was undoubtedly and openly a pirate. They had always frequented Charlestown, selling their loot there and getting immunity from the law in return for good bargains, and now, since Blackbeard and Stede Bonnet had been pardoned and Governor Eden had tacitly struck a bargain with the former, who was still carrying on his old trade but slyly, now, I say, the town swarmed with pirates who swaggered on the streets, drank rum and roared sea-songs in the taverns, and openly boasted of ships boarded and loot taken. However, they were careful not to offend the townspeople for, however much the inhabitants desired the pirates' trade, there was a certain point beyond which they would not allow them to go, even to retain the profits of trade. And the pirates themselves were greatly desirous to keep the port of Charlestown open to them, for if it were closed there would be no place where they could dispose of their plunder, nearer than the Dutch West Indies, so they disported themselves with as much decorum possible to them while in port and the merchants of Charlestown winked at their deeds on high seas and grew rich off the proceeds of piracy. So it was in Charlestown in 1718.

As I passed a tavern of the lower sort, one of those which was patronized a great deal by smugglers and pirates, I heard a clamor of shouts, curses and the tinkle of breaking glass and the next minute a man was catapulted from the door and hit the cobblestones with a thud, a dirk flying from his hand and tinkling on the stones. Instantly the door of the tavern was filled by the bulk of a huge red-faced man who cursed and shook a cutlass at the first fellow.

"Try to cozen an honest man, would ye?" he bellowed. "I'll teach ye Simon Baddlesmere's not the man to trifle with, ye varlet!"

The other, a small, wiry old fellow, with straggly gray whiskers, got to his feet, recovered his dirk and seemed in the favour of renewing the argument, but on observing the cutlass in the innkeeper's hand, and the angry faces peering over his shoulder, he merely hitched his trousers and spat toward the inn.

"A fine lot ye are," he commented, sarcastically. "You wi' your red mug and bull voice and the rest o' th' cowardly vagabonds and ragamuffins that guzzle in th' slovenly rum-puncheon ye call an inn! Keelhaul me, I thought 'twas a decent grogshop or I'd never gone there!"

His abuse infuriated the innkeeper, who gave a bellow and charged out of the door brandishing his cutlass, and followed by just such an assortment of idle guzzlers as the old man had described.

I expected the old fellow to flee, but he stood his ground boldly, poised on the balls of his feet and holding his dirk in such a manner that I knew he had some skill in knife-fighting. Moved by a sudden impulse, I stepped between him and his assailants.

"This has gone far enough," I said. "What is the disagreement?"

"Disagreement?" roared the innkeeper. "Why, this beggarly knave drank rum in my inn like any king and refused to pay his score, and then when I but demanded my just pay, he drew knife on me and cursed me in mine own inn!"

"How much is the score?" I asked.

"Five shilling three pence," was the sulky reply.

"Always a liar, eh Simon?" the old sailor remarked dryly. "The score is but three shillings."

"Here is the money," I said, handing it to him. "Now get back to your rum barrels."

The innkeeper turned sulkily back to his inn, followed by the others. The sailor laughed scornfully.

"I'm main grateful for what ye did fer me, mate," he said, turning to me. "D'ye mind if I walk up the street wi' ye, or whichever way you're steering?"

"Certainly not," I replied, studying him with interest. He was about medium height as I have said, lean and wiry of build, slightly bowlegged, with a leathery face fringed by straggly, gray whiskers. His eyes were gray and twinkled. He was dressed in the rough clothes of a common sailor. Suddenly he began to curse the innkeeper.

"Keelhaul me, it ain't comed to a purty pass when a gentleman o' fortune like me can't get a swig o' grog in Charlestown without plankin' down the silver! Why, I went into that Chinaman's hut of a grogshop and took a few glasses of rum, and not of the best either, though it sold for the top price, and then when I set my glass down and started to leave, why that innkeeper, the son of a double-Dutchman, he ups and says he, 'Where's the money for my rum?' I says, perfectly polite, 'Why, mate, not bein' flush just now, I'll drop in and pay you after next cruise.' And what does he do but swear at me and try to throw me out. And when I took out my knife, he called a lot of ragamuffins and they all boarded me and slung me overboard. And you know the rest. Shiver my tops'yls!"

The old fellow interested me. I paused at a tavern door.

"Come in and have a drink," I invited, and he accepted with alacrity.

He gazed at me meditatively over the glasses, started to speak, then hesitated. Finally he said, "Live in Charlestown?"

I told him no, I had a plantation in Virginia.

"You'll have seen a great many seagoing men, I make no doubt?"

"Why, yes, certainly."

"Then maybe you've seen," here he eyed me cunningly, "a seafarin' man wi' the flag o' Spain tattooed on his right breast? A tall, big man wi' strange eyes that look right through ye and the flag o' Spain tattooed on his right breast, wi' a dragon curled around the staff."

"I never saw such a man," I answered.

"Ah," was his only comment as he retired to his ale. Then, "Listen mate, if ye ever sight the craft I just spoke of, the seagoin' man wi' the Spanish flag and dragon tattooed high on his right breast, close to the shoulder, why you just tip me off, will ye mate?"

Then, "Ah," and back to his ale when I said I would. At last he leaned back and looked me up and down. Then he spoke abruptly.

"Mate, you've done handsome by me, real handsome I calls it, keelhaul me! And what's more, I like your trim. I like the cut o' your jib and the spread o' your sails. I got a scheme afoot but I'll have to have help, and the man that helps me will be rich, keelhaul me if he won't! Now you look like a proper man. Are you hitched? Married?"

"No."

"Good! Any money?"

"Enough for me."

"Then by Davy Jones it's enough for me! Mate, you're the man for this job! What might your name be?"

"Stephen Morgan."

"Morgan!" he exclaimed in great excitement. "Morgan! Any relation to Sir Henry Morgan?"

"His grandson," I admitted.

The old sailor sat gazing at me with great respect, almost reverence. Then he rose hurriedly and pulled me to my feet.

"Quick, captain," he exclaimed. "Come on, come on. Some place we can talk. Hurry! I got a grand tale to tell ye!"

I paid for our liquor and we stepped out in the busy streets of Charlestown. He led the way down the streets to the waterfront and then down the quays until we came to an old, deserted dock. After looking about suspiciously, he seated himself on the edge of the wharf and beckoned me to do likewise. I complied, wonderingly.

"To begin, cap'n," he said, filling his pipe with strong tobacco, "I knowed your grandfather well."

"You did?" I asked, somewhat surprized.

"Ay, that I did. I sailed wi' him while he were on the account. Ah, lad, there were a man! No such men as he nowadays. Brave as a lion he were. Keelhaul me, but I can see him as plain as I sees you. Tall and elegant, taller than you be, cap'n, standing like a king on the quarterdeck, wi' his cocked hat an' fine coat wi' the jeweled butts o' his pistols peepin' out o' the pockets and his golden hilted rapier at his belt. Ah, he were a man! There were some as thought he couldn't be a fightin' man because he always dressed so neat and dapper. L'Ollonais' mate was one o' them. They met in a tavern in the West Indies and the mate sneered at Morgan for a dandy. They had words and the mate reached for a pistol. But before his hand could touch the butt Morgan had run the man through. Then he wiped his blade as calm as you please and went back to his wine. Ah, if ______ had seen him at the taking o' the plate ship off Caracas in South America, he wouldn't ha' crossed the cap'n so quick like. I mind him standing in the bows wi' his sword in his hand, wi' his face pale and eager. And the voice o' him when he roared, 'Give them a broadside and then close and board!' And he was the first man to leap on to the Spaniard's deck. And he was a fine navigator, too."

"You must have been young then," I remarked, interestedly.

"Ay, that I was, mate. Cabin boy I was. And though I say it as shouldn't, not bein' a boastful man, you won't find a better cabin boy than me between England and the West Indies. Cabin boy I were when he sailed from Jamaica wi' Mansvelt, but I was bos'n when the king pardoned him. But this wasn't what I wanted to tell you. You mind when Cap'n Morgan took the city of Panama?"

"Yes, and immediately afterwards deserted his men at Charges, taking with him all the best ships and most of the treasure. A fine trick to play on men that had followed him through thick and thin."

"Lad, you shouldn't speak that way of your grandfather," the old pirate said reprovingly. "He were more of a man than you'ull ever be and, besides, weren't most of the men Frenchmen? Weren't they grumbling against the cap'n and plotin' mutiny? Eh? Answer me that now!"

"How should I know?" I inquired, amused at the sailor's heat. "I wasn't there."

"Ay, but I were. Now don't interrupt me no more till I finish wi' this yarn. Well, I was with the cap'n at the taking of Panama, and a rare fight it were, what with the fortifications and the Spanish arquebusiers and the Indian archers. Ay, and a rare town it were too, with oodles and oodles of loot. One hundred and seventy mule loads o' treasure we took out of the town, jewels and plate and silver and pieces-of-eight and Spanish doubloons. All the Brethren of the Main gathered at Charges, the appointed rendezvous to divide the booty. And here the trouble began. Many of the men wasn't satisfied wi' their share but must have more, and they accused Morgan of takin' more than his rightful share and of cheatin' them, and there were plots and mutiny and suchlike until Cap'n Morgan, he ups and says to the few as was loyal to him, says he, 'These men are tired of me. They want a new leader. They want to be rid of me and, by thunder, they shall be.' And that very night he sailed away with the best ships and nearly all the loot, taking with him me and the others that was loyal to him, havin' stove in the other ships so that the mutineers couldn't follow. We sailed for Jamaica."

Here he paused to refill his pipe and I asked, "How did Morgan get hold of the loot?"

"Why, at the first, when the men began to quarrel over it, he took into his ship all of it, so the men wouldn't fight over it and maybe steal it."

"Why, then," I exclaimed, "he had it all planned from the first."

"Very likely," replied the old sailor serenely. "He were a great hand for looking ahead. Well, we sailed for Jamaica and we hadn't covered half the vy'age when the topsy'ls of a fast sailin' craft hove in sight agin' the skyline. Morgan called me to the quarterdeck. He was that companionable and I was bos'n then and had powerful keen sight. 'Hawkins,' says he, 'what ship is that?' handin' me his telescope. I looked. It was still far away but I says, 'Cap'n, I'd say she was either *The Dolphin* that we left stove in at Charges or else a British man-o-war.' Just then the lookout in the mizzentops shouted, 'Land ho!' Morgan says, 'Mutineers or man-o-war's men, they'll never get a look at this plunder. Clap on all sail for the land!'

"In no time we drew up alongside the land, a long low-lyin' island with lots of trees and swamps and such like. We rounded the place until the whole island was between us and the man-o-war. (For that's what she turned out to be.) Then Morgan ordered a boat sent overside and he went ashore. Him and me and three sailors and two boatloads of loot. Five of us went ashore. Two of us came back—me and Morgan. Morgan would a' come back alone but he knew he could trust me, and besides I had a musket. Morgan drew a map of the place we hid the treasure wi' the longitude and latitude of the island set down complete. He always intended to come back for the loot. Well, we'd hardly shipped the boat and weighed anchor when around the shoulder o' the island came the man-o-war, swoopin' down on us like a cormorant, sails spread and decks cleared, for she knew Morgan's ship. We had a fast-sailin' craft and for a while she couldn't get in range of us but she was gainin' fast when a squall hit us, and when it cleared we was headed for the open sea, runnin' before the wind wi' all sails set and the man-o-war was three leagues astern and losin' ground all the time. Soon after, Morgan was pardoned by the king and made Deputy-Governor of Jamaica, and he didn't have time to go after his loot what wi' the duties of his office and puttin' down piracy. An' he didn't forget his friends, either, for he made me first mate on a ship he fitted out to send against the Dons. He made a bargain with us. Kirby was cap'n, I was mate. He furnished the ship and kept the warships off us and we gave him a third of the profits. Kirby had been captain of one of Morgan's ships while the cap'n was on the account and he knew about the loot. But Morgan always sent us in some other direction so we didn't get a chance to look for the island. No one knew the location but Morgan. 'Kirby,' he says one day, 'when I can find leisure I'm going after that loot. I'll go in your ship and share it fair with the crew and you.'

"Well, one day Morgan sent for Kirby and me and we went to his fine governor's house, the finest in Jamaica.

[. . .]

[What follows is a newly discovered page that appears to be from an earlier draft of the story. This page is handwritten on lined paper; the preceding was typed.]

[. . .]

"Reef the mainsy'ls," he shouted.

"Reef them yourself, I replied, indignantly. "You're the captain of this craft, and, anyway, I don't know how."

He cast me a reproachful look.

"Ah, lad, that the grandson of old Cap'n Morgan shouldn't know how to reef a sail! Well, take ye the tiller and I'll do it, but 'tis a pretty pass when the captain of a ship must haul and steer on his own craft like any other common A. B. mariner!"

[. . .]

"So there I was..."

(untitled and unfinished)

So there I was. Stranded in a strange land, a land that no one knew existed. The reason I was there was, I could always drink whisky or let it alone and usually I drank it. I was mate on the blackbirder *Belle of Glasgow* and we were beating back from the New Hebrides with a cargo of black boys bound for the Australian plantations. The captain, Angus MacKenzie, a tough old Scotchman, left me in charge of the ship and went on a drunk. The second mate and I were they only whites on board and we navigated the ship until we found the captain's private store of real Scotch whiskey. We were fed up on trade-gin and when I came out of that drunk, the ship had drifted clear out of the regular routes into seas where we had never been before and old Angus had come out of his drunk and was stamping and cussing on the deck, partly because the second mate and me had let the ship drift out of all reckoning and mostly because we had drunk up all his Scotch whisky. He swore and put us in irons but we laughed at him. I left him and the second mate trying to find our latitude and longitude and went on deck. I went to the for'ard locker to see if the whisky I had hid was still there. It was. A full quart bottle and four quart bottles of trade-rum. I put three bottles in my pockets and held the other two in my hands. I wondered if the whisky still tasted the same. I took a swig. It did. Then I got to wondering if I could still like traderum after drinking Scotch whisky. I tasted it. It was still suited to my taste. Then I wondered how they would taste together. I thought that I would go to my cabin and get some tobacco but the next thing I remember I was sitting on the end of the bow-sprint, singing. Then I woke up and I sure got a surprise. The sun was just coming up and I was lying on a kind of a raft—and the ship was nowhere in sight. And away off to the east I could see land. I sat up and wondered. I concluded I must have fallen off the ship and it sailed on without me. The raft was just a tangle of drift wood. I either landed on it when I fell overboard or else had sense enough to swim until I reached it. I took a piece of board and used it for an oar, steering for the land. I soon reached it. There was a long, shelvy, sloping beach that ran back a few hundred yards to a forest that was strangely free of undergrowth. For all I knew there was a whole tribe of cannibals lurking among the trees but I was going ashore, anyway. I was hungry and thirsty and I could see fruit growing on the trees. I dragged the raft up on the beach and made for the trees. I was surprised at the number and variety of fruit. Guavas, coconuts and pineapple were in abundance. There were lots of good-sized pebbles on the beach and I knocked the fruit off the trees with them. I felt refreshed after I ate the fruit and began to take notice of my surroundings and an inventory of my means of maintenance and defense. I had on more clothes than I had when I got drunk. Then I had been bare-footed and hatless. Now I not only had on socks and shoes but a pair of leather puttees, a broad-brimmed hat and a pea coat. I must have dressed up while drunk. Probably when I went after the tobacco. I wondered if I had gotten the tobacco. My pockets were weighed down by something. I began to feel in them. My fingers encountered cartridges. Boxes and boxes of them. I took off my coat and laid it down. The cartridges had made me think of my guns and I wondered if they were wet. I always wore two down in those seas—Colt single-actions, a .45 and a .44-40, with the holster-ends tied down. I took them out and examined them. They weren't and hadn't been. I must have landed on the raft when I fell off the ship. Then I went through my pockets. There were two bottles of trade-rum, full bottles, and the bottle of Scotch whisky, nearly half-full. Then there were five boxes of .45 cartridges, four boxes of .44-40s, a box of .575s (the captain had a Hollands' .575 that he used for a whale gun), and a double handful of cartridges for the pistols. Then there was a short, heavy machete with a blade not quite a foot and a half long and no sheath, a cigar lighter, a ball of heavy cord. Not a sign of tobacco. I remembered that the box of tobacco and a carton of ammunition had been side by side. I had been too drunk to distinguish between the two and had filled my pockets with cartridges instead of tobacco. Then I must have rummaged around, put on the extra clothing and put the other things in my pockets (for all of which I was devoutly thankful) and then came on deck and fallen overboard. I was pretty well able to take care of myself. So satisfied on that score I began to look over the scenery. I could not tell much about it. Just beach and sea and trees. I climbed a tree that seemed taller than the rest and when I gained the top I had a fine view. I saw that I was on a kind of peninsula that stretched from a mainland in a kind of rough V shape. I was on the narrow extremity and it widened as it neared the mainland. It was thickly wooded and I was astonished at the number of fruit bearing trees. There seemed to be a break in the woods just where the peninsula joined the mainland. Then the forest rolled away into the distance and

[...]

"Help! Help! They're murderin' me!"

(untitled and unfinished)

"Help! Help! They're murderin' me!"

Mike O'Brien stopped short at the mouth of the black alley he was passing. There are many secrets in the noisome and mysterious native quarters of Makassar into which it is best for a stranger not to pry. Best to ignore the weird wails and shrieks that sometimes rack the ears from darksome places, and try to forget what they may mean.

But Mike O'Brien was a fighting man with a fighting man's reckless impulsiveness. He bounded into the alleyway, groping in the blackness, his great body tensed for action, his mighty fists knotted into iron sledges. He made out a vague struggling clump in front of him—heard a gasping for breath, caught the dim glimmer of a knife. Then he leaped like a huge tiger and struck terrific blows. He felt flesh and bone give before his hard fists and blood spattered his arm.

A keen edge licked along his shoulder, slicing his ragged shirt, and then one of his powerful smashes connected squarely and he saw a dim bulk crash into the filth and refuse of the alley-way. The other—or others—melted away from him, slinking into the gloom like phantoms.

"Lend a hand, mate," gasped a labored voice at his feet. "The swine have knocked the breath outa me!"

Mike stooped and lifted one of the prostrate figures. The other he let lie.

"Outa here, quick!" grunted the rescued man, and together they made their way into the comparative light of the sordid street. Mike looked curiously at his companion. He was a lean, wiry man of middle life, with a straggling beard shot with grey. He had the look of a beach-comber as to clothes, but his keen frosty eyes were not those of a vagrant. This man sized Mike up and down; he saw a splendid animal of a man, whose mighty chest showed like that of a bronze image through his tattered sleeveless shirt. O'Brien was the typical type of Irish-American fighting man—dark, with volcanic blue eyes brooding under heavy black brows. Broad shouldered and deep chested, he was at once lithe and massive, combining the strength of a bull with the quickness of a cat.

"I know you," said the older man. "You're Mike O'Brien that was with the *Water-snake*. I seen you fight in the waterfront stadiums different places. You on the beach now?"

"Almost," growled the fighter. "I had a row with old Bully Hurley, my cap'n, and he discharged me. I lost most uh my pay at roulette and I can't find a berth seems like."

The other seemed not to have heard.

"We need another man to work the sloop," he mused. "And you're a fighter—we can use you. But we can't pay you nothin' yet."

Mike laughed shortly and turned away with a shrug of his massive shoulders, but the older man caught his arm in a nervous grip that bit like a steel vice.

"Wait! You don't know what you're passin' up! It's the biggest thing you ever got a chance at in your life! Come down to Dutchy's Bar—I'll spill it to you."

At Dutchy's Bar, a sordid den far down in the mazes of the waterfront, the older man looked about suspiciously. A half-breed listlessly polished the bar with a dirty rag and at the back a sodden drunk slept with his arms and head on a table. The stranger bought two bottles of beer and carried them back with him to another table. There were no glasses; the men drank out of the bottles.

"My name's Sloan, 'Aroo' Sloan."

O'Brien nodded. He had heard the name—one connected with shady dealings and strange trading among island kingdoms.

"I've got two pals, Red Masters and John Roach. We haven't much money, but we've got hold of a sloop—a crazy old craft but she'll carry us as far as we want to go. We need a fourth man; I like you. I've heard you spoken of as a square dealer. You're different from the general run of beach-combers, the lousy rats! If you say the word, it's share and share alike!"

"I dunno what you're talkin' about!" complained Mike.

"I'll tell you, mate!" Sloan leaned forward and lowered his voice. "It's treasure we're after!"

Mike laughed shortly. "Pipe dreams, old timer. I've heard them tales before. What is it this time—a pearl cache or a floatin' mint gone ashore?"

"No! No!" Sloan's eyes were lit with an avid gleam. "Lean closer and I'll tell you. I found a old sailor dyin' on the beach at Surubaya. He'd seen the treasure! But nobody would believe him and he had leprosy—nobody would go about him. But I listened to him and tended to him while he lasted and he gave me a map he's made. I burned it, but before I did, I copied it on a very much smaller scale. Where it's hid, nobody knows but me! And mate, it was a true tale he told me! The treasure is on a certain island in the Banda Sea. He was wrecked on that island and he stumbled onto the treasure. But there was a terrible race of people guarding the treasure, and when he'd start talkin' about 'em, he'd kind of go off his head and wander in his talk. But I gather he escaped 'em some way and took to sea in a open canoe he'd stole from 'em. Far at sea he was picked up by a Dutch trading schooner and they laughed at his tale—said he was crazy. And he was showing signs of leprosy then, so they dumped him on the beach to die.

"But mate, I know he spoke the truth! I've heard old tales of that treasure, all my years in the island. Vague whispers and hints and old legends! Others has too, and they found I had a map. Bully Harney and his gang—Tom Richards and Bill Slade and Juan Diego, the half-breed. It was Juan and some of his native friends that set on me in that alley. They want the map—the fools, to think I'd pack it with me. But they'd a killed me if you hadn't interfered."

"What is this treasure?" asked Mike. "All my life I've heard talk of such stuff but I never believed in it."

[. . .]

The Shadow in the Well

(untitled synopsis)

The tale is laid on an island on the Spanish main, 1711. The pirate ship is anchored offshore and all the crew are on shore. Steve is a captive, bound hand and foot to a tree. John Groshawk is the pirate captain, the former one having been killed in the fight in which Steve was captured. Nell Brent, a woman pirate, has saved Steve's life. The pirates have a map showing hidden treasure, left on the island in 1580 by a strange and bizarre figure—a pirate who dealt in magic and witchcraft. Groshawk announces he will go inland searching for the treasure and he orders Nell to remain on the beach. She reaches for her pistols but is seized and disarmed and left with the men on the beach, who remain to watch for a Spanish man-o-war reported in those waters. Groshawk goes inland with Make Bellafonte, Bill Deal, Juan the Butcher, Jeremy Fletcher, La Coste, Jim Worley, Peter Ord, Dick Bain, Ash Stark, and Joab Godfrey.

They vanish into the woods and the others go around a point of land to gamble in the shade, taking Nell Brent with them. She slips away and comes back to where Steve is tied. She offers to free him if he will aid her and he agrees. She has just freed him when Solomon Deas comes upon them. Steve, a powerful man, strangles Solomon and takes his cutlass. He and Nell go in the woods and meet Mike Bellafonte, sent back to the beach by Groshawk for sledges. Seve and Mike fight and Mike is slain.

Steve and Nell go on and come to a great black temple in the midst of a swamp. They enter the columned portico and come into a large chamber, in the midst of which is a large black altar. Attempts have been made to shatter it, in the belief it was hollow. Corridors open from this chamber and down one they see the glimmer of torches. They follow another and eventually come to a right angle, where there is a well, its mouth level with the floor. They hear the pirate crew behind them, and hide in the tunnel. Groshawk is swearing because Bellafonte has not returned with hammers to break open the altar. At about this time a man arrives with word that Steve and Nell have escaped, killing Deas and Beallafonte. Groshawk sends him back after hammers, and meanwhile he wishes to explore the black, mysterious well. Jem Worley is lowered into the well on a long rope, and suddenly screams comes up from below. The rope goes slack and comes up without him. Le Coste leans far over and throws a lighted torch down the well—suddenly screaming, clapping his hands over his eyes and pitching headlong into the well.

The nerves of the rest are shaken. And they turn into another corridor. Nell insists on following them, just out of the torchlight, and for some time they wander trough dark corridors, finding nothing. A shout informs them that the pirate sent for the hammers has returned and they go back and break open the altar, finding nothing. Angered, they return to the well—and suddenly a monstrous thing appears from it, which slaughters Groshawk and all his men. It attacks Steve, whose cutlass is futile against it, but Nell strikes it with a lighted torch and it shrinks away. Steve seizes the torch and it flees before him into the well. Steve and Nell flee from the place and join the other pirates who are cowed by the unnatural happenings. They all go aboard and sail away.

The Shadow in the Well

(unfinished draft)

John Groshawk gnawed the ends of his thin drooping moustaches and stared at me in his evil, gloomy way, and I glared back at him. For albeit I was his prisoner and bound hand and foot in the midst of his cut-throat band, I hated the bloody pirate too much to fear him.

"Another cord to his wrists," he ordered, and Mike Bellefonte drew the knot so tight that the strands bit into my flesh.

"There, by Judas," said he with an oath. "These ropes will hold even Big Steve Clarney."

"Good enough," quoth John Groshawk. "Let him hold up that palm tree while I give ye your orders."

"You'd best loose his bonds a little," said a softer voice. "The cords have near cut him to the bone."

"Enough from you, Nell Brent," growled Groshawk. "One 'ud think, by gad, ye were soft over this Irish lout."

Her answer was a sizzling volley of oaths that brought a thin sour smile to the buccaneer's lips.

"But there's such a thing as common humanity even in the Red Sea Trade," she concluded.

"Not in John Groshawk's crew," he answered. "Belay that guff—if I catch you trying to loose his cords in secret, I'll string ye up by your thumbs."

It was not Nell Brent's way to swallow such talk meekly, but her gaze dropped sullenly, and muttering angrily beneath her breath she hooked her thumbs in her wide silken sash and stood sulkily like a spanked child.John Groshawk turned to his motley crew, and I, glowering at them all, must needs admit that it was a colorful and strange scene.

John Groshawk dominated the scene—tall, rangy, long-legged, with his cold hawk-eyes, thin jutting nose, drooping black mustachios and cruel mouth. He stood with lean legs in their Cordovan boots braced wide, lean hands on the pistol butts that projected from his striped sash, narrow head jutting forward on his lean brown neck, with his cocked hat pushed back and showing the gaudy bandanna which covered his skull beneath. His ear-rings were hoops of gold and their jeweled pendants swayed as his sneering lips moved.

A little to one side, intent on his words, but as an actor who feels half out of the picture, stood Nell Brent, with her sulky face and gay garments. Her cocked hat had been discarded in the shade of the palms and the gleams that filtered through the broad leaves struck glints of bronze from her unruly black hair. She was a study in silk—tight silken breeches above soft leather knee-boots, a silken shirt worn under a brocaded jacket, a silken sash about her slim waist, holding jeweled dirk and pistols. Her wide purple eyes were clouded and moody; evidently this famous girlpirate, heroine of so many broadsides, chanties and songs ashore, was none too sure of herself.

Directly in front of Groshawk stood the crew, a villainous gang—Mike Bellefonte, with his bull's shoulders and short black beard—Le Coste, the Frenchman, tall, lank, with tarnished finery and nervous hands—Juan the Butcher, the Costa Rican half-breed, with his bare yellow skull and rotting fang-like teeth showing beneath his thick negroid lips—Peter Ord, drawling, fastidious, with his air of a gentleman fallen in evil ways—Solomon Deas, with his leering vulture face and bare splay feet—gad, what a devil's crew!

"Well, John," drawled Peter Ord, "you've brought us all ashore—what now? Where do we search for Jacob Trant's treasure? Are you sure this is the right island?"

"It's the isle, right enough," grinned Groshawk. "The same one drawn by Trant's own hand on the map I took from the Spaniard—and it all yellow wi' age and stained wi' blood. There's no mistake."

"What about this treasure?" clamored Ash Stark. "We've followed ye blind since Cap'n Bisley was killed, John Groshawk, and ye took command, as havin' been first mate. We've passed up good prizes and shook off that Spanish man-o'-war—ye've led us here far beyond the track of sea-farers—now we want to know why!"

"Aye!" rose a shout. "Give us the lay, John!"

"Be silent!" Groshawk's head jutted at a more aggressive angle and his jaw snapped like a steel-trap. "Don't raise your tongues to me, ye spawn of the wharves! And remember, it's Cap'n when ye speak. Well—I'll tell ye. How many of ye have heard the name of Jacob Trant, cap'n of the Black Toad?"

No one answered; they all knew of the name, and bare feet scuffed the turf uncertainly.

"What's he to do wi' us, Cap'n?" spoke up Bill Deal. "And him dead and in Hell for more than a hundred years?"

Groshawk smiled thinly.

"Let me tell the tale of Jacob Trant over again to jog your memory, belike. He was a Dutch pirate who delved in alchemy and black magic. A true warlock, were he! He sailed on the Main belike before Hawkins and Drake, and much plunder he took on all the Seven Seas—aye, he sailed to India and to Cathay, and took toll of all shipping.

"At last he was taken in Amsterdam and tried, not for piracy, but for being a wizard, and was condemned to be hanged. All night he sat in his dungeon, reading in a black book none but he understood, while in the square outside they planted the stake and heaped the fagots. And in the grey of dawn he rose and laughed, and the guards who heard him laugh fell down gibbering in black madness. His chains fell from him and at his touch the stout oaken doors crumbled and rotted away, and he came out from his prison. His ship, wi' the grim black demon painted on the bows, lay close guarded at the quay, and Jacob Trant came upon the wharves laughing as no mortal man ever laughed. He laid his hands upon the soldiers who guarded the wharves and they shriveled and lay dead on the wharves like dead wood charred by the flames o' Hell. And Jacob Trant went aboard his ship alone, and alone he cast off and put to sea. The king's ships pursued him, but a great wind sprang up and hurled them back to land, shattered and broken, and in the whirling chaos they saw the last of the Black Toad, flying into the teeth of the wind, with Jacob Trant standing at the wheel, his long black beard flying and him howling a wild chant that rose above the thunder of the waves. No living man saw Jacob Trant again, but he left something behind him—a map which was found in his cell after his flight. It was given to the hangman to burn, but he sold it to an English sailor who feared not black magic, for a shilling. The sailorman was murdered in a Bristol dive and a wench took the map from his body—so the tale goes—and gave it to a Portuegee, her lover. He was drowned at sea, belike, but some whim o' fate cast the map in its case ashore on the Slave Coast and there it rested for half a century in a Benin ju-ju hut. A black man stole it and wore it about his neck for a charm; he was shipped as a slave to Bernuda and after his master had beaten him to death for some trifling fault, his master took the charm and discovered its meaning. He was fitting out a ship to go search for the treasure when a Spaniard murdered him for the map. And the Spaniard was on that prize we took off Turtle Point."

"How d'ye know all this?" broke in Peter Ord.

"Because, ye mincin' fool, I've been on the track o' this bit o' parchment for a half score years, ever since I had it from the lips o' that Dutch hangman's son, that Jacob Trant left a map. I've gathered bits here and there about the world as I've traveled over it, from old crones and sea-farin' men who'd heard o' Jacob Trant's map. And I know. Now the map's ours, and I tell ye, all the gold that Harry Morgan took would look like a heap o' shillings beside Jacob Trant's loot o' Cathay and the Indies!"

He suddenly drew a roll of yellow parchment from his pocket and unfurled it with a dramatic gesture. "Look there, ye sea-rats!" They crowded about and I craned my neck to see. I could tell that parchment was very old, yellow, dim, darkly stained in places, and crusted from sea-water. The lines of the map were very much faded, as was the scrawling script; in one corner of the parchment squatted a vague, bulky object that somewhat resembled a toad.

"What's that thing, John?" uneasily asked Dick Bain.

"That's the Black Toad, same as was painted on the ship's bows."

"This writin's all in Dutch," grumbled Ash Stark. "I can't make nothing o' it."

"Nor I. That's Dutch, and Old Dutch at that. That Dutchman Yon could make out enough to tell me the latitude and longitude and all, and he might ha' made all the writing out, but he was killed along o' Cap'n Bisley, you know, when we took the *Bristol Girl.*

"But this is the island, no doubt about that. Yonder's the bay wi' the long spit running out to the south, and the in-curve o' the shoreline below it, see? And this mark in the center o' the isle must show where the loot's hid."

"Look's like a castle or something," muttered one of the men.

"Now we'll do this," said Groshawk authoritatively. "Some of you have got to bide here to keep watch for that Spanish warship that may be following us, for aught we know. The others will go wi' me to look for the plunder. Bellefonte will go wi' me, and Bill Deal, Juan, Jeremy Fletcher, La Coste, Jem Worley, Peter Ord, Dick Bain, Ash Stark and Joab Godfrey. The rest o' you bide here and keep watch. If you see aught suspicious, signal me wi' three musket shots."

"What of me?" burst in Nell Brent suddenly, her eyes smoldering; she was not accustomed to being ignored thus.

"You'll stay here wi' the men," said Groshawk.

"I'll see ye damned first!" she exclaimed. "I take orders from no man!"

"Ye'll take 'em from me," he answered coolly. "Bisley's dead, that humored ye like a spoiled baby—I'm cap'n here and you'll—"

Like a flash she reached for her pistols, but Mike Bellefonte had stolen up behind her and he caught her in his huge arms, picked her up, screeching and kicking, as if she were a child, and disarmed her. On her feet again, she stood, fists clenched, white with fury, but silent, as if nonplussed.

Groshawk appropriated her weapons. "You're a pretty lass, Nell, but too saucy. You'll take a deal of taming before you'll be fit for John Groshawk's mistress. Now, lads, we're off to comb this cursed island. Bide ye here, and watch the ocean—and watch Mistress Nell. If ye let her go near Steve Clarney I'll flay ye alive. As for big Steve—I'll see to him when I come back."

"You black swine," I snarled. "Had I but a hand free I'd give you your needings, you damned, cowardly, cringing spawn of the gutters—"

"I ha' no time to listen to your Irish blarney now, Clarney," said he with a grim smile. "Treasure's in the wind; when I come back, though—"

He laughed meaningly, which was more sinister than a spoken threat. A word to his rogues and they shouldered picks and muskets and trailed out behind him. The column passed into the shadows of the forest and vanished.

The sun had climbed higher and its rays struck through the palm leaves.

"There's deep shade around yonder point of land, only some fifty paces away," said Solomon Deas. "Let's seek it; let the Irish ape stay here and fry—he'll be frying in Hell soon enow, anyway. And, Nell, my dearie, ye'll come wi' us," he concluded, with a disgusting leer, laying his filthy hand on her arm. She snatched it away as if stung, her hand instinctively seeking her empty sash.

"Keep your vile claws off me," she snapped. "I'll go where I choose."

He grinned savagely. "Don't be putting on airs about us, my fine lass, or I'll tan the seat of your silken breeches with my belt. Come along!"

Nell was livid with fury and I thought for a moment she would leap at him with her teeth and nails, then her shoulders slumped and she walked ahead of the crew sullenly. She seemed bewildered, incapable of coping with her problem. Her status in the crew had changed greatly since the death of Captain Bisley. That lean old sea-eagle had allowed her almost incredible liberties and had laughed at her swaggerings and strutting. Then the whole crew had treated her with respect tinged with fear; Groshawk was of a different mind and the men reflected his attitude. She was unarmed and they no longer feared her.

The girl and the pirates disappeared around the short point and I presently heard voices raised in oaths and argument as they diced and drank. The palm leaves no longer sheltered me from the sun which beat fiercely on my unprotected head. I reflected that if I was forced to stand so for many hours, John Groshawk would be spared the trouble of butchering me.

Then as the voices rose louder and oaths clashed, Nell came hurriedly around the point and ran swiftly and silently toward me. She reached me and spoke swiftly: "Listen to me and do not speak until I finish! I stole away while they quarreled, but they will be after me in a moment! Swear to aid me against that bastard of a Groshawk and I'll free ye. Remember, you owe me your life—I kept them from throwing you overboard when you were taken in the seafight and refused to join them—I ha' kept you safe since then and done all I could to ease your captivity—"

"I swear," I broke in on her chatter. "Woman-like, you'd bring up my obligation to you—but I'd join hands with the Devil to ruin John Groshawk."

Thereat she swore between her teeth, but I felt her swift fingers working at the knots. They loosened—slipped from my numb wrists—

"Slide into the sand and lie still!" came her fierce whisper, and I obeyed without knowing why. From under lowered lids I saw Solomon Deas approaching, cutlass in hand, his hateful leer on his face.

"So ye'd free the great lout, eh?" he sneered. "Just as John warned us. What will ye give me not to tell Groshawk—what means this? Why does the great fool lie there like one dead?"

"He is dead, you fool," answered Nell. "Ha' ye never heard that this tropic sun kills men? And here he's stood wi' his scalp uncovered to it. Bend and look at him if you believe me not."

Grunting incredulously, Deas bent over me, his shaggy head close to my face, his vile breath in my nostrils. That was all the chance I needed. As a hawk grips a sparrow I caught the throat of Solomon Deas and crushed the yell that sought to rise to his lips. He had forgot the cutlass in his grasp. He dropped it and tore at my hands with his naked fingers for an instant—but only for an instant. Then blood gushed over my fingers and Solomon Deas went limp. I rose, flinging the corpse off me, and saw Nell looking at it, wide-eyed.

"By Satan!" she whispered. "You tore his throat out! And I had feared your hands too numb from your bonds."

"Never too numb to crush the life out of a snake," I grunted, picking up the cutlass. "Let's begone before the other rogues miss you. What now?"

"We'll follow Groshawk," said she. "If we can find the treasure ahead of him, I'll dictate my own terms—the beast! I'll heave his heart's blood yet. I've sailed the seas since I was sixteen and no man's yet put an insult on me and lived over-long to boast of it. Come!"

We went swiftly into the deeper shadows of the forest and as we went, Nell cast her eye up at me as one might eye a giant mastiff.

"By Satan," quoth she, "free of bonds you seem even more powerful than before. I wonder that we took you alive when we captured the *Bristol Girl*."

"You had not," I growled, "but that Bellefonte smote me a coward's blow from behind with a musket stock and knocked me senseless. I'd ask naught better than to meet him in equal fight—"

"You'll have your wish," said she with a grim laugh, "for here comes Mike through the woods alone!"

We had traversed the dim silent fastnesses of the shadowy woods and were emerging into a small glade—and across that glade from the other side came Mike Bellefonte. His bearded mouth opened as he saw us and he halted stock still. With a growl of fierce gratification I advanced toward him and he, nothing loath, stood his ground and drew his only arm, a cutlass similar to the one I bore.

That fight was short and bloody. He cut tremendously at my head and I parried and hacked back savagely. He ducked clumsily, and as my blade sang viciously over his head, he slashed at my belly. A quick leap backward saved me, though the edge slit my shirt, and I struck a terrible overhand blow, with every ounce of my beef behind it. Bellefonte had no time to parry it; he caught my whistling edge on the flat of his blade which shivered to sparkling splinters, and my next stroke split his skull.

"One debt paid," I growled, shaking the sweat out of my eyes, and the red drops from my blade. "Lead on to John Groshawk."

Nell's eyes gleamed. "You ha' the right spirit," quoth she. "I like you better and better."

"Like or hate, it's all one to me," I answered. "I'll play this red game to a finish; lead on, Miss Buccaneer."

Her expression changed and she stamped her little foot.

"You Irish rogue," she cried. "I'll ha' ye know that better men than you ha' fought and killed one another to kiss my hand."

"I've no doubt of it," I answered, "but I'd never kiss your hand and your red lips so near."

She looked uncertain, and then laughed. "You tack faster than the wind changes; you'd make a chancy lover."

"'Tis no place to be speaking of light matters," said I sternly, "and a dead man at our very feet; may the saints rest his soul in the Hell where he's gone; come, let's be off."

She shook her head with an expression of bewilderment and gestured me to follow her.

The trees grew taller and thicker. What light filtered in through the tangled branches was dim and illusive. Through a realm of shadows we moved silently forward and presently the terrain changed; the trees thinned and the ground became rougher, sloping up to low hills. We mounted these and saw before us a sort of plateau, grown densely with tall trees, and through the waving branches we glimpsed what looked like a building of black stone. A somber silence brooded over all. We came out upon the plateau and looked about curiously.

[...]

Black Vulmea's Vengeance

(earliest known draft)

Chapter .1.

Out of the cabin of the *Cockatoo* staggered Black Terence Vulmea, pipe in one hand and flagon in the other. He stood with booted legs wide, teetering slightly to the gentle swaying of the lofty poop. He was bareheaded and his shirt was open at the neck, revealing his broad hairy chest. He emptied the flagon and tossed it over the side with a gusty sigh of satisfaction, then focused his somewhat blurred gaze on the deck below. From poop ladder to forecastle it was littered by sprawling figures. The ship smelt like a brewery. Empty barrels, with their heads stove in, stood or rolled between the prostrate forms. Vulmea was the only man on his feet. From galley boy to first mate the rest of the ship's company lay senseless after a debauch that had lasted a whole night long. There was not even a man at the helm, which was lashed securely.

In that placid sea there was no hand needed on the wheel. A light but steady breeze billowed the sails gently. Land was a thin blue line to the east. A pure blue sky held a sun whose heat had not yet become fierce.

Vulmea blinked tolerantly down upon the prone figures of his crew, and glanced idly over the larboard side. He grunted with the sudden jolt of surprize. A ship filled space in what he had expected to see naked ocean stretching to the skyline. She was little more than a hundred yards away and was bearing down swiftly on the *Cockatoo*, obviously meaning to lay alongside. She was tall and square rigged, her white canvas flashing dazzlingly in the sun. From the main truck the English flag whipped red against the blue. Her bulwarks were lined with tense figures, gripping boarding pikes and grappling irons, and through her open ports the astounded pirate glimpsed the glow of the burning matches the gunners held ready.

"All hands on deck!" yelled Vulmea groggily. Reverberant snores answered the urgent summons. All hands remained as they were—on deck indeed, and motionless.

"Wake up, you lousy dogs!" roared their captain. "Up, curse you! A king's ship is at our throats!"

He might have shouted to the gulls wheeling above. With a curse he lurched in a reeling run across the poop to where a swivel gun which stood at the ladder head, commanding the deck. Seizing this, he swung it about until its muzzle bore full on the rail of the approaching cruiser. He squinted along its barrel as if he were aiming a musket.

"Strike your colors, you damned pirate!" came a hail from the trim figure that trod the warship's poop, sword in hand.

"Go to hell!" roared Vulmea, and knocked the glowing coals of his pipe into the vent. The falcon crashed, smoke puffed out in a white cloud, and the charge of musket balls with which the gun had been loaded mowed a ghastly lane through the boarding party clustered along the cruiser's bulwark. Like a clap of thunder came the answering broadside and a storm of metal raked the *Cockatoo's* decks, turning them into a red shambles. Spars splintered, ropes parted, sails ripped, timbers smashed, and blood and brains mingled with the pools of liquor spilt on the decks.

And a round shot as big as a man's head smashed into the falcon, ripping it loose from the swivel and dashing it against the man who had fired it. The impact knocked him headlong across the poop where his head hit the rail with a crack that was too much even for an Irish skull. Black Vulmea sagged senseless to the boards. He was as deaf to the shouts of the conquerors and the stamp of victorious feet on his red-streaming decks as were his men who had gone from the sleep of drink to the black sleep of death without knowing what hit them.

CAPTAIN John Wentyard, in the main cabin of his Majesty's cruiser the *Indomitable*, sipped his wine and set down the glass with a gesture that in another man would have smacked of affectation. Wentyard was a tall man, with a narrow, pale face, colorless eyes, and a prominent nose. His rather somber costume contrasted with the glitter of his officers who sat respectfully about him.

"Bring in the prisoner," he ordered, and there was a satisfaction in the cold glitter of his pale eyes.

They brought in Black Vulmea, between four brawny sailors, his hands manacled behind him and a chain on his ankles that just was long enough to allow him to walk without tripping. Blood was clotted in the pirate's thick black hair, and crusted a cut on his shoulder. His shirt was in tatters, revealing a torso bronzed by the sun and ridged with great muscles. A faint grin played on his lips, and there was no mercy in their stares, and he seemed not at all abashed or intimidated. He met the stern stare of the captain and his officers and showed no sign that he was affected. His gaze was level and reflected only a sardonic amusement. Wentyard frowned. He liked for his captives to wince, to cringe before him. It made him feel more like justice personified, looking down unemotionally on the sufferings of the evil, from a great height.

"You are Black Vulmea, the pirate?"

The other nodded coolly.

"I suppose you will say," sneered Wentyard, "that you hold a commission from the Governor of Tortuga? These commissions from the French carry no weight with the officers of his Majesty's navy. You—"

"Save your breath, lad," Vulmea grinned hardly. "I hold no commission from anybody. I'm not one of these swashbucklers who hide behind the name of buccaneer. I'm a pirate. I've sunk as many English ships as well as Spanish—and be damned to you, heron-nose!"

The officers gasped at this effrontery, and Wentyard smiled a ghastly, mirthless smile, white with the anger that he restrained.

"You know that I have the authority to hang you out of hand?" he said. "I am not forced to take you back to Kingston for trial."

"I know it," answered the Irishman softly. "It won't be the first time you've hanged me, John Wentyard."

"What?" The Englishman stared.

A flame grew in Vulmea's blue eyes and his voice changed subtly in tone.

"On the Galway coast it was, years ago, captain. You were a lieutenant then, under Perrott. There was a skirmish and the Irish lost—poor, ragged, half-starved peasants, against full-armed English soldiers and marines. After the fight there were the usual hangings. And there was a boy who crept into a thicket to watch—a lad of ten. You spied him, John Wentyard, and had your men drag him forth and string him up alongside the kicking bodies of the others. I was that boy. I've looked forward to this meeting, John Wentworth, you English dog!"

Vulmea lips still smiled, but the veins knotted in his temples and the great muscles stood out distinctly on his manacled arms. Ironed though the pirate was, Wentyard involuntarily drew back, daunted by the hate that blazed from those savage eyes.

"How did you escape your just deserts?" he asked coldly, recovering his poise.

Vulmea laughed shortly.

"Other peasants were hiding in the thickets. As soon as you English left they came out— and not being civilized Englishmen, but poor, savage Irishry, they cut me down when there was still life in me. We Gaels are hard to kill, as you men of Perrott learned to your cost."

"You fell into our hands easily enough this time," said Wentyard.

Vulmea grinned.

"Who'd have thought to meet a king's ship in these empty western seas? It's been weeks since we sighted a sail, save for the pinnace we took yesterday, with a cargo of wine, bound for Panama. It's too far south for Spanish ships to be frequent. We've had no luck with prizes, and when the lads wanted a drinking bout, who was I to deny them? We drew out of the lanes the Spaniards mostly follow, and thought we had the ocean to ourselves. I'd been sleeping in my cabin for some hours before I came on deck to smoke a pipe or so and saw you."

"You killed seven of my men with your fire," harshly accused Wentyard.

"And you killed all of mine," retorted Vulmea. "Poor devils, they went to hell without knowing what hit them." Through the stern windows he could see the topmasts of the *Cockatoo* just sinking, hulled by the close-range broadside.

He grinned again, with a hard contraction of his cheek muscles. His toes dug hard against the floor, unnoticed even by the men who gripped him on either side. The blood was surging through his veins, and the feel of his great strength was upon him. He knew he could, in a sudden, gigantic explosion of strength, tear free from the men who held him, clear the space between him and his enemy with one bound, despite his chains, and crush Wentyard's skull with a smashing swing of his manacled hands. That he would die an instant later mattered not at all. In that moment he felt neither fears nor regrets—only a reckless, ferocious exultation and a cruel scorn of these stupid, blinking Englishmen about him. He laughed in their faces, joying in the knowledge that they did not know why he laughed. So they thought to chain the tiger, did they? Little they guessed of the devastating power that lurked in his swelling thews.

He began filling his great chest, drawing in his breath slowly, imperceptibly, as his calves knotted and the muscles of his arms grew hard as iron. Then Wentyard spoke again, checking the spring before it started.

"I am commissioned to either hang you when captured, or bring you back to Kingston to stand trial there. I can act at my own discretion. It makes little difference, whether you hang at my yardarm, or on the Kingston wharves. But if you wish to gain a few months of life, I might agree to take you to Kingston. On one condition."

"What's that?" Vulmea's tensed muscles did not relax; his great chest expanded gently.

"That you tell me the whereabouts of the pirate captain, Van Raven."

In that instant, while his tensed muscles went pliant again, Vulmea unerringly gauged the man he was dealing with and changed his plan. He smiled.

"And why the Dutchman, Wentyard?" he asked softly. "Why not Tranicos, or Villiers, or Montbars, or a dozen others, of greater renown than Van Raven? Is it because of the treasure he reputedly took from the Spanish plate-ships? Aye, the king would like well to set his hands upon that hoard and no doubt a rich prize would go to the captain lucky enough or daring enough to seize it. Is that why you came all the way around the Horn, John Wentyard?"

"We are at peace with Spain," answered Wentyard acidly. "As for the purposes of an officer in his Majesty's navy, they are not for you to question."

Vulmea laughed at him, the blue flame flickering in his eyes.

"Once I fought a king's frigate off Hispaniola," he said. "I sank it. Damn you and your prating of 'His Majesty'! But if it's treasure you want, I can show you where to lay a finger on a hoard that would make the Dutchman's loot look like a peat-pool beside the Caribbean Sea!"

A pale spark seemed to snap from Wentyard's colorless eyes and his officers leaned forward tensely. Vulmea grinned. He knew these navy men were credulous as landsmen and merchantmen were in regard to pirates; they believed the wild tales told of the vast treasures accumulated by the rovers. Coolly he regarded Wentyard, plumbed the avarice of the other's hard soul, and said: "This treasure lies near the coast of Ecuador. Four years ago Dick Harston, the English pirate, and I heard of a mysterious tribe of Indians dwelling in the highlands, and possessing great stores of gold, and of precious stones as well.

"We landed at a certain nameless bay, and, guided by an Indian, marched inland with five hundred men. To make a long tale short, we found the tribe, scattered the warriors and marched back toward the coast with our loot—fifteen mule-loads of virgin gold, three mule-loads of jewels!"

The flame grew in Wentyard's eyes. His white hands knotted about the slender stem of his wine glass.

"A day's march from the coast, we camped near the ruins of an old heathen temple. And there we fell out over the division of the spoil. We came to blows, and presently, whilst we fought among ourselves, there came a scout running with word that a Spanish flotilla had anchored in the bay, driven our ships away, and sent nine hundred men ashore to pursue us. We hid the treasure in the old temple, and scattered, each band for itself. Eventually I, with my crew, made my way back to the coast and was picked up by my ship which had fled from the Spaniards.

"Harston gained his ship with a handful of men, after skirmishing all the way with the Spaniards, who chased him instead of us, and later was slain by savages on the coast of California.

"I never had an opportunity to go back after the loot. It is still there, and I'll show it to you, in return for my life."

"That is impossible," snapped Wentyard. "The best I can promise you is to return you to Kingston, where the governor will do as he likes, with you."

"Well," said Vulmea, "maybe the governor might be more lenient than you."

Wentyard did not reply, but spread a map in front of the Irishman.

"Where is this bay?"

Vulmea indicated a certain spot on the coast. His arms were partly released while he marked it, and Wentyard's head was within reach, but his plans were changed, and included a chance for life—slim, but nevertheless a chance.

"Very well. Take him back to the brig."

Vulmea went out with his guards, and Wentyard sneered coldly.

"A promise to a rogue is not binding. Once the treasure is aboard the *Redoubtable*, gentlemen, I promise you he shall swing from a yardarm."

TEN days later the anchors rattled down in the nameless bay Vulmea had described.

It seemed desolate enough to have been the coast of an uninhabited continent. Dense jungle crowded the narrow strip of white sand that was the beach. Gay-plumed birds flitted among the broad fronds. But a dim trail led back into the twilight vistas of green-walled mystery.

Dawn was a white mist on the water when the landing party marched down the trail—thirty marines under the command of Wentyard himself, and their prisoner, his legs free, but his hands bound before him, and a rope made fast to them with one end in the grip of a brawny seaman whose other hand held a cutlass ready to chop down the prisoner if he made any move to escape.

"Fifteen men are enough," Vulmea had told Wentyard. "Here are no Spaniards anywhere near."

"I wasn't thinking of Spaniards," answered Wentyard coldly. "I am providing against any attempt you might make to escape."

"What of savages?"

The pirate laughed.

"Go beyond the Cordilleras if you seek real savages. There are Indians, almost white, who take men's heads and shrink them no bigger than your fist. But they never come this side of the mountains.

As for the race that built the temple where we hid the jewels, they have been extinct for saints only knows how many centuries. There is no gold to bear away, only jewels, that one strong man could carry."

"One strong man," murmured Wentyard, licking his lips at the thought of the wealth represented by a load to stagger a strong man. "What of this trail?" he asked suspiciously.

"It was an old Indian road, which hasn't been used in centuries ago, save Harston and myself, and the Spaniards which pursued us. You can see where the young growth has sprung up above the scars of the axes with which we cleared a way."

Wentyard nodded. They tramped stolidly along on through steaming heat, and when the sun hung still high in the jungle branches, they came to the mouth of a ravine. Neither Wentyard nor any of his men had glimpsed the furtive, shadowy shapes flitting along through the jungle on either hand. Vulmea was aware of their presence, but he only smiled grimly and said nothing.

At last he halted at the mouth of a ravine and pointed down it.

"That's the roadway that leads to the old temple. At the end stands the ruined walls."

"On, then!" snapped Wentyard, fanning himself with his plumed hat. Sweat trickled down his face and under the collar of his crimson, gilt-embroidered coat.

They marched on between walls fringed with fronds. The jungle ran densely along the rims of the ravine. The walls were perhaps forty feet high, the ravine some fifty feet wide. A low growth of vegetation carpeted the floor. The walls were sheer in most places, but in others natural ramps ran down into the ravine. Presently Vulmea stopped. Some yards further on the ravine bent around a rocky shoulder. From the other wall stood out a corresponding shoulder.

"That used to be a gateway," said Vulmea. "That rock on either hand is masonry. A gate stood there."

From the jungle at the mouth of the ravine something twanged sharply. There was a whistle that ended in a thud, and one of the men dropped with an arrow through his throat.

"The devil!" yelled Wentyard. "Dog! I thought you said there were no Indians hereabouts!"

Vulmea laughed scornfully.

"Poor-spirited dogs that slink in the hills beyond jungle. Don't you see them skulking among the trees? Give them a volley. That should do them."

Wentyard barked out an order, for he too glimpsed brown figures moving among the green foliage. Fourteen muskets crashed, and the bullets rattled among the leaves, cutting through the twigs. A few severed fronds drifted down; that was all. But the smoke had not lifted when Vulmea, snapping the cords he had patiently worked on all day long, knocked his guard staggering with a buffet under the ear, snatched his cutlass and was gone, running like a cat up the steep wall of the ravine. They gaped after him with empty muskets and Wentyard's pistol banged futilely. From the green fringe along the ravine rim came a mocking laugh.

"Fools! You are in a trap! There never was any jewels! The Indians caught me here once before and butchered all my crew, as those skulls in the grass testify. You'll never hang me!"

"Dog!" yelled Wentyard furiously. "You told us there were no natives here!"

"I told you the headhunters never came over the mountains," answered Vulmea. "They don't, either. I told you the people who built the temple were long extinct. That's so, too. I didn't tell you that a tribe of nameless brown devils live in these jungles, and have lived here for centuries. I think they were the ones who exterminated the people that built the temple. Anyway, they wiped out my men, and the only reason I got away was because I'd lived with the Savages of North America for so many years I learned all their cunning and woodscraft."

"And you'd abandon white men to savages!"

"It goes against my principles," the Irishman admitted. "But I'm not such a fool as to sacrifice my life helping men who want to hang me. I feel sorry for your men. That's why I urged you to bring only a few. If you had brought five hundred the result would have been the same. I wanted to spare as many as possible. As for you, you filthy dog, you forfeited any consideration you might demand as a white man. I took my chance. It might have been me that arrow struck."

Just as Wentyard wondered if there were no Indians on the wall above them, the foliage was violently agitated, there was a yell, and down came a naked brown body, all asprawl, revolving in the air. It crashed on the floor of the ravine—a brawny warrior, naked but for a loincloth of bark and bronze armlets and anklets. He was deep chested, broad shouldered and muscular, the features not unintelligent, but hard and brutal. He had been slashed across the neck.

The bushes waved briefly and then again, which Wentyard believed marked the flight of the Irishman along the ravine wall, pursued by the companions of the defeated warrior, who must have stolen up on Vulmea while the pirate was shouting.

But Wentyard had his own problems.

His men were falling about him under the whistling arrows. He started to fall back, then hesitated, fearing that the ravine beyond the bend was filled with warriors. The broken stones afforded some refuge, and he placed his men there. Arrows showered down on them from the walls of the ravine, and they fell one by one. It was just at dusk when the rush came, naked brown bodies flitting through the shadows, and suddenly forming a wave that flooded the ravine. The muskets tore lanes in that wave, but it came on and engulfed the white men in a snarling, slashing, clubbing chaos.

Wentyard broke away and fled, blood smeared on his arms, dripping from his sword. He fired one of his pistols full in a painted face surmounted by a feathered crest, saw it vanish in red ruin. He clubbed another with the empty barrel, ran one through and fled down the ravine. It lay empty before him. Beyond the turn he saw the ravine widen out; stone walls, almost hidden by vines and creepers, rose, pierced with blank windows and doorways. His flesh crawled with the momentary expectation of a thrust in the back. He ran into the nearest door and turned at bay, crouching, panting, fumbling with his other loaded pistol.

He was in a room of stone walls, with grass growing up through the cracks between the stones of the floor. Other doorways led into similar rooms. Silence brooded over the place. Through the broken roof he could see the rim of the cliff a few yards above the top of the wall. The temple or palace stood in a stone-walled bowl, almost choked with rank vegetation. He did not believe anyone had occupied the ruins for centuries.

He crouched at the doorway, pistols in hand, waiting, but no rush came. He feared an arrow from the foliage on the cliffs, but none came. The leaves did not rustle. Hunger and thirst tortured him.

When night fell he feared the stealthy creeping of naked warriors down the ravine. But none came. When it was dark he stole along it, but was driven back by a rush of spearmen who lurked in the mouth beyond the bend. He barely regained the ruins. Did they fear his pistols? They had not shown any great fear of the muskets of the marines. Why did they not rush the ruins and cut his throat? Were they saving him for a grimmer fate?

Dawn broke clear and hot, and all day he lay suffering from hunger and thirst, tormented by gnats and insects, waiting for the rush that did not come. He was starving and desperate. He dozed fitfully that night, heard a scuffle and rushed out to find a fantastically garbed black man laying dead before the door. His skull had been split. He was a Cimaroon, one of the slaves who escaped the Spaniards and reverted to savagery. Evidently this man had lived with the Indians, and had not been held from his enemy by whatever ideas prevented the Indians from entering the ravine.

Wentyard could not escape. He could not climb the walls. He investigated the ruins, finding them merely a succession of ruined walls, roofless and doorless. He could tell nothing about the bas-reliefs on the walls.

Dawn found him frantic. His pistols had been stolen in the night, when he had slept, despite the feeling he was being watched. He awoke with cold sweat, feeling that some hideously evil thing had passed close to him in the night. He thought he saw a swaying shadow hover an instant in a doorway and then silently vanish. Then he found his pistols had been stolen, but his sword was left.

At dawn he found fruit and water in a stone vessel just inside the inner door. He ate ravenously, and later in the day found more food, this time meat in a vessel—stewed monkey meat he believed, but he ate it ravenously.

The sun was hanging in the jungle trees when he turned to confront Vulmea, who stood before him with drawn cutlass.

"You!"

Aye! I've been spying on you, waiting for you to starve. But I decided to kill you myself. That's why I stole your pistols."

"And you spied on me last night," snarled Wentyard.

"Not I. I was sleeping up on the cliffs. If anything spied on you it was one of the spirits which haunt this place. The Indians won't come in here. That black man I killed would have cut your throat, though. I brought you the food because I wanted you to be strong. Now on your guard!"

A clash of steel and Wentyard's blade whirred into a corner.

"Bah!" Vulmea threw aside his sword. "Can't you even fight?"

He slapped Wentyard viciously first on one side of the face and then on the other, and when the Englishman sprang at his throat, he knocked him sprawling with a savage smash under the heart. Wentyard groped inside his shirt, drew something out and began to weep.

"What the hell!" Vulmea jerked it away from him, amazed to see what could bring tears from John Wentyard. It was a miniature portrait of a young woman and child. It was cracked and crumpled from the blow, but their softness and gentleness was evident.

"Your wife and daughter?"

Wentyard nodded, mutely. The breaking of the portrait he had always carried over his heart seemed to have broken his spirit.

"Hell, I never knew that. I'll get you out of this. We can climb the cliffs, but there's a cordon of Indians strung all about the place, for a mile in each direction. I could get through them, but you couldn't. I know a way though."

Vulmea led Wentyard into what must have been an ancient aqueduct. It was high enough for a man to walk upright. On their way they encountered a huge anaconda, which Vulmea slew, and after many adventures, emerged on the beach, where Vulmea showed Wentyard his ship, and turned away, not trusting the Englishman.

Humor

A Pirut Story

"What ho! me harties," sez kaptin Alfonzo Goofus as he sees a ship puttin outa port. "What ho," sez he. The kaptin wuz a pirut ez may posibly bin suspishuned. "Stand by to go about," sez Alfonzo Goofus.

"Nuthin doin," anserd the captin uv the aposin ship.

"An why not," sez Alfonzo. "Gimme no back talk dangone ye."

"Do yore stuf," sez the captin, "but look out."

"Why," sez Alfonzo?

"Becoz," sez the captin, drawin hisself up to hiz full hite.

"We're American citizens, by golly!" baffled sez Alfonzo.

Yet curse not gentle reader, for by such stuff did Josh Billings and many another so-called humorist achieve fame.

Bill Boozy was a pirate bold

Bill Boozy was a pirate bold,
He never washed his neck.
He chawed a wad of chewing-gum
And spat upon the deck.

Sez'e', "No more we'll stuff ourselves
With quarts and quarts of rum,
Lashed to the mast,
The color's fast,
Yo ho, and a pack of gum!"

At the Inn of the Gory Dagger

At the Inn of the Gory Dagger, with nothing to win or lose,
With pistols thrust in their girdles and boots,
guzzled the pirate crews.
There was Bill with the tattooed buttocks, and Tom with
the timber leg,
And Barbarous Mike from Liverpool — oh, he was a tough,
tough yegg!
Our goblets banged on the table tops, our laughter rose in
a gust.
And now and then a shot cracked out and someone kissed
the dust.
It made a man right nervous, ducking the cutlass cuts,
And every so often someone yelled with a sword
thrust through his guts.
The hot oaths cracked the ceilings, the goblet burned at
the lip,
And we reveled and killed one another in goodly fellowship.
Then up from a wine-stained table, shouting for five
more beers,
Rose Eve of the Sash of Crimson, the queen of the buccaneers!
And over across the tavern room, with a bellow coarse
and rude
Rose Murderous Mike who called himself king of
the Brotherhood!
"Here and at once," Eve shouted, "We 'ull settle this case
for all!
"With the slash of a keen-edged cutlass or the crack of a
pistol ball!"

For there was a feud between the two as who should rule
the seas.
Eve stood with her skirt of scarlet that did not reach her knees.
She wore fine boots of leather that left her white knees bare,
A sleeveless, low-necked jacket, and a ribbon in her hair.
Around her slender and shapely waist was wound her
crimson sash,
Therein was a slender rapier, keen as a riding lash.
Murderous Mike was a mighty man, in knots his muscles
stood,
He'd the name of the hardest bastard in all of the Brotherhood.
His arms were like the masts of a ship, bulging and iron strong,
And 'twas said of him that his penis was nineteen inches long.
"Hold everything, bold messmates," said Anaconda Bill,
"Ain't they no way to settle this, without you got to kill?
"Oh keep them deadly weepings alongside of your pants,
"And settle it the peaceful way, along o' gymes o' chance."
"This is too deep for peaceful games," said Mike, "It will
not do!
"For mumble peg or tiddledy-winks, or matching nickels
too!"
"Out sword, you crumby son-of-a-whore," Eve challenged
high and shrill,
"And I will cut your liver out and fry it on the grill!"
"Each man to his own weapon," Mike answer straightway
made,
"I will not use a sword or gun to master a saucy jade."
"Then what, in the name of Satan?" Eve tossed aside
her sword,
And all we buccaneers stood still, a wondering gaping horde.
He caught her close in his iron arms, while she cursed at
her helplessness,
And he slapped her buttocks down on the board and
lifted up her dress.
Then he drew forth his penis — an ox it would have felled —

And when Eve saw the size of it, she opened her mouth
and yelled.
But though she kicked and struggled and did her very best,
Once it was fairly in her, she did not seem distressed.
And while we yelled and cheered them on, there on the
board began
As fierce fought battle as ever was waged by woman and man.
A test of strength and endurance, till the roof began to spin,
And still he could not wear her down, and he would not
give in.
They jazzed till the sun came up in the east, they jazzed till
the sun went down,
Their muscles cracked and their brows were set in a
death-or victory frown.
The moon came up and the moon went down and the
matter was still in doubt,
But she was growing stronger and he was wearing out.
And as the east was growing red, and the light of day came in
He tumbled off her onto his back and gasped, "Oh Hell,
you win!"
And the sun that rose and glimmered over the distant leas
Looked on a humbled chieftain and the mistress of the seas!

ROBERT ERVIN HOWARD (1906-1936) grew up in the boomtowns of early twentieth-century Texas, eventually settling in Cross Plains where he lived for the remainder of his short life. Deciding early on a literary career, he spent the bulk of his time crafting stories and poems for the burgeoning pulp fiction markets: *Weird Tales*, *Action Stories*, *Fight Stories*, *Argosy*, etc. Howard's literary reputation was assured with the publication of "The Shadow Kingdom" in 1929, which featured a unique blend of Fantasy and Adventure which has since been termed Heroic Fantasy. The creation of Conan the Cimmerian in the pages of *Weird Tales* has earned him lasting recognition.

RUSTY BURKE has been championing Howard and his works for more than a quarter century. He edited a number of early chapbooks for Necronomicon Press, was founding editor of *The Dark Man: The Journal of Robert E. Howard Studies*, and was series editor for the Wandering Star, Del Rey, and Bison Books editions of Howard's works. He has written numerous articles, essays, and introductions about REH and compiled several references for Howard scholars. He annotated Howard's *Collected Letters* for the REH Foundation Press, and serves as President and Chairman of the Foundation. He lives in Washington, DC, with his wife, artist Shelly Wischhusen.

ROB ROEHM has edited more than a dozen Howard-related books for the REH Foundation Press as well as a couple with his own Roehm's Room Press. He has won multiple awards for his research and writings in a variety of Howard-themed publications. He has traveled to every location in the United States that Howard mentions visiting—from New Orleans to Santa Fe, and dozens of Texas towns in between—verifying and expanding our knowledge of Howard's biography. His research has also uncovered lost Howard stories, letters, and poems. He writes about these discoveries, infrequently, at howardhistory.com.

PAUL HERMAN, long-time engineer and intellectual property attorney, began publishing REH in 1999 via his own Hermanthis Press and later, Wildside Press; he has edited well over one million words. His etexts have been the starting material for a significant number of REH books published in the last 17 years. His REH bibliography, *The Neverending Hunt* became the new standard when it was first published in 2006, and is the basis for the HowardWorks website. His wife of 38 years, Denna, continues to tolerate his hobbies. Paul currently resides in Weatherford, Texas, a few miles from Robert E. Howard's birthplace.

MARK WHEATLEY holds the Eisner, Inkpot, Golden Lion, Mucker, Gem and Speakeasy Awards and nominations for the Harvey Award and the Ignatz Award. He is also an inductee to the Overstreet Hall of Fame. His work has often been included in the annual Spectrum selection of fantastic art and has appeared in private gallery shows, the Norman Rockwell Museum, Toledo Museum of Art, Huntington Art Museum, Fitchburg Art Museum, James A. Michener Art Museum and the Library of Congress, where several of his originals are in the LoC permanent collection.

STÅLE GISMERVIK has been passionate about REH since discovering Conan in 1990. He established one of the earliest and largest Conan-focused websites, and currently manages the comprehensive REH resource at reh.world. Ståle also administers the Robert E. Howard Foundation website and its Press counterpart, and oversees the curation and editing of Foundation eBooks. Recently, he has taken on the role of preparing the new Ultimate Books for publication. His work contributes to the preservation and promotion of Howard's legacy.

www.ingramcontent.com/pod-product-compliance
Lightning Source LLC
Chambersburg PA
CBHW060707190726
48289CB00002B/582